DESIRE AT DAWN

Visit us at www.boldstrokesbooks.com

By the Author

Every Dark Desire

Broken in Soft Places

Desire at Dawn

DESIRE AT DAWN

by
Fiona Zedde

2014

DESIRE AT DAWN
© 2014 By Fiona Zedde. All Rights Reserved.

ISBN 13: 978-1-62639-064-5

This Trade Paperback Original Is Published By
Bold Strokes Books, Inc.
P.O. Box 249
Valley Falls, NY 12185

First Edition: June 2014

CREDITS
Editor: Cindy Cresap
Production Design: Susan Ramundo
Cover Design By Sheri (graphicartist2020@hotmail.com)

Dedication

To all my readers who loved *Every Dark Desire*
and wanted more. This is for you.

CHAPTER ONE

The human security guards were easy prey, and Kylie took them like a gift. When they attacked her on the roof of the museum, she fought back and laughed. She punched and clawed, gushing blood and breaking bones, twisted away from them, and jumped off the fifteen-story building with their taste still on her lips.

The falling happened slowly, night rushing up into her face, a million stars burning above her, the floors of the building darting by. The full skirts of her midnight blue dress drifted up around her hips like the petals of a dark flower. Then the ground was at her feet. She landed in a crouch, sprang up, and ran.

Earlier, she'd been careless. Perhaps deliberately so as she had walked slowly through the museum, allowing the humans to see her, a brown young woman with feral eyes, prettily dressed in the designer frock her mother had gotten for her, but still out of place among the glittering humans in their sequins, pearls, and money worn casually like air. The museum was relatively small. Only a half dozen or so rooms with glassed-in displays of jewels, gold, and other old things that meant more now than they ever did.

In the gallery where Kylie stood, the light was bright on the square glass cases and over the people walking through the wide room. She breathed in their artificial and human smells. The delicious copper and sunlight flavor of the blood she'd taken from a pair of tourists barely an hour before was still on her tongue when she spotted the necklace she wanted.

So she'd smashed the glass case, snatched the diamond and ruby necklace from its velvet pedestal, and ran.

Triumph sang through her. The ruby necklace she'd stolen was a cool weight against her hip, tucked away in the hidden zippered pocket of her dress, a false feeling of security as she sprinted into the cool clutch of evening.

Buckhead, Atlanta, on a Saturday night. Partiers decorated the streets like silken ribbons. The beautiful and the very much alive.

She sprinted into an alley and emerged on the other side in a crush of humans. They were laughing, happiness hovering over them like the best and rarest of perfumes. A wedding, a bride and her party, tumbling onto the steps of a hotel, their clothes an explosion of tulle in the night air. An evening wedding.

Just like the one her mother had had with Silvija. She stopped, the memory of the moonless night almost seven years ago making her stumble. Her mother with a woman. Her mother married.

Someone bumped into her from behind.

"Are you all right, honey?"

A woman's concerned voice touched Kylie, then hands floated to her shoulders. Kylie flinched away with a growl. She caught the frightened gaze of the woman who snatched her hand back and stared at her with wide eyes.

As a human, she would have been ashamed of acting like that. As herself, she wanted to tear out the woman's throat and feel her kindness pouring over her tongue. Even in her most extreme daydreams as a girl in Jamaica, Kylie never thought she'd be this. She pushed through the crowd, darted into traffic, and left the humans' happiness behind.

She caught a flash of her reflection in a shop glass. She saw a narrow strip of a girl with wild hair and tortured eyes, the dark blue dress fluttering against her skin in the wake of her own breeze. She stopped. The humans were looking, taking note of her mad dash through the streets, a flush of scarlet in their beige lives.

Once she'd jumped off the fifteen-story building, the guards from the museum hadn't stood a chance of catching her. But still, she felt like something was chasing her, a forever feeling of restless anger and fear that only dissolved with the coming of the sun and oblivion. Or when she risked her neck for baubles that didn't matter.

She walked slowly now, hips swaying, feeling the brush of the stolen ruby necklace with each step she took. The coolness of a late fall breeze stroked her face and thickly coiled hair as she walked down Peachtree Street—past the glittering high-rise condominiums, the Fox Theatre, an occasional car with Southern rap music blaring from its stereo—to Ponce de Leon Avenue with its feral looking hookers and the Krispy Kreme donut shop. She headed toward Little Five Points, an area of town she'd liked as soon as she saw it.

Her cell phone rang. She took it out of the hidden pocket where it rested with the necklace, and glanced down at it, although the caller could only be one person.

She greeted her mother in her most neutral tone. "Good evening."

"Where are you, Kylie?" Her mother's husky voice fluted high with worry. "The sun will be up soon."

"I'm fine." But she looked up in surprise at the touches of gray in the otherwise dark sky. Garlic and holy water of vampire legends didn't affect her at all, but the sun would burn her to cinders. "I'm in Jersey." The lie came easily to Kylie's tongue.

"Then you can make it home before sunrise."

"I'm not sure," she said. "I'll try."

But of course, she was nearly six hundred miles away from the clan home. A plane ride. A car. A brisk run. She'd turn to ashes in the sun if she tried to make it back before dawn.

Her mother seemed to sense something. Kylie could almost see her pausing whatever she was doing, her fingers frozen on the zipper of one of her brightly colored, figure-hugging dresses as she got ready for bed. "Kylie, don't be careless and expose yourself to danger. Come home. Or find a safe place to rest for the day."

Despite the fierce words, her mother's tone was soft with concern. Kylie wondered if she'd practiced it before calling.

"There's no danger here," she said with the ruby necklace brushing her hipbone. The sky grew even lighter above her. "I'll be back soon," she said. "Everything is good." Then Kylie hung up.

Mama. A stranger. But still always Mama.

Sometimes, she didn't know that stranger who occasionally hugged and kissed her. Her mother was alternately cold and kind, filled to bursting with a guilt Kylie wanted no part of. A distant mother who had all the time in her endless life for Silvija, her wife, but never for Kylie. Not really. She shook the useless thoughts from her head, stuck the phone back in her pocket, and began to hunt for a place to spend the day.

On the way to shelter, she got distracted by the beauty of night giving way to daybreak around her. It was a time she had loved as a human, darkness drifting away to allow the faintest traces of pink on the horizon, a stroke of the vivid color signifying the stark rise of the light. Kylie squinted against the weak light. She wasn't like her mother who could stand it past sunrise. Once, she'd seen her sit on the top floor of their Central Park penthouse apartment, hidden in a shadowed corner as the sun rose, its light creeping toward her on cat feet while she watched it all with that smooth and impassive face of hers. Kylie knew her mother had been badly burned before, but Belle was not afraid.

Her mother was strong. Kylie was not. If nothing else, the sun taught her that.

Rising dawn. People were still on the streets, their laughter and music leaving Kylie spellbound. It was late, but so many of the humans were about. She thought she would get used to that in New York, a city of endless night and endless activity. Even just before daybreak, the streets were alive with their particular energy and bite. But here in Atlanta, it was different; there was a Southern slowness, a delicious leisure to the streets, the conversation, the voices. There was no rush, simply a meandering with the smell of incense winding through their clothes.

The pink brightened in the sky, then, slow as a dream, changed to amber. The light brushed her forehead and she leapt back, gasping at its sting, a hornet's piercing prick. Kylie threw her arm up to protect her face. She scuttled backward until her spine slammed against brick.

Despite shouting at her mother many times over the years that she wished she were truly dead, Kylie fought for her existence with every sight of the rising sun. Operating on pure instinct alone, she ducked into a nearby alley. She turned and dug fingers into the red brick and climbed up, scrambling up a brick building and to the screened-in second floor balcony. It was locked. She cursed and climbed higher, her fingers and the toes of her flats hooking into the exposed brick.

Kylie bypassed the fourth and fifth floors, something calling her higher to the top floor of the building. That balcony door was unlocked. She slid quietly in, letting the thick linen curtains fall behind her.

In the sudden silence, she heard her breath, felt her chest in panic. Kylie's cheeks prickled with shame, although there was no one around to see it, to see her, a vampire who hadn't needed to breathe for seven years, get frightened into drawing air. She cut off the unnecessary breathing and calmed herself.

She realized then that she was in a woman's apartment.

The hush of the apartment was loud compared to the grumbling wakefulness of the city down below: the buses already growling through the Atlanta streets, cars zooming past with their lights still on to combat the failing darkness. Across the street, the café already had its shades raised while figures moved behind the glass in preparation for a new day.

Kylie lifted her head to draw in the scents around her, a habit that Julia, another member of the clan, always teased her about.

"We're vampires, not wolves," the little imp always said.

She shook away the extraneous thought and focused on her surroundings. She crept deeper into the apartment that was shrouded heavily in darkness. She remembered the lessons that her mother taught her, how to be light, to move so delicately that not even the air was disturbed.

Although it was a typical lofted apartment, the place was old. What someone else might have labeled antique with its wooden floors and the trapped scent of dozens of lives, many of them decades past.

It had a large living room with a couch, coffee table, TV, and bookshelves, and a kitchen separated by a breakfast bar and lush, padded stools. Thick tapestries in rich shades of burgundy and tourmaline and gold lined the walls. The stairs lead up one level to the open bedroom fitted with a queen-sized bed. Pillows of various sizes covered one side of the bed, none of them matching, inviting a solitary sleep, not the embrace of two or more lovers. Flowering tiger lilies sat on the bedside table. They exhaled a delicate perfume that trailed through the entire apartment. Everything was in shadow.

The woman sleeping next to the island of pillows was thin; her body made only the slightest rise beneath the deep orange sheets. Her hair was very short, cut in shining, black coils that framed an interesting rather than pretty face. Redwood skin, high forehead, wide nose. A plump mouth that Kylie imagined might have been used very often for kissing. She looked no older than thirty-five.

There was a sadness in the room that pulsed against Kylie's skin. She hissed a silent breath of surprise. Pain like this she understood. Everyone else Kylie had ever known seemed to bury their pain in pretty boxes, putting them under beds or displaying them as antique trinkets on bookshelves. But not this woman. She wore it as plainly as her face.

Kylie wanted to pull her awake. To tug on the flesh of her face to see if it was real, this pain of hers. But she did not. Instead, she sat hidden in the bedroom until the woman's sleep was assured, then she walked through the entire apartment, touching the woman's things, feeling out this stranger with her naked suffering. The woman smelled fragile, of hot female things as well as her delicious sorrow.

Kylie was sated, her body full of blood and nearly warm from her early evening feeding on two deliciously naïve tourists. Their blood pulsed through her body, a warm comfort like the fresh mint tea of her human childhood. She felt her tamed hunger lying content on its belly and tucked away in a darkened corner. Walking through the strange woman's bedroom with its tempting smell, she was grateful for her hunger's rest.

Despite the flash fire of sunrise beyond the windows, Kylie wasn't tired. She wanted to further explore the woman's apartment, explore the woman herself who exuded such a seduction of feeling. But she knew if she stayed awake, her impulsive nature would lead her to do terrible things. So she forced herself to find rest.

She burrowed inside the woman's surprisingly large hall closet, finding a space behind a curtain of dresses, thick sweaters, and coats put away for the season. Kylie padded the floor with the thick winter blankets she found and pulled some over her to find some semblance of warmth.

At rest in the padded darkness, her skin felt uneasy. Cold and itching from the need to be pressed against other skin, another symptom of the sickness her maker had left her with. She needed to sleep with other vampires, needed their warmth while she slept in order to rest through the day.

But because she had no choice, she did without.

CHAPTER TWO

At sundown, when the woman left the apartment, Kylie walked out of her closet. The small space was even quieter than before. It was an odd absence of human sound, simply the electrical drone of the refrigerator, a persistent drip from the toilet, and the hum of traffic beyond the closed doors of the balcony. Already, she missed the woman's soft breaths.

The balcony was open, with only the screen door pulled to allow in the cool fall breeze and the cacophony of scents from the still-bustling neighborhood. Fresh coffee. Pizza. Hot grease from a nearby fast food restaurant. Spilled beer on the streets. Piss. Vomit. Spilled semen.

Kylie looked around the room and drew in a deep breath. She drew in the sad scent of the woman that was in its own way more seductive than any perfume, human or vampire. Without stopping to reconsider her actions, she unzipped the ruby necklace from its hidden pocket in her dress and hid it in the closet, slipped it into the floral shoebox snuggled against the quilt on the top shelf.

Kylie carefully left the woman's apartment and slid down the building wall that faced the street then she slipped quickly into the alley. Her feet hit the ground, the practical ballet flats connecting with a delicate tap. She straightened, ready to head for the airport, call a taxi, and leave this place that had attracted her simply because of the necklace in the museum. She looked up, seeing the jutting side view of the sixth floor balcony she'd just left. She thought of the ruby necklace she'd hidden.

Go. Her common sense told her. Go to the airport and go home. Sleep in your bed. Rest with your family. But the woman's scent haunted her, made her pause in the alley. What was it that made her so unhappy? Like Kylie, did she have a mother at the root of her sadness? At the thought of Belle, she took a calming breath.

And decided to stay.

The whys of it echoed in her mind as she slipped from the alley and onto the main street, joining the flow of pedestrians fresh from work and off to their first drink of the night. Kylie felt almost human walking across the main street, Moreland Avenue, next to a pale girl with a Mohawk who strolled arm-in-arm with her bald and pierced girlfriend. A man with dreadlocks and a guitar strapped to his back crossed the street in the other direction and gave Kylie a considering look. He threw a faintly interested leer at her slim body in its party dress, at her wild hair she had fluffed after rising from her pallet on the closet floor. She glanced back at him then away, feeling the usual disinterest when someone looked at her sexually.

She crossed to the other side of the street where a small café sat just on the corner. The scent of strong coffee and chocolate cake greeted her at the door. A woman walked from the café with a glass of mango juice. She set the juice down at one of the three wrought iron tables that were already occupied.

Kylie sat at the last empty table.

"Hi there." The woman who had brought the juice greeted her with a smile and eyes that flickered over her with curiosity. "Can I get you something, honey?"

The woman was of average height with glistening ocher skin and wide, interested eyes. A lion's mane of natural hair bloomed around her face. She smelled like coffee and fresh baked bread, with a hint of the female musk between her thighs. Kylie's canines tingled. She licked them and tamped down the mild hunger.

"A small coffee, please."

"Of course, honey. Just you wait there one tiny minute." The woman disappeared into the shop and reappeared a few minutes later with Kylie's drink. She put a five-dollar bill in the woman's hand before she could walk away.

"You can pay later, darlin'. You might want something else."

"It's okay," Kylie said, refusing the money the woman tried to give back to her.

After the woman went away, she settled back into the hard iron chair with her hot coffee. She didn't touch the drink. As a human girl, she hadn't felt one way or another about coffee, mainly drinking tea at home. But she discovered that once she had been transformed from girl to beast, the smell of coffee, rich and dark and full bodied, was a comfort to her.

No one bothered her. She sat and watched the evening pass by, ignoring the twitching need inside her to rush back to home's very necessary comforts. She hadn't slept all day, and her body felt the lack. But Kylie was more interested in the sad human woman than in her body's discomforts.

Evening blanketed the street, the corner, the neighborhood where she sat. The coffee on her table grew cold, but the scent did not diminish. And all the while, she watched the street for a sight of the woman. Her stranger.

It wasn't long before she saw her, barely three hours later. A slender woman with low-cut natural hair and an air of fragility about her. She wore sandals, a long multicolored skirt, and a thin white blouse under a red, bolero style jacket. The woman carried a cloth shopping bag over a slender shoulder. Kylie deliberately sniffed. She'd bought strawberries, spinach, a grapefruit, and bundles of asparagus.

The woman looked all around her as she walked, her head moving like a periscope, taking in everything from the cloud-strewn sky to the bums on the streets, the dreadlocked musician playing on the corner for money, maybe even Kylie herself from her café perch. But even as the woman watched everything around her, her steps remained purposeful and sure. She took the keys from her skirt pocket and opened the outer door to her building, then stepped inside. She kept walking into the vestibule, leaving the door to fall shut behind her.

Kylie listened to her progress through the building.

Her heartbeat was strong and sure, a strange counterpoint to her frail looking body. Her breathing accelerated slightly as she walked up the stairs, heart thumping at a faster rate. Her palm rasped against the banister while her skirt brushed the ground with each step.

She could hear the woman at her apartment door now, keys jingling. She pushed her door open then closed with a weak squeaking of its hinges. A vague tingling between her shoulder blades drew Kylie's attention away from the woman.

Someone was watching her. She blinked. Her posture remained perfectly relaxed, but every movement ceased as she took in the sounds, smells, and sights in her immediate field of vision and periphery. She could feel unfamiliar eyes on her, and the tingling between her shoulder blades getting worse.

But Kylie kept her eyes on the woman's door, one hand relaxed near her cold coffee, the other lying on her thigh. She only smelled humans. None of the vampire kind were close enough for her to smell. Did that mean it was a human watching her? The thought relaxed her. She released a breath and flexed the hand on her thigh. It was only a human. She shrugged off the unease like a dirty cloak.

If there was anything Silvija and Belle had taught her since being with the clan, it was confidence in the strength of her own body. She felt nearly invincible at times. Not always against other vampires but definitely in comparison to a human. A human who would find it just about impossible to harm her.

This feeling of invincibility was something that Silvija had often warned her against. And this was a caution Kylie ignored. What could a human do to her? She flicked her fingers in the air, dismissing the danger. Kylie looked up at the woman's window. The echoes of a light glowed from behind her curtains. Beyond her sight, the woman moved about the apartment in the midst of her evening rituals that Kylie longed to see.

Her phone rang, a quiet sound that Violet, the tech wizard in the clan, told her was inaudible to human ears. Kylie answered the call.

"Hello, Mother."

For a moment, there was only silence on the other end of the line. A reprimanding lack of sound.

"Kylie, we were expecting you home last morning." Her mother's voice was low and tight. Worry with a trace of anger.

"I'm okay, Mother. I wasn't able to make it back before morning. I found somewhere to lay low for the day."

"And someone?"

The tone made Kylie bristle. Her mother always wanted to know if she had slept with anyone, either human or vampire. "No. No one." It was none of her business. Just because her mother was having regular sex that made her forget about everything and everyone else didn't mean Kylie needed to do the same.

"You must be exhausted then. Come home. I don't know where you are, but it's not good for you to be so far from us."

"I'm fine, Mother. There's no need for you to worry." If worry was even what Belle was feeling about Kylie's disappearance. Since being joined with her mother and her new family, Kylie thought it was more a matter of ownership, Belle wanting the world to know she had a daughter and her daughter was here with her among the clan. This creature that was twice of her blood.

"I do worry, Kylie. Come home."

Kylie waited a beat before replying, toying with the idea of staying away even longer. "Okay. I'll be there before bedtime."

Her mother released a breath. "Good. See you soon."

When Kylie hung up the phone, she had no intention of doing what her mother suggested. But, against her will, she remembered the unpleasantness of the long morning in the closet, unable to sleep all day, the heaviness in her body, and the dimmed reflexes that came from not getting enough rest.

She'd already spent a restless last few nights at home, chafing in the confines of the Manhattan penthouse once she'd decided she would try for the ruby and diamond necklace on display in the Atlanta museum. A necklace once worn by a long dead Russian czarina.

It had been beautiful on the television. In person, it was even more so, a chain of rubies, each four carats, each surrounded by a ring of small diamonds and linked by four-petaled diamond flowers. It was something Kylie would never consider wearing, but the challenge of taking it had pulled her from her boredom, distracted her from the resentment and anger that seemed to always live in her chest. Then she had done it. Child's play.

But with one call, her mother had pulled her mind back to the anger and unease. And as much as she didn't want to go back to them just yet, she knew she had to. She narrowed her eyes to peer through the woman's curtains. But she was still out of sight. Kylie turned away from the woman and got up from the table. Between her shoulders prickled again, but she shrugged off the eyes.

Fuck off.

She looked around her on the street, daring any of the humans to make a move against her. She would tear their hearts out and drain the useless organs dry. Scowling, Kylie slid a dollar under her coffee cup and started to walk.

Chapter Three

Kylie opened the door to the clan's stronghold with her key, typed in the alphanumeric code, and waited a few seconds while the security system verified her identity with a voice scan.

Their security was tight. Not just because the clan leader was paranoid, but because almost eight years ago, most of the vampires had been wiped out and the house where they lived completely destroyed. The security breach had been an internal one, someone they all trusted, so Silvija had created fail-safes throughout the entire structure of their new home, continuous scans and secret contingencies that ensured no single clan member had the power to open up the stronghold to danger.

"Welcome, Kylie," chimed the security system's feminine, electronic voice.

The door clicked open with a heavy, unlatching noise, like a bank vault. Beyond the thick, modern-looking door was another door. This one made of mirrored glass. She typed in another code. The glass lifted, finally allowing her access into the nineteen-room penthouse apartment that housed the clan.

The house was massive. A three-level penthouse in the skies of Manhattan with ten bedrooms, windows in every room except the bathrooms, and a large gathering space at its center where clan members could rest their eyes from the world. All the windows were three inches of reinforced, bulletproof mirrored glass that went from clear to black at the touch of a button or the right verbal command.

From the outside, the house looked like a white and glass cube perched on top of yet another high-rise in the city. Terraces surrounded each level. An observatory, helicopter pad, and sparring deck were on the roof, and there was an outdoor pool on the second floor. The offices—Silvija's and the security room with their weapons and live feed on the security monitors—were on the highest floor.

Home sweet home.

She didn't make it very far down the long, wide hallway before she heard the sound of footsteps hurrying in her direction. She linked her hands behind her back, striving for nonchalance while she simultaneously hoped and did not hope it was her mother. Breath left her throat when Belle rounded the corner.

"Kylie."

Her mother was beautiful. One of the most beautiful women Kylie had ever known. She had a long neck, tilted cat eyes, and a full mouth made for scowling rather than smiles. A strong beauty. As a child, Kylie remembered feeling almost blessed when her mother, sullen and gorgeous, smiled just for her. Belle was taller than most of the women in their small Jamaican district and even most of the vampires in their clan. Except Silvija, of course. Her slim, willowy body was on display in simple blue jeans and a yellow blouse that looked like sunlight against her dark skin. Her kitten-heeled shoes tapped against the tiles with each step. Today, she wore her hair in small, tight braids in a snaking pattern on her elegant head.

Despite the emotional distance between them, Kylie felt a spurt of gladness. A remnant of the years of being without her, when Belle was living as a vampire a world away and Kylie was growing up without a mother. Twelve years of her absence.

"Mother." Kylie gave her mother the smile she thought Belle wanted.

She wasn't prepared for the hug, the arms that swept around her and pulled her against a body smelling like the Caribbean Sea. Of home.

"I was worried," Belle said. "We all were." Her voice was low and tender, her Jamaican accent still thick and warm.

Kylie looked behind her mother, knowing, before her eyes confirmed it, that there were no others rushing out to meet her after her night and day's absence from New York. Kylie smiled, a tight stretching of her lips. "I'm all right. Nothing is going to happen to me."

Belle pulled back, looking down into Kylie's face. She touched her cheek, stroking the tender skin under Kylie's eyes with a thumb. "Sometimes I think you want me to worry for you."

Kylie gave her that smile again. "Never."

"Where were you? It shouldn't have taken you so long to come here from New Jersey." Her mother watched her, a light of curiosity in her eyes. No suspicion, merely waiting for her question to be answered.

"I just lost track of time, that's all." She pulled back from her mother's embrace and started down the hallway. Her mother fell in step beside her.

Without speaking, they walked together to the main gathering room, a type of family room that had all the particular comforts of the eight vampires who shared the penthouse: Silvija, Belle, Julia, Ivy, Violet, Liam, Rufus, and Kylie.

In the middle of the large room, Kylie's chair hammock was suspended by bolts from the ceiling. One quarter of the floor space was covered in Julia's bearskin rugs, overlapping white and brown bear pelts from animals the small vampire had killed with her bare hands and fangs.

One wall was nothing but bookshelves and, built into the actual shelves, two seating spaces facing each other, especially created for Violet and her twin, Liam. Rufus's seventy-inch flat screen TV took up space on the high wall above a scattering of half a dozen armchairs. In a large corner of the room sat a platform bed, neatly made and with a chessboard sitting on a wooden tray in its center. Silvija and Belle's never-ending game.

Belle sat on the bed and Kylie sank to the floor at her feet, deliberately not sitting in the space her mother shared with her lover. The tiles were warm through her dress. She pressed her palms to the floor on either side of her thighs, reminded of the small closet where she had spent the previous day. The scent of sadness. The shoebox that smelled like dried flowers. A delicate feminine shape under the sheets.

"I hope you're being careful when you lose track of time," her mother said. "Please. I don't want anything bad to happen to you." Her voice was low and soft, her eyes wandering over Kylie's face with love.

Kylie allowed herself to bask in its warmth. She bit the inside of her lip, a childhood habit of distress she never got over. She was suddenly overwhelmed by the urge to throw herself in her mother's lap and confess everything that happened in the last few hours. "You shouldn't worry, Mother. I'm fine. I always am."

Her mother leaned back into the headboard, slipped off her shoes, and curled her knees up in the bed. "I'll always worry for you, Kylie. You're my baby. That will never change, no matter how strong you get, or how old."

Her eyes were warm and luminous in the artificial lights in the room, and for a moment, Kylie felt like the center of her mother's world with Belle's attentions firmly fixed on her.

She smiled. "I—"

Silvija's aggressive scent invaded the room seconds before she appeared in the doorway. "Belle, they're having Shakespeare in the park tomorrow night. You should come with me." Her mother's lover looked at Kylie with a slight smile. "Ah, Kylie. I'm glad you made it back. Your mother was getting gray hairs over you." She slipped gracefully into the room, effortlessly powerful in her bare feet, loose jeans, and a V-neck T-shirt.

Kylie touched her mother's knee, already withdrawing with the presence of the clan leader. "I think she's fine now."

Silvija sank down into the bed beside Belle and pressed a kiss to the crown of her head before draping her long body across the large surface. Kylie felt out of place, as if she were no longer needed. She got to her feet.

"I'll see you later."

"You don't have to go anywhere," Silvija said.

"I know, but I need a shower. It's been a long night and day." Without waiting for either of them to reply, she left the room.

Halfway to her room at the upper level of the penthouse, she paused, wondering if she was overreacting. Even after seven years of living with the clan and with her mother, she had never adapted to the situation with her and Silvija. The two were lovers. They were married. They loved each other in a way that Kylie couldn't even begin to imagine. But knowing that and letting go of her jealousy were two separate things.

Her mother was with another woman. That was disorienting enough after everything she'd learned about love and relationships in Jamaica. But worse than that, her mother only seemed to have time for her wife, and none for her own daughter. Kylie bit her lip, then turned to go back to her mother, to apologize and try to be part of the family everyone else seemed to be happy to share.

The door was open, just like she left it, but Silvija and her mother were closer now. Belle sat in front of Silvija with her head bowed, a hint of a smile on her face while Silvija loomed behind her, hands on Belle's arm, her mouth near Belle's ear. She spoke softly, but Kylie heard every word.

"I'm going to peel off your outer layers, slowly." Silvija's voice came in an intent growl. "And feast on you until there's nothing left but the juice on my chin."

Kylie froze in the doorway, unable to look away from them. Belle laughed, but the sound quavered, like a violin under the first stroke of the bow. "I didn't know you were a cannibal too," Belle murmured as Kylie forced herself to turn and jerkily walk away.

Her face was cold with embarrassment. After all these years, their intimacy still bothered her, still disturbed any amount of peace she'd gained while being with the clan. She consciously lost Silvija's response in the quick tap of her feet against the tile. Sometimes their happiness was just too much to bear.

Kylie turned blindly down the hallway heading toward her room. Senses scrambled, she didn't realize there was someone else there until it was too late. Too late to avoid the crashing of bodies, hands on her arms steadying her. Ivy.

"Hey! Where are you running off to?"

The tall soldier, Kylie had never known her as anything else, steadied her with rough hands. Her always roving eyes moved over Kylie's face, throat, and body, seeking information and cataloguing it. Cataloguing *her*.

Ivy's slightly tilted almond eyes, a reminder of Asia, dark in her butter brown face, warmed slightly as they assessed Kylie. It should have made her uncomfortable, but strangely, it didn't. Her coolness was neither friendly nor off-putting. It kept Kylie not precisely at arm's length but at a distance comfortable enough for Ivy to see her while not allowing them to touch in any real way. It was safety and Kylie understood that.

Ivy's brother had been killed in the clan war, and rumor was that she'd never been the same since. She worked hard, never played, never smiled; everything she had or was she kept in service to Silvija and the well-being of the clan. She didn't wear her loss on her face, but Kylie felt it nonetheless.

She drew back from Ivy's grasp the same time Ivy released her.

"I'm not running anywhere," she said.

Just then, Kylie realized that Ivy was dressed for a workout. She'd pulled her long black hair in a single braid down her back. A loose gray shirt and pants covered her slim and muscular frame. Her feet were bare.

Ivy raised an eyebrow. "In that case, you should come upstairs with me. It's been a while since we've sparred."

After the day she'd had, Kylie didn't think that would be a bad idea at all. "Give me a couple of minutes," she said.

Kylie dashed to her room to change while Ivy continued on to the roof. Within fifteen minutes, she had joined the others on the roof, dressed in her own sparring clothes—black yoga pants and matching tank top. She pulled her hair back in a thick braid at the back of her head.

The entire rooftop, broken up into three spaces—the helipad, observatory, and terrace—was theirs. The wide expanse of the terrace was carpeted in artificial grass and bordered by lush climbing vines that needed nothing to thrive under the New York sky. It was fall, but the flowers were still green and thick, cradling a few pale blossoms that perfumed the night air. The long iron benches had already been shoved aside to the edges of the roof to make room for them.

"The prodigal returns," Violet teased her.

Her bald head gleamed under the moonlight, her beautifully round body a deadly distraction in the black leotard.

"Glad you made it back home in one piece," Rufus said. Their resident rock star.

He was usually away on tour or in the studio recording his latest album. It was rare for him to be home, and Kylie enjoyed his presence precisely because it was such an uncommon thing.

He gave her an understanding look that nearly undid her. Out of everyone in the house, he had always seemed to see her for what she was, not what they wanted her to be. He was never judgmental, only sat and waited to see if she wanted to unburden herself. Most times, she did not, and he didn't seem to mind.

He was dressed in an outfit similar to Ivy's, loose and all gray, the material flowing gracefully over his slender but powerful body. His long dreadlocks were pulled back from his face into a tight bun.

Rufus, Violet, and Liam had all been assumed dead after the explosive destruction of the clan's old home, but the three resourceful beasts had kept themselves safe then found their way back to Silvija not long after Kylie was turned. Kylie was glad. She couldn't imagine her existence without them.

"Ready?" Ivy asked.

Rufus threw a punch at her in answer.

It was a dance they all knew well. Punch and duck and lunge and parry. A fist to the rib or face if you were slacking. Kicks connecting solidly against a shoulder, a thigh. Grunts of pain, triumph.

Silvija demanded that everyone in the clan have sparring sessions at least once every week. There were no set pairings. They all fought each other on their testing ground, and fought full-out, not pulling punches or kicks, to make sure they would be ready in case an enemy came for them.

It had been hard for Kylie at first, raised in a home of peace and Bible study, where a charming smile was the only thing needed to conquer a bully's fist. But there was no room for passive resistance among the beasts. She learned quickly enough to kick as hard as the rest of them, to bounce back from a vicious hit, to ignore the splash of her own blood and jump back in to give as hard as she got.

She threw herself into it now, hammering her fist into a careless Rufus, ducking low when he tried to regroup and slam an elbow into her face. Kylie laughed.

"You're going to have to do better than that, old man!"

Rufus was quick. He tapped her kidneys before she could dance away again. Kylie grunted, the pain sharp and immediate, then clenched her teeth hard. She twisted away to slam a roundhouse kick to his chest. He staggered backward a few steps, then grinned savagely.

"Nice!"

Kylie played with them for another hour or so, the time slipping easily through her fingers, her body sustaining blows then immediately regrouping. But all too soon, the initial euphoria and distraction soon drained away until she felt too large for her own body, the energy snapping under her skin, unused. She stopped and caught a fist to the temple. She winced and danced back, shaking away the pain and the brief flare of stars behind her eyes.

"I'm done," she said, holding up her hands in surrender.

"We're just getting started!" Violet bounced on the balls of her feet, her hands clenched into fists, her sneakers slapped hollowly against the padded floor.

"I know, but—" Kylie shook her head, unable to express the feeling of restlessness, of wanting more, stirring in her.

She'd felt it when she walked in on her mother and Silvija in the living room. It had seemed to disappear once she started sparring, but as the initial adrenaline rush wore off, the feeling returned. She was distracted and twitchy once again.

"I have to go," she said.

She turned and left them, opening the door to the cool darkness of the penthouse. Opaque glass walls. Thick blond brick. The hum of the technology keeping them secure.

Kylie gripped the banister to the curving chrome staircase that led down to the topmost floor and the piano, white tiled floors, and tall windows letting in a glittering view of New York by night. The aches and pains from her sparring session were already fading away as if they had never been. She leapt the last few steps, her bare feet thumping against the cool tile.

Clicking footsteps sounded from nearby. The smell of hothouse flowers. Then Julia appeared from one of the rooms down the wide hallway. The vampire who had turned her mother was slender and beautiful with her bald head and midnight skin. Tonight, she looked particularly elegant and available in a clinging, off the shoulder black dress. A large gardenia lay perched over one ear and deep purple lipstick emphasized her full mouth.

Her gaze over Kylie was both predatory and wary. "You look ready to fuck something," she said.

Kylie jerked back from her, disgusted. Her hands curled at her sides, and she thought of the supreme satisfaction that would come from slamming Julia against the wall. The thick sound her body would make as it hit the pale brick. Her flower falling from behind her ear, the petals separating and scattering under Kylie's feet. She took another step back. Julia's smile widened.

"I'd offer to pluck your little flower for you, but your mother would probably kill me. For real this time." Her eyes raked Kylie again. Then she tucked her purse under her arm, blew Kylie a kiss, and kept walking past, heading downstairs, probably on her way to a party.

Kylie froze in her wake, listening to the disappearing sound of her heels on the tiles.

You look ready to fuck something. Julia's words echoed in her head.

No! She didn't want that. She never wanted to surrender herself so completely to another person, to such an animal act, the way her mother had. It was a surrender that seemed to obliterate all care or thought for anyone else except the lover.

She spun away from Julia's phantom presence and headed to her room. Even though she'd been sweating before from her sparring session, it was only now after seeing Julia that she felt dirty.

Kylie took a long shower, lingering under the hot spray until the large bathroom swirled white from steam. After she was dry and dressed, she sat on her bed to ponder the conundrum of the Atlanta woman.

She was away from the woman, but might as well have brought her back to New York the way she occupied her mind. Kylie worried her lip between her teeth, trying to decide what to do. She hadn't made it very far in her mental ramblings when an odd sound came to her.

Moaning.

An odd mix of pleasure and pain, arousal and fear. Before she could second-guess herself, she left her room and walked toward the noise, glad for the distraction from her own thoughts.

The noises took her farther down the hallway and down the stairs to the second floor of the penthouse. She heard a heavy slap and a muffled shout of pain, soft whispers. Abruptly, she realized it was just sex play. But the odd nature of it—the tortured sounds, an unusual smell (of gasoline?) she caught on the air—made her curious.

She found the source of the noises in Ivy's bedroom.

Julia, Violet, and Ivy. They were in the center of the large room, naked and playing with fire.

Ivy was tied and gagged, her long body bent over at the waist on a thick wooden table. She lay on her belly, her arms stretched wide and handcuffed to opposite corners of the table. Her spread legs bared a smoothly shaved pussy dripping thick juices down her thighs. Someone had twisted her long hair into a tight bun.

Julia viciously spanked Ivy's ass and grinned as the soft flesh rippled from the blow. This must have been the party she had been rushing off to. She still wore the white gardenia over her ear, but she'd stripped off the elegant dress in favor of a white dildo strapped to her hips with a matching leather harness. She spanked Ivy's ass again, then squeezed the taut flesh.

Violet, standing near Ivy's shoulder, held up a long match. A flame bloomed from it, bright and deadly in the large room. She touched it to the glistening flesh of Ivy's back, and blue flame rushed in a line over the brown skin. Violet waited precious seconds before killing the flame with a single sweep of her hand.

They were playing in front of the large mirror that stood on the wall across from the bed. The mirror reflected back the three of them at their play. Only Ivy watched in the mirror, her eyes wide as she stared at what Violet was doing to her.

"You like what you see?" Violet asked Ivy before she lowered the match again.

Ivy whimpered behind the gag. Beads of sweat dotted her face and strands of hair clung to her forehead. Her body, coated in what smelled like white gas, glistened in the light from the room's dim lanterns.

Ivy's upturned ass faced Kylie, so did the mirror. She could see everything. The warrior's damp face, wet pussy, the tight flex and release of her leg and calf muscles when the flames sank too deeply into her flesh. Ivy's legendary control was gone, given up to the service of pleasure and the peaceful oblivion of mindless physical submission and release.

Although it wasn't Kylie's first time watching other vampires have sex, it never ceased to amaze her how rough they were with each other, how they seemed to hurt each other, hurt themselves, and love it.

Ivy moaned around the gag. Tears splashed down her cheeks, but her expression was one of fear and bliss, a strange ecstasy. Her flesh looked like that of a phoenix as the fire jumped onto it and slithered over her flank before disappearing under Violet's quick hand. But Ivy did not try to get away. She only stared in the mirror at what the other two were doing to her, her tears flowing, pussy dripping.

Julia, with her thick white phallus bobbing from her hips, came close to the table on the opposite side from where Violet was doing her wicked work. Moaning, she dipped her fingers into Ivy's pussy from behind and stroked her cock with the other hand.

"You're so wet for us, baby," she murmured in her low and carrying voice.

From outside the room, Kylie watched in dread and amazement. Fire alone couldn't kill a vampire, but burns took the longest to heal and were some of the most painful injuries Kylie had ever experienced. She must have made a noise because Julia's head jerked toward her.

Julia grinned and continued her slow stroke of Ivy's pussy, latching her eyes to Kylie's, her lips parted at the wet sound of her fingers plunging deep inside Ivy's juicy cunt, then retreating. She gripped a muscular ass cheek, and raked her long nails across the flesh until the smell of blood exploded in the room. Kylie's teeth pulsed dimly in her mouth.

Still watching Kylie, Julia stroked Ivy's clit and Ivy moaned behind the gag, jerking her slick brown body in reaction to whatever Julia was doing to her. Violet set her lower back on fire again then swept her hand across the swirling pattern of blue flame and extinguished it. She looked fiendishly happy and aroused, her eyes brighter than the lights in the room.

She moved as fast as lightning, touching flame to several different parts of Ivy's body, watching them swirl, blue and deadly, over the glowing flesh before putting them out.

Julia broke her stare with Kylie to step behind Ivy. She parted the slick and swollen lips with one hand, while holding the bone white cock with the other. Slowly, she slid the cock into Ivy's pussy. Ivy moaned, shoving her hips back for more.

"Such a pretty pussy," Julia murmured.

Then she started to fuck Ivy. Slowly. The shaft of the dildo emerged from the tight pussy, slick with Ivy's juices. Then she fucked her faster, slamming her into the table with the force of a jackhammer while Violet twirled blue flames all over Ivy's shoulders and back.

It was like a dream, or a nightmare, of fire and sex. The smell of arousal and impending satisfaction floated in the room along with the scent of gasoline, tears, and blood. Julia grunted as she fucked Ivy into ecstasy. The sounds of their passion grew louder in the room, the slam of the table against the floor, flesh against flesh, moans and grunts.

Abruptly, Violet extinguished the flame on her match, yanked the gag out of Ivy's mouth, and leapt on top of the long table with her thighs spread. She shoved her pussy into Ivy's mouth, her eyes rolling up into her head as Ivy latched on to her clit and began to suck.

Kylie stepped back from the doorway, swallowing heavily, and turned around to go back to her own room. Their love play was hard, so rough. Was that the only thing out there for her now that she was one of them?

The question plagued her all the way to her room.

Chapter Four

Hours later, Kylie lay in her bed still listening to the sounds of fucking; the lust in the penthouse never seemed to end.

She could tell who it was by the sound of their breath, by the scents coming at her through the house. In the bedroom one floor and not enough walls away, Rufus and Liam took each other. They were loud and vicious. There were sounds of flesh hitting the wall, gasps, the smell of blood, a hoarse scream from Liam. From farther down the hall she could smell Silvija and her mother, but she quickly turned her attention away from them and their always amorous tendencies. Any room with the two of them had the potential to become uncomfortable simply because of the way they were with each other—tender and hard at once, lovers who loved and loved passionately.

Kylie curled up in her bed while the lights of Manhattan—its office buildings, the searchlight from a passing chopper, other apartments in the sky—blazed at her through the windows. She loved that no one could see her while she lay in her big bed and watched. About a mile away, a couple in an equally tall building insisted on making love with the windows open. So even when Kylie was trying to avoid the concupiscence in her own house, she was faced with an anonymous version of it just outside her window.

To the discordant music of Liam and Rufus's vicious passion, she watched the tamer human couple. The woman, pale and slender on all fours in the black satin sheets. Behind her, her lover yanked her long black hair back, baring her slender neck as he wrapped the hair slowly around his fists, pulling her head farther and farther back. Kylie could practically smell the woman's excitement.

Her male lover's arousal was easy enough to see. His thick penis thrust into the air as he reached between her legs and prepared her with his hand. Kylie watched them, trying to feel something other than a vague curiosity about what the woman's cleft felt like, if she were truly enjoying herself or just pretending. Minutes later, she pressed the remote on her bedside table to darken the window and pull the thick curtains over the glass.

She'd never had sex with anyone, but nothing that she saw around her made her want to change that. She knew that her mother and Silvija enjoyed each other. Everyone in the house did. Their rituals of blood and sex were practically a prerequisite to starting the night. But she was cold to it all. She watched humans sometimes, even felt a vague agitation under her skin, but there was no one she'd ever seen who made her want to get down into the filth with, get wet and growl and become truly beastly to reach a mutual sexual goal.

Her bedroom door opened behind her, and she smelled Liam, freshly showered. She didn't have to look over her shoulder to see that he wore his robe, long black silk that held the scent of his recent shower and his own skin. He touched Kylie lightly on the shoulder and slid into the bed in front of her, making himself the littlest spoon. He relaxed against the sheets with a sigh. A few minutes later, Violet came in. She too smelled of the shower with no hint at all of what she'd been doing with Ivy and Julia. She slid behind Kylie, the biggest spoon, resting her cheek against the bent curve of Kylie's back.

She felt her own body relax, already anticipating the sweet oblivion of sleep.

"Little Kylie." Violet squeezed her tightly. "It's good to have you back. You know worry isn't good for my complexion." She giggled, always the playful one.

Kylie smiled and squeezed the hands around her stomach. "I'd never want to mess up that gorgeous face."

Violet and Liam, twins who looked nothing alike but shared the same childlike spirit, never came to her smelling of sex. And she was grateful for that more than they would ever know. They knew she didn't want sex or any flirtation; they had understood Kylie instantly all those years ago when the question of sleeping arrangements came up.

With them, she was able to fulfill her basic need to be cradled against other vampiric flesh while she slept, without worry of being taken advantage of during the day. She didn't know what she had done to receive such kindness from them, but she was grateful.

"It's a good thing this gorgeous face of mine is forever," Violet said in reply to Kylie's earlier comment.

"Quiet time," Liam mumbled in his near-sleep and reached back to pinch his sister.

Violet flinched and snapped her teeth at him. "Watch it, boy."

Kylie smiled and settled down even more between the twins. Soon, she dreamed.

CHAPTER FIVE

I'm going to be gone for a while." Kylie said the words softly so as not to disturb Silvija who was still sleeping—or at least pretending to—on the other side of the large bed she shared with Belle.

The room smelled of their recent lovemaking, but Kylie ignored that. What she had to say to her mother was more important than any discomfort she had with their intimacy.

Belle sat up in the bed, holding the sheet against her bare breasts. "Why?" She lightly touched Kylie's hand resting on the bed between them. "Have you been so unhappy here?"

Kylie avoided looking at her mother. The question challenged her to tell the truth, to rediscover that brief connection they'd had the previous evening before Silvija interrupted them. Kylie shook her head.

"It has not been easy," she said finally.

Her mother looked stricken. Then her face smoothed itself out. "You know I never wanted this for you." The words left her mouth in a whisper.

Instantly, they were both transported back to that evening in Jamaica when Kylie had come sliding down the hill. She remembered clearly the first surging rush of blood in her veins. How she had felt both hot and cold at the same time. Invincible and vulnerable, needing her mama with a fierceness that had stolen every rational thought from her head. She had killed her own grandmother to get to Belle.

Kylie blinked. She still needed her mama.

But during the separation when Belle had been taken by the vampires and Kylie was left with her grandmother, they had lost the easy connection they had with each other. Every conversation was a struggle, every suggestion from Belle was a chance for Kylie to rebel, every glance of Belle and Silvija's happiness just reinforced how she had none of her own.

Kylie swallowed past the painful lump in her throat. Then she pulled back instead of going closer, tugging her fingers back from beneath Belle's.

"It doesn't matter," Kylie said. "I'm here now."

"Yes, but for how long?" A tight smile touched her mother's lips when Kylie didn't respond. "Can you at least tell me why you're leaving?" Regret and sadness colored her voice.

Kylie bit her lip, still unable to say a word.

"Okay. Be careful." Belle caressed the lushness of Kylie's hair, tugging at the coils near her ear then releasing them. "If you need anything, please call me."

Nodding, Kylie reached out, a spastic movement of her fingers, and touched her mother's bare forearm. "I'll be back soon."

❖

Kylie arrived in the woman's Atlanta neighborhood in the late evening. Ten o'clock, Monday night. There was a light crowd on the streets in soft disarray from the remnants of the work day. Happy-hour-wasted executives and long-skirted assistants spilled from the bars and headed for home. Hard rock music thudded from a nearby bar.

Kylie paid the driver and got out of the yellow cab then stepped back from the curb right in front of the woman's apartment. She adjusted the backpack on her shoulder to straighten her thin T-shirt belted into loose-fitting jeans. She tugged the light fall jacket closed over her breasts.

It was a jacket she did not need. But long ago, Silvija and others in the clan advised her to be mindful of what humans were wearing and mimic them. Jackets for the cold, short sleeves for the hot. Vampires didn't feel the extreme heat or cold so had to rely on watching their surroundings and the humans in it for cues on what to wear and how to act in certain situations.

There was a light on in the woman's apartment, the chirp of conversation from a television show. It sounded like the woman was walking around the apartment, wearing the same path in the hardwood floor, instead of paying attention to the television.

Something in Kylie beat faster at the thought of seeing the woman again. Although it seemed ridiculous now that she had made such a long journey simply to see a human she'd never spoken to, she trembled with eagerness.

Kylie didn't wait for traffic to subside before stepping into the street to cross to the other side. Cars honked. A couple holding hands on the street corner gave her a curious glance before quickly looking away.

She crossed the street to the woman's apartment and glanced over her shoulder before leaping up and scrambling up the dark face of the building to the sixth floor balcony. The woman was inside. She could hear her quiet breathing, smell that delicious fragile sadness of hers.

On the balcony, Kylie slipped her backpack over both shoulders and leaned against the railing, looking down over the street as if she belonged there. No one had seen her quick climb to the balcony. She didn't quite move faster than the human eye could detect, but she knew her speed would trick them into thinking they were seeing things. From her own experience before she had been turned, she knew the trick well enough. One moment, a creature was in one place, and the next, it was in another.

Even after seven years, she was still not able to think of herself quite in those terms. The first time she saw one of them, the fear nearly ran down her leg in a scalding shower. Her mother. She had beat Julia bloody, slamming her body into a tree until Kylie thought for sure Julia, whom she had initially thought was creepy and a little forward, was dead. But even as Julia trembled and bled from Belle's abuse, a light flashed in her eyes, like she was enjoying the blood gushing from her body nearly as much as Belle was.

"What are you?" Kylie remembered crying out, heart racing in her chest as she stared at the mother she hadn't seen in over thirteen years.

Belle, cold and blood-splattered, only said, "I am nobody you know."

Kylie had no idea that later she would be one of them. Vicious. Bloodthirsty. But even with her transformation, she did not truly consider herself one of the vampires. She was still Kylie, an almost orphan who once had a grandmother she loved. Kylie nibbled her lower lip until she drew blood.

As if responding to her sharp but fleeting pain, the woman inside the apartment whimpered. Kylie heard the sound of tears, sobs tearing from a delicate throat, then the rustle of clothes. The woman's footsteps headed away from the balcony. Seconds later, the sound of the shower broke the silence, the delicate tapping of water flooding against tile.

Kylie slipped into the apartment then and went immediately to the closet where she had spent that singular night. She made herself comfortable in the small space while the woman finished up in the bathroom. Within minutes, a cell phone rang. The human walked quickly into the bedroom, wrapped in a towel, to answer the call. Drops of water slid from her body and splashed against the floor. Kylie heard each drop and licked her lips, suddenly thirsty.

"Hello?"

The woman's voice was a surprise. Deep where Kylie had expected light. Like a teacher's. A voice used to commanding respect in a classroom or lecture hall. Southern. Hot and firm at the same time. "Yes, this is Olivia." She paused, listening to whoever was on the other end of the line. "Of course I'm all right. Are you sure you didn't mean to call my mother?"

Seconds later, she disconnected the call without saying anything else. The small phone clacked against the bedside table when she put it down.

Olivia. She silently tasted the name on her tongue. *Olivia.* She pursed her lips on the first syllable, licked her palate on the second, bit her lip on the third as she said her name. *Olivia.*

Olivia didn't move when she put the phone down. Kylie imagined her staring into space, her large eyes unblinking under the inky brush of dark lashes. In the closet, on the improvised pallet, Kylie wondered what it would be like if Olivia looked at her. What would she see?

Then Kylie heard Olivia rouse herself from wherever she had gone in her mind. The mattress sighed when she sat on her bed, drying her body with a towel. She smoothed lotion into her skin before slipping between the sheets on her large bed. Olivia did not fall asleep immediately nor did she read. Kylie would have heard the sound of pages turning, anything other than the slow, even breathing and stillness.

Kylie tried breathing as Olivia breathed, consciously raising her ribcage to the delicate sounds of Olivia's respiration. It was another two hours before she slept.

❖

Kylie slipped from her hiding place, knowing she would not be able to sleep during these peak night hours. After fighting so long for sleep, Olivia held on to it with the ferocity of a child. She lay still under the sheets, not stirring at all when Kylie crept through the apartment.

Everything about this existence was still new to her. The strength of her body. Its hungers—her eyes flickered to Olivia—especially its hungers. Her teeth tingled, a pleasant ache that spurted saliva in her mouth and made her fingers curl into a cool fist. She had taken a man at the airport, so she wasn't hungry. She remembered well how it had been to tear into his neck and suck on the hot fount that jetted into her mouth. What she felt for Olivia was not that.

It felt so different from simply wanting a meal. There was that hunger yes, but there was also a possessiveness. She wanted no one else to have this woman. She wanted to touch her and to be the only one to experience that privilege. Kylie tilted her head at the mystery of it, confused at her own desire.

To distract herself from it, she looked around the bedroom, seeking out details she had missed the day before. The bedroom's brick walls were covered in lush tapestries of the same gold and burgundy color scheme as the rest of the apartment. But where the living room was littered with books, travel knickknacks, pieces of art that smelled like they'd come from different countries, there was nothing personal in the bedroom. No family photographs, school trophies, or well-worn blankets. Simply the massive bed with a leather bench at its end, a deep red throw on the bench, two shoulder-high bookshelves that created an artificial doorway into the bedroom. A game of Scrabble set for two players sat neglected on the leather bench, and a large mirror in its heavy-looking antique wooden frame hung on the wall opposite the bed. Nearly everything looked new.

Despite the lack of personal touches, the bedroom felt warm. A pulsing heat that welcomed her, intruder that she was.

On the bedside table sat a book with a dark purple velvet cover. A journal. Kylie picked it up and opened it to the page marked with a green ribbon.

Everything exists between one moment and the next. An ill-timed step into the street. A marriage proposal. A phone call. "You have cancer." The words rang unacknowledged in my head as if meant for someone else. The doctor said other things, her tone an endless cheerleading parade, outlining the benefits of my type of cancer, a cancer she preferred since there was a greater chance of defeating it. How could she be so cheerful delivering this news?

But the alternative—pitying condolence—was worse. "We can get this thing gone," she said. "We'll get it out with a lumpectomy, chemotherapy, and radiation for six weeks every day, and everything will be fine."

But now I'm not fine. As I write this, I feel the tears coming up to choke me. This isn't fair. What did I do wrong?

Kylie closed Olivia's journal. Her thumb brushed the thick purple velvet cover, stroking it gently as she watched the woman sleep. Dying. Olivia was dying.

She looked up from the journal to the woman on the bed. Sleep softened the lines in her face, made curves of the angular body mostly hidden under the dark sheet. The mirror reflected Kylie's image back at her, a literal thief in the night, snooping through the private thoughts of someone who did not know her. Kylie scowled at herself in the mirror and saw a fiend scowl back. Sharp teeth resting lightly on plump burgundy lips. Her wide eyes, heavy-lidded and harmless in her round face. The thick dandelion of hair that brushed her shoulders.

In the bed, Olivia shifted.

Kylie stilled. She thought of what it would mean to die. For real. As an eighteen-year-old in Jamaica, living with her grandmother who had sheltered her from everything, death was just another word. Even after Belle had disappeared from their lives when she was so young, it had never occurred to her that she was truly gone. Kylie had not seen her mother's body—or any dead body—to impress upon her the horror and permanence of death.

And now that she was a vampire and death did not touch her at all except the kind that she delivered herself, she found it nearly impossible to contemplate it seriously. But here was the human woman, Olivia, sick and dying. She quietly replaced the journal on the bedside table and walked away from the bed. But she did not leave the room. Kylie dropped to the thick rug on her belly, head spinning as she imagined Olivia dead.

A flare of scent flashed her eyes up, narrowed them. She leapt to her feet and rushed silently through the apartment and to the balcony.

Ivy.

The other vampire stood in the darkness outside of Olivia's home wearing black. Kylie could smell gun oil and tempered steel. She carried a gun and at least one knife.

Kylie drew the door shut. "What are you doing here?" She kept her voice low.

"Following you." Ivy was matter-of-fact about her presence on the balcony of Kylie's human. "Belle worried that you would get into trouble."

"How much trouble can I get into staying with a human?" Kylie drew herself up to her full height, which was at least three inches shy of her mother's six feet. "I'm as safe here as if I were at home."

"Someone is watching this apartment."

Kylie twitched with surprise. "What?"

Ivy raised an eyebrow, declining to repeat herself.

"Are you sure?" Kylie looked around the building, seeing only the familiar café, the humans going about their lives. Panhandlers, drunks, hippies, a few hipsters with their eighties haircuts and clothes.

"Someone has been watching this apartment." Ivy spoke slowly as if to make sure Kylie understood every word. "I'm sure they saw me climb up here from the street. I'm sure they're watching us now." Then she frowned, narrowing her gaze at the apartment. "This place smells funny."

Kylie opened her mouth to ask Ivy again if she was sure about them being followed. But she had been wrong when she asked her that the first time. Ivy, if nothing else, was precise. She was careful and methodical, serving as Silvija's right hand while Kylie had been with the clan.

"Did someone follow you?" Ivy asked.

She shook her head although she wasn't completely sure. None of the humans from the museum where she'd stolen the necklace had followed her as far as Little Five Points. They hadn't followed her at all. She hadn't sensed or smelled any other vampires tracking her. Both times in Atlanta, all she'd detected was humans. Harmless, inconsequential humans.

"What have you done aside from follow this human?"

Kylie didn't bother to deny what Ivy stated as fact. "I didn't do anything else." She didn't think Ivy would take an enlightened view of her theft from the museum.

Ivy stared at her with blade sharp eyes. "Nothing else?"

"Nothing." Kylie didn't look away, didn't flinch.

The excursions to galleries, stores, and shops were her own secret indulgences. Shiny things she took and gave away or discarded, depending on her mood. Suddenly, a dark shape vaulted over the balcony. She hissed and drew back, fists flying up before she recognized Violet.

"They are watching this building, and definitely this apartment in particular," Violet reported. "They didn't follow me when I left." Then she wrinkled her nose as if she caught wind of a bad smell. She hitched a dismissive shoulder then winked at Kylie. "Hey, little one."

Kylie looked from one to the other, not quite knowing what to say. They looked so certain of what they had reported, but why would someone be watching Olivia? Why would someone be watching her? She thought again of the things she had taken before and wondered if she had brought trouble to Olivia's front door. She bit her lip and leaned back against the brick exterior of the building while Olivia slept peacefully inside.

"It's probably nothing," she said.

Ivy crossed her arms. "Your mother wants you to come home."

Kylie's jaw tightened at the unexpected statement. "Why?"

"You know why," Ivy said the same instant that Violet gave her a significant look.

"This is a crazy little town, Kylie." Violet's purple eyes flashed in the dark. "If someone is watching the human, they could see you. But if someone is watching you…." She let her voice trail off.

But she'd painted a vivid enough picture with those simple words. There was no need for her to go on any more. Kylie's mind supplied well enough the image of someone, on the hunt for her, gutting the woman and drinking her blood. Collateral damage. Kylie shifted restlessly against the rough brick.

"I'm not leaving." She crossed her arms over her chest to match Ivy's posture.

"You don't have a choice here, Kylie." Ivy's voice was firm.

Desperation clutched at Kylie's throat. Being with this woman gave her the most peace she'd had in a long time. She didn't want to give it up just because her mother said she should.

"I'll always have a choice."

Someone's phone rang. Ivy's. Kylie shamelessly eavesdropped. "Yes?"

"Leave her." The words from the other end of the line surprised everyone on the balcony. "If she wants to stay with the human, let her stay. We don't imprison people here. At least not very much." A hint of a smile appeared in Silvija's voice. "Keep an eye on whoever is watching, but let her stay with the human if that's what she wants. There's nothing happening here in New York. Leave Violet and come home."

Ivy didn't argue. "Of course." She looked at her watch. Probably checking to see if she had the time to catch the last New York flight. "I'll be back before sunrise." She hung up the cell phone.

"Okay." She raised an eyebrow at Kylie. "You heard Silvija." She gave a brief and pointed nod at Violet. "Enjoy your time away from home."

Then she turned and leapt off the balcony. Seconds later, she was on the ground and melting into the mass of humanity walking through the neighborhood. Kylie bit the inside of her lower lip, frowning. She felt Violet's unhappy eyes on her. She didn't like the idea of being away from her twin. As much as they often fought, they hated to be separated. And now, because of Kylie, she wouldn't be able to see her brother for who knew how many nights.

"You don't have to stay," Kylie said.

"I don't?" Violet looked briefly toward the interior of the apartment where Olivia slept. "Little bit, you haven't been paying attention to how we live if you believe that." She shook her head, the sadness taking over her face, darkening the usually merry eyes. "I'm not going to throw Silvija's orders back in her face. You're so much more like your mother than you even realize."

But Kylie refused to discuss her mother, how she did not know her, despite the handful of years they had spent together in this gilded cage. She unhooked her teeth from her raw bottom lip and ran her tongue across the flesh as it healed nearly instantly.

"There's no trouble here with the woman. You can just go back to New York and tell Silvija that."

Violet only sighed, flicking her gaze impatiently over the humans wandering the streets. She was getting hungry. "There's a little hotel about a mile from here." She took a card from her hip pocket and held it out to Kylie. "I'm staying there for the day, maybe longer if Silvija says so. Come when it's time to sleep." She ran a hand over her shiny head and found a smile that even Kylie could see was forced. "I'm heading out for a nibble. Wish me luck."

Kylie clenched her jaw, hating that she was the cause of Violet's separation from her brother. "Okay." She took the card and shoved it in her jeans pocket.

Violet waved then jumped over the railing, following the same route that Ivy had taken.

Kylie watched her for a moment before turning her attention to the rest of the street, the tumble of activity. Humans going about their evening. Her fingers clenched briefly in the red brick of the balcony, scraping into the stone. Was that all she had to worry about? If not, who would want to trouble her, and why?

CHAPTER SIX

Olivia was crying. This was no ordinary bout of tears. It was wrenching sobs. Gasping tears that jerked her body, phlegm running from her nose, her slight frame rocking back and forth on the floor. Her thick orange robe sagged around her narrow shoulders. She pounded her fists against her thighs as her face curled in on itself, lips trembling, thick lashes damp and heavy with her tears. Her eyes were animal, swollen and red.

Her sadness filled the room, bloating the space with its nauseating heaviness.

Kylie stood in the shadows. She watched, not knowing what to do.

She had just come in from an evening's hunt with Violet and was well fed and ready for more details of Olivia's life, determined to ignore the improbable threat that the mysterious, lurking humans posed. But instead of another field trip into the heart of Olivia, she found a wreck in the living room. Olivia, collapsed into a pool of sorrow on the floor, her laptop in front of her showing photo after photo from an Internet search she had just done. On the screen, photos of women with their breasts cut off. Single mastectomies. Double mastectomies. During the surgery, after the surgery, endless photographs. Bloody tissue. Flat, scarred chests. Clear, fluid-filled tubes that fed away the dripping waste from beneath hacked flesh.

It was obvious that Olivia couldn't look at the pictures anymore. She was a ruin. She screamed and cried. She touched her breasts, dug her fingers into them as she stared past the computer screen, inconsolable.

CHAPTER SEVEN

❖

I know you're there." The voice, soft but sure, came from the figure huddled in the bed. Her eyes searched blindly in the darkness. Kylie watched her, the flitting eyes, the small and getting smaller body under the sheet.

No, you don't, Kylie thought as the eyes calmed when no answer came from any corner of the apartment. Olivia relaxed into the sheets. The pulse stopped rapping at her throat. Despite her half knowledge that she was being watched, Olivia's breathing regulated, then slowed. She fell into sleep.

❖

Every night, Kylie woke up pressed against Violet, their scents mingling as they lay in bed and talked, Violet sharing with her how much she missed her brother, Kylie feeling badly enough that she couldn't stay and listen to the sadness for long. She left to go find Olivia as soon as she could.

Most evenings, Olivia wasn't at home. Kylie crept in and waited for her. Resting in the friendly shadows of the apartment, nosing through Olivia's things until Olivia appeared, often with fresh food for dinner, most times with a look of exhaustion and even deeper sadness on her face.

Once Olivia appeared, Kylie watched her go about the activities of her simple yet strangely elegant life. Knowing she was on the cusp of death, Olivia did everything deliberately.

Whatever job she had before, she'd left it. Despite the chill in the fall air, she spent many of her days in a pool. Probably one indoors. Kylie could smell the chlorine on Olivia like a harsh perfume every time she came home. On days when she didn't make time for the pool, she came home with groceries, just a small collection of things. Sometimes, it was only one thing. A bag of red grapes. Freshly ground coffee in a white paper bag. A loaf of olive bread.

And Olivia, Kylie was coming to learn, was forgetful.

Sometimes, she would pull the door shut behind her but leave her keys dangling from the lock. Or she would forget her wet umbrella in the hallway, neglecting to bring it in to rest in the umbrella stand just inside the door. Once, she rushed off to meet someone but left half the lights on. Kylie had come into the apartment that was as bright as a Sunday afternoon.

Kylie put these small things away for her. Turned off her lights. Picked up an umbrella that had fallen across the threshold so Olivia wouldn't trip when she came home. Even though Olivia didn't notice, it pleased Kylie to do these small things and made her feel truly a part of Olivia's life.

On most evenings, Olivia looked through an album of photos, pausing on each page, touching the photos through the plastic. Her face was at its most contemplative in those moments. Not sad. Not happy. She simply looked as if she were looking at her past through a fogged lens. Removed.

The humans in the album were ordinary looking enough. Attractive in their own way, many of them shared features in common with Olivia. They ran the gamut from milk white to deepest ebony, looking fierce and fearless in the photographs rather than happy. There were a lot of them, at least a dozen reappearing in multiple photos, and they loved to wear some type of camouflage.

An older woman often appeared next to Olivia in the photos, usually wearing camo like the rest but never smiling. In one photo that Kylie stared at most often, the older woman sat at a picnic table between Olivia and a man who looked like a pale version of them both. Olivia was small and delicate in her white blouse as she said something to the woman, her hand raised in mid-gesture. The man in the photo frowned at the two women, looking as if he wanted to be anyplace other than where he was.

On nights when she couldn't sleep, Olivia sat on the balcony, carefully watching the sky, waiting for the sunrise, her slight form still and attentive. Sometimes she took a book out there to read; other times she had her journal where she wrote her thoughts, a line of observation, a remembered line of poetry.

Kylie liked to read the journal afterward and pretend they'd had a conversation, pretend that what Olivia wrote was to her and all she had to do was decipher the words and whisper her replies in Olivia's ear while she slept.

Although she was floundering in the open sea of unfamiliar and frightening emotions, desperately looking for something steady to hold on to, Kylie couldn't justify watching Olivia. Couldn't justify keeping Violet away from her brother and the rest of the clan. But she didn't want to stop. She couldn't.

CHAPTER EIGHT

Kylie was eager to see Olivia. The sun had barely set before she slipped out of her guilt-ridden hotel bed to find her way to Olivia. She was so eager that she almost knocked over a human, a tall male, who had insisted on standing in her way. He had pale skin, broad shoulders, and the hard eyes of a soldier. But she didn't want to waste time proving to him that she was the harder one, so she let him have the sidewalk and hurried on to her destination.

On Olivia's balcony, she paused. Inside the apartment, she heard Olivia. Her quiet breathing, the rustle of bedclothes, a delicate sound of agitation.

Was she all right?

She slipped inside the apartment. But even as she moved beyond the curtains and across the cool floors in concern, part of her recognized what it was. Hitched breath, hands on flesh, a warm body moving on top of cotton sheets. Olivia was masturbating.

Kylie gasped in recognition, a silent sound that was lost in the soft moan and sigh, the hiccup of breath, Olivia's bare thighs sweeping across the sheets. Lifting. The delicate place between her legs exhaling a musky and womanly scent as it swallowed the black phallus Olivia was using on herself. Kylie licked her lips. She slipped up to the lofted bedroom, keeping herself in shadows, watching.

Olivia had started a long time ago, possibly before sunset, and definitely alone. She was naked on the bed, her slender body writhing beautifully in the sheets. There was something both lovely and primal about her movements. This was a moment Kylie had not allowed herself to dream about, but as she watched, she realized it was a dream come true.

Her body was slight and thin, with one breast scarred and nearly half the size of the other. She had wide nipples and a flat belly that glistened with sweat and dipped and clenched with her efforts. She gripped a black dildo in her fist, moving it with distracting ease in and out of her lushly wet pussy. Kylie licked her mouth watching the swollen lips flutter around the dildo, the soft pink heart, the pussy lips, and mound like fresh nutmeg shavings.

"Ah!"

Olivia threw her head back into the pillow, her neck arched and stretched, the small breasts heaving. The nipples were puckered and hard. Kylie imagined them wet from her mouth and unconsciously circled her hips on the floor. One pillow tumbled from the bed. The sheets rustled with Olivia's movements; the springs in the mattress sighed as she fucked herself hard with the black dick, hips flying up to meet her own thrusts. Her body was painted wet with sweat.

Kylie's eyes latched on to Olivia's pussy where her hands worked furiously, one ramming the dick into her soaked cunt while the fingers of her other hand made tight and hard circles around her clitoris. Her body dripped its juices on the sheets. Soft, needy noises spilled from her lips.

Kylie felt rooted to the spot, unable to move. Olivia fucked herself with a desperation and passion that she'd only seen with women and their lovers. But Olivia was her own lover, and she made love to herself with a lush fervor that made Kylie jealous. Goose bumps floated over Olivia's skin. The scent between her legs grew stronger. Her hands on her clit and on the dildo moved faster. She gasped and moaned and writhed on the bed, her body a symphony of erotic beauty.

Kylie tried hard to ignore the blossoming interest between her own thighs. But it was hard when her panties were soaking wet, and she found herself pressing down into the floor, searching for relief for the ache, wanting to touch the source of that sweet discomfort but not knowing quite where to begin. As pleasurable as it looked, it also seemed painful, a loss of control, an undoing.

Olivia's toes curled against the mattress, her thighs pressed wide open. The dildo clenched in her fist dipped in and out of her with a wet, carnal sound.

"Ah! God!" Olivia cried out then flung a hand across her mouth, her hips still making hungry circles in the bed, the dildo still fucking her pussy. She jerked in the bed as if struck by a live wire, calling out again under her clenched hand.

Kylie could hear Olivia's heart racing, her pulse. The breath shivering in her throat as she slowly came down from her orgasm. Her bare body was a feast for Kylie's hungry eyes.

Watching her, Kylie was agitated. Between her thighs was a soaked forest, aching for things she'd only seen but never experienced. Olivia rolled over in the bed, away from Kylie, curling up on top of the sheets with fingers curled under her nose, smelling herself. Kylie sat watching her for a long time, before she slid quietly from the apartment and went to kill something.

CHAPTER NINE

After a mostly unsatisfying hunt, Kylie made her way back to Olivia's apartment. She stood in the middle of Olivia's darkened apartment smelling herself. Maybe she should have gone back to the hotel to shower. It was not so much her own scent that she could detect but the stink of the other human woman she'd taken. The woman had been slender and strong, reminding her of Olivia. Kylie had left her alive.

From the bedroom, she heard Olivia stir. Heard her take a deep breath then emerge from sleep, heart immediately beginning to race.

"I smell you," Olivia said.

Kylie bit her lip and stood absolutely still. Then she opened her mouth to confess, to apologize. Ready to fly back off the sixth floor balcony.

"You smell nice."

The voice was muffled by the pillow, but Kylie heard Olivia as clearly as if she had shouted through a megaphone. Olivia took another breath. She pulled a pillow close to her chest, sighed into it, and fell back asleep.

CHAPTER TEN

K ylie thought she was being subtle. Clever even. But apparently, not enough.

"Is it strange that I talk to you when I'm not even sure you're here?" Olivia turned slightly toward the darkened corner of her kitchen as if to watch Kylie, who was wrapped in shadows and lying on the floor of the bedroom above. "Probably," she said after a thoughtful silence. "Whether you're here or not. Sometimes it hardly matters. You listen. You don't judge. You make room for me. When I've always doubted I deserve that space."

Olivia turned down the blue flame under her small pot of soup. The now familiar combination of smells—miso paste, scallions, soba noodles she made every other day—pulled Kylie, inexplicably, into a sense of comfort and ease. She crouched on the lofted bedroom floor with its clear view of the kitchen below and watched Olivia pour the steaming mixture into a bowl.

"It's the small things now," she said with her eyes still closed. Olivia held the bowl balanced in palms protected from the heat with a black cloth napkin. Tears slid from her closed eyes. She drank the soup and tears flowed while Kylie watched, the carpet pressing against her belly, scratching at her cheek.

This was the first time Olivia had talked to her since telling Kylie she smelled nice. It disconcerted her, but tripped a strange sort of happiness in her chest as well. She wasn't as unwelcome as she'd first thought; maybe Olivia even enjoyed her illicit company and the vague comfort of that discomfort. If there was any such thing.

Kylie worried her lip between her teeth again as she watched Olivia and felt the weight of the room where she lay, the rug pressing into her through her clothes. It was odd, but she felt more welcome in Olivia's small set of rooms than she ever had at the clan's massive penthouse apartment in New York.

Maybe because here, you are not fighting for attention that will never be yours, a low voice at the back of her mind said. She shook it away and refocused on Olivia. But seconds into her contemplation, a scratching sound came from the balcony. Kylie lifted her head.

"Come out," a lower than a whisper voice called out for her ears only.

It was then that she realized there was a new scent nearby, a scent that did not belong on the balcony or even in Atlanta. Salt air and sea grapes. Her mother.

She barely gave herself time to feel startled before she flew up from her prone position on Olivia's rug and crept down the stairs, feeling like a parody of a cat burglar as she used both her vampiric speed and quietness to flit quickly past Olivia in the kitchen that only had the stove light on, leaving everything else in darkness.

The doors to the balcony squeaked open, but she ignored the sound, hoping that Olivia was too caught up in her misery to notice it. The linen curtains billowed in the slight breeze and brushed at her back. She stepped outside.

Belle. Standing in a red and white polka dot dress and high heels, her thick hair parted down the middle and pulled back from her face in two neat waves at the back of her neck, she looked like a 50s pinup model. Her lips were bright red, so were her short nails. She spared Kylie a single glance before balancing a hand on the edge of the balcony and leaping off. Her dress billowed up, then she was on the ground and looking up at Kylie, waiting.

After a brief look back at Olivia who didn't seem to notice a thing, she followed her mother out into the darkness.

At eight o' clock, the neighborhood was already lively with the evening crowd. Slow-moving traffic with bright headlights illuminated the long street and shops on either side. An unending stream of humans flooded the sidewalks.

"What are you still doing here, Kylie?" Belle walked with her hands in the pockets of her dress, the heels of her shoes delicately kissing the sidewalk.

They moved side by side down the narrow walk. A man with a neatly trimmed beard and too much alcohol in his blood walked toward then slipped between them, disappearing from where they had come.

Kylie unconsciously mirrored her mother's stance though she didn't look nearly as beautiful and dramatically feminine. In her jeans and gray T-shirt, her unimpressive height of barely five feet nine, she felt less than, a dainty and almost unworthy creature. She shrugged off the feeling.

"I like it here," she said in response to her mother's question. "That's why I'm still in Atlanta."

"The human is dying. I can smell it."

Kylie nearly stumbled on the smooth sidewalk. "I know."

"Then what are you doing here? Either kill her or fuck her and move on. Or give her your blood and make her one of us."

Kylie hissed on a breath of unwelcome air. "I could never do that." The thought of making Olivia what she was actually sickened her. She shook her head. "I'd rather see her dead than turn into what I am."

She felt her mother's gaze. "Is this really such a terrible existence?"

"You know it is." Kylie couldn't look at her. "I've never wanted this. I feel like a monster."

"I thought you'd get past that."

"Have you?"

"Yes." Her mother drew a breath. "I have. I've had to."

Of course she would say that. She'd been living an ideal life with Silvija. Killing and fucking and rubbing their happiness in everyone's faces.

"I can't," Kylie said. "I may do what I have to do, but I hate myself every time a human takes their last breath in my arms."

"Maybe you're doing it wrong then," her mother said. "They shouldn't die in your arms but in the dirt where you found them. That's the surest way to get emotionally entangled." Belle looked her over again with keen eyes. Searching.

Did she know that what Kylie said was merely what she wished and not what was? She wished she was caring and gentle, as human as she once was. Instead, all she felt for them was hunger. She thought briefly of Olivia and clenched her back teeth at the surge of lust that moved through her.

They were on the jogging path now, empty of everyone except the occasional passing drunk or homeless person. Distantly, she could make out a few inhuman scents. Other vampires in the area she had noticed before but had not bothered to find.

"You smell like your human, you know." Belle spoke into Kylie's deliberate silence.

"She isn't my human," Kylie said the words before she could stop herself.

Moonlight glinted off her mother's teeth as she laughed softly. "If you haven't claimed her yet then it's only a matter of time."

"I'm not like that!" Kylie snapped. "Not like you and—and her." They both knew the "her" she was talking about.

Her mother looked at her again but with something more complicated in her gaze. They'd never talked about sex before, had never discussed that Belle was now living with and having regular sex with a woman. Something she would have never dreamed of doing in Jamaica.

The few times her mother had tried to talk with Kylie about anything approaching the subject, she had shut her down, saying that her grandmother had taught her everything she ever needed to know about getting naked with another human being.

"Don't be so closed minded, daughter."

Kylie hated it when Belle called her that. It sounded as cold as "stranger."

"I'm not being closed minded." But she was being something. Wasn't she the one who had watched Olivia touch herself and taken her own private pleasure from watching Olivia's mindless bliss? Wasn't she the one who wanted…more?

Her mother merely smiled, a bare movement of her painted lips. "Come have dinner with me tonight."

Pleased surprise flitted through Kylie's body. She felt it like a rod through her spine. "Um…Okay."

Her mother laughed again. The breeze lifted up, billowing her skirt around her knees, bringing her scent that was like home brushing against Kylie's face. Sometimes looking at her was almost unbearable. She was so beautiful yet so distant. Farther away, it seemed, than even when she had been missing in Jamaica and Kylie only relied on her grandmother for a steady diet of love and tenderness.

Kylie and Belle moved into the hidden areas, away from the streetlights and toward the shadows that the unwise and the criminal had slipped off to. The fall air was crisp, perfumed with the scent of dying leaves and wood fires. Belle nodded, hands still in the pockets of her delicate looking dress. She turned her head away from Kylie. Her face shifted in the silvered darkness, becoming harder with the scent of a possible prey. Kylie smelled it too. Enticing.

The scent was beyond the homeless men huddled under the overpass. A pair of them Kylie could hear talking about women in the neighborhood they'd like to fuck. It wasn't the group of young girls walking home together after a late-night movie, their laughing gaggle of voices riding the night. It wasn't even the single man, a lone nighttime jogger, making his way on the path, secure that no one would trouble him, would dare compromise his masculinity. He wasn't enough for the two of them. Or was it that feeding on one person would be much too intimate an act for them to share? Kylie shied away from that thought and focused instead on the most enticing meal available to them.

No more than half a mile away, a photographer and his subject were taking advantage of the bright moon to photograph Atlanta by night. Kylie could hear them. His instructions, the young girl's ready compliance, the sigh of her clothes as she turned this way and that. She smelled the makeup and powder on the girl's skin, the hint of sweat under her clothes. Kylie licked her lips.

Her mother kicked off her pretty high heels and toed them under a flowering bush. "Ready?" Her voice was a low purr.

Kylie nodded. They walked together toward their prey, silent. Kylie thought she should do well to remember that moment. Except for one disastrous night nearly seven years ago when she'd first joined the clan, she and her mother never hunted together. Never. That first time had been a trauma that neither of them wanted to relive. So it had been Rufus who taught her to hunt, Rufus and Ivy. And at times, they all hunted together, swarming in a pack on some unsuspecting group in the feast of a city that was New York, but even then, Kylie and Belle stayed away from each other.

On that long ago night in Jamaica, the moon had been high and full overhead. A salt-scented breeze rustled through the soaring trees in the front yard of the cottage where the clan—Belle, Silvija, Julia, and Ivy—stood in a loose circle, waiting.

On her first full night as a vampire, fear and excitement battled for dominance inside Kylie. After years of separation, she was with her mother again, and Belle's love promised to make up for everything Kylie had lost along with her human life—sunlight, mangoes, her grandmother.

The night before, she had woken up from a nightmare only to realize that it was real. In a fit of hunger, she had split open her grandmother's throat and drank her up like fresh tea. Her first blood, the sweetest she'd ever had, but also the one that brought her the most pain.

Kylie was fragile, on the edge of falling apart because of what she had done to her grandmother. She stood under the moonlight at her mother's side, feeling like a beast, unworthy and ashamed. Perhaps sensing her turmoil, Belle touched her face with hands that smelled like the earth.

"This is what we do," her mother said.

Kylie trembled in the grip of remorse and relief, gladness and guilt, not knowing quite what to do. Belle removed her hands but kept her eyes on Kylie's, her velvet brown gaze filled with as much guilt as Kylie felt.

Then Belle blinked and turned away, linked hands with Silvija who had been watching them with concern. Their hands squeezed then let go. Kylie looked away from them, uncomfortable with the sight of them touching.

Silvija turned, moonlight creating shadows and beauty on her full-lipped face. "Let's go."

Then the clan was off, loping over the damp grass, through the yard, and down the hill. There was human scent in the air and Kylie followed, running full speed. The wind rushed against her face, tugged at her clothes. The night was like another world. Scurrying insects and the smell of fear, animal footsteps darting away from the clan, the heady perfume of orchids.

Before too long, she smelled smoke in the air, the sign of a fire not too far away. There was singing and bare feet stomping in the dirt, conversation and laughter. The smell of ganja. Some humans were having an outdoor party.

The clan broke it up. Kylie and her new family burst into the ring of hippies and wannabe Rastafarians with their long, manicured dreads and mediocre marijuana. The humans froze in mid-dance around the fire. Seven of them. Two women. Three were dancing while the others sat around the fire, smoking and talking.

Belle struck first. Or maybe it only seemed that way because Kylie was watching her mother closest of all. She sliced through the small group like a blade, jumping over the high tongues of flame to seize one of the women who only had time to lurch to her feet in shock before Belle grabbed her hair, jerked her neck back, and slashed into her throat with razor fangs.

The woman fought Belle, flailing her thin arms, scratching at her mother's face. Belle broke her arms, a sound like twigs snapping. She gave a shriek of agony. Belle lashed a hand over the woman's mouth and continued to feed, mouth slurping at the ragged gash in her throat. Blood spilled down the woman's neck and splashed on her rainbow-colored, crochet dress.

The woman dropped to the ground and Belle went with her, sucking at the gushing fount without stopping. She was on her knees, the woman's head and neck cradled in her arms in a parody of caring while the human's legs twitched in the dirt. Belle raised her head, revealing bloodstained lips and curved teeth. She stared at Kylie who had frozen in the clearing in horror.

"Come drink," Belle said. Blood sprayed from her lips as she spoke.

"No!" Kylie backed away from the sight of her mother, the killer, who was enjoying the human's pitiful struggles, holding her on the brink of death so the blood would remain sweet. Inviting Kylie to—her stomach heaved. She threw up its measly contents in the dirt while all around her the others killed, enjoyed, feasted.

Kylie dropped to all fours near the fire, wet strings of blood hanging from her lips, the smell of smoke and spilled blood, shit and piss assaulting her from all sides. She squeezed her eyes shut, still seeing her mother at her bloody feast, ripping out the woman's throat. Then it was her grandmother who swam before her eyes, dead and drained from the night before. And finally, Kylie saw herself.

She didn't hate the carnage around her. Instead, she felt the spurt of wet hunger in her mouth, felt how badly she wanted to take her mother's place at the human's throat. Her stomach lurched again.

But that night was in the past. This was now. And although she had her fears and contrary desires, Kylie wanted tonight to be better. She wanted to accept her mother and herself as what each was. As usual, she wanted something more.

Quietly, she crept at her mother's side. They moved like ghosts, the pavement like a perfect spring under her feet. The moment her feet touched the ground, the concrete conspired to push her up and forward again, until she was moving as fast as a bicycle, a fact that even now continued to astonish her, how fast she could run, how strong she was, how suited to killing her body had become.

It wasn't long before she and Belle found them. Pavement became stone then grass. An abandoned house appeared on the hill. It had been burned and was now a ruined shell with kudzu growing over its charred frame, blackened doorways, even its chipped concrete steps. Kylie stopped to watch them and her mother did the same. As always, she fought that split second of jealousy, of déjà vu, whenever she was about to take a human. Their life was so valuable, but so transient. A thing that was so strong one instant, then gone in a flash. Swallowed, burped, and quickly forgotten.

Kylie savored their humanity and the thought of taking it from them. She suspected, though, that her mother was meditating on something else entirely. Belle watched the model while a predatory and pleased smile played on her red lips. The model was pretty enough and vulnerable-looking. Thick black curls spilled down the side of her throat in a scented fall while her pale skin glowed in a tight rubber dress that would make it nearly impossible for her to run. Even if she ran, there was no place for her to go.

Kylie's hands curled at her sides as her lips parted in anticipation, making room for the slow and almost erotically painful lengthening of her feeding teeth. The inside of her mouth was wet. She was suddenly starving.

Belle nodded toward the girl. "Take her."

She didn't have to say it twice. But at the sound of her voice that Belle did not bother to hide, the humans looked up in surprise.

"This is a private photo shoot," the man said with irritation.

Kylie grinned. "We like private."

She clenched her fists, pounded them once against her thighs, and sprang. She cut quickly through the darkness, giving up the anonymity of watching them for much, much more direct involvement. It didn't take long for the pair to see what was going on, how unwise it was for them to be walking through the darkness as if they owned it. The night was the territory of beasts. Not men. And certainly not humans.

Kylie's feet sprang across the grass. Puzzlement then fear flashed in the girl's eyes that tried to track Kylie's quick progress toward her. Kylie almost remembered what it was like to watch the eerie vampiric speed from human eyes—blurs of movement, slashing teeth, a savage death. Or sometimes a quick one.

Kylie grabbed the girl from her shrinking crouch in the charred doorway, shoved her head aside, and pulled the pulsing artery swiftly to her mouth. Her skin popped like a cherry, releasing its hot nectar into Kylie's mouth. The blood gushed over her tongue, a warm flood of nourishment, coppery and intoxicating. Yes, the girl had taken something, had been drugged. Kylie tasted the trace bitterness in the blood, a fleeting thought before she staggered on her feet.

"Oh!"

Kylie dropped the girl against the wall and spun where she stood, eyes blinking.

She was distantly aware of her mother and the photographer. Belle dragging the camera from his hands and smashing it against the stone steps. A hand clenched tightly over his mouth to stop his screams as she ravaged his throat. Even in her savagery, she was elegant, sensuous.

Her mother moved as if she were made of light, her body like a thousand fireflies in the dark evening. The sound of her gulping down the human's blood was like a song, its rhythmic bass thumping loudly in Kylie's head. Belle didn't waste a single drop. She pinned the man's bucking body to the ground with the easy weight of her own, dropping on him like a spider, her dress floating around them, partially hiding his body from view as she fed from him. She muffled the sounds of his terror beneath her hand.

"Stop it."

The girl's voice was feeble, but it was there. She sagged against the wall, her neck sluggishly bleeding, her eyes glassy and wide. Improbably, her nipples were hard against the rubber dress, and Kylie could smell the thick rise of her pussy's scent in the night. But Kylie shook her head. She did not want that. But the girl wanted her. Even dying, she reached for Kylie, one hand held out in supplication, the other tugging at the tight neckline of her dress.

"Kiss me!" the girl gasped.

Her mother looked up from her feast. "Give the girl what she wants, Kylie."

"No." Kylie shook her head and fought against the effect of the drugs rampaging through her blood. "I told you, I don't do that."

Her mother looked over her shoulder at Kylie again, blood staining her lips an even richer red. "Don't judge what you don't know." Then she bent her head to finish her meal.

Kylie stood under the bright moon watching her mother kill. Perversely, seeing Belle drinking up the man's life essence made her not want to kill the drugged young woman. Under Violet's counsel, she had left some of the humans she'd fed from alive, taking only just enough blood to sustain herself, drinking from whores who were prey in the night as they waited for their next john, the homeless who offered her sex but whose blood she took in exchange for a few dollars in a dimly lit alley, licking their musky necks until they forgot about the pain of their lives for a few precious minutes. It wouldn't do to alert the police about a predator on the loose, Violet told her. They might actually try to do something about it.

If she stayed in Atlanta long enough, Violet would turn her back into a human yet. Against the wall, the human woman was faint from blood loss, but she still reached out for Kylie. The temptation to finish her was strong, but with Belle there beside her she simply could not do it. She didn't want her mother to see how much of a beast she'd become, how much like Belle from that long ago night in the Jamaican hills.

Her mother rose from her feast, licking her scarlet lips. "Finish her," Belle said. "Or take her someplace where she would be found and tended to. You took a lot from her and she is already skinny." She waved a dismissive hand at the girl's rubber-clad body.

Kylie righted herself as the effects of the drugs lessened and she was able to see without every movement being light-streaked and too beautiful to look away from. She took the girl in her arms and carried her toward civilization.

She left her on the front steps of an apartment on a well-lit doorstep. She would be found. She would be cared for. Kylie and Belle walked away from the woman and found the bright sidewalk leading down a narrow residential street and toward a small nightclub where Kylie could hear music pounding through thick walls. Traffic zoomed steadily past on the main street ahead of them.

"Now what?" Kylie asked.

"Now we enjoy what is left of the night."

Kylie drew back, surprised.

"I'm hurt. You don't want to spend some quality time with your own mother?" There was a teasing lilt to Belle's voice, but there was something else moving behind it too. "I know things have been strange for us since you've been with the clan, but I thought that by now you'd have sorted out your feelings and…" Her mother tapered off.

"Nothing changed for me. Sometimes I look at you and I don't know who you are. The thing I see in front of me is so different from the mother I used to know." Kylie clamped down on her lip, surprised by her own honesty. Maybe it was the last of the drugged blood talking. But she didn't stop. "It feels like I just got here. I still feel like we're strangers."

That was not what she had meant to say. She wanted to bridge the gap that had sprung up between her and Belle. She wanted to be closer to the woman who had given birth to her. But from the age of five until eighteen, she thought her mother was dead. Now, here Belle was back in her life with a new name and a savagery that was as alien to Kylie as the sharp teeth and the scent embedded in her skin.

As much as she wanted the connection to happen between her and her mother, she felt like she kept running into her mother's shield. Or she was using her own shield to ram into her mother again and again, trying to get Belle to surrender the love that Kylie so desperately wanted. But that was no way to gain peace.

"Would it be hard to end this distance between us, daughter?" Belle walked at Kylie's side, barefoot and elegant, her tall figure illuminated under the slivered moon.

Daughter. Kylie cringed at the word.

"Mother, it feels like the hardest thing I've ever tried to do."

CHAPTER ELEVEN

Kylie was late. Olivia had just fallen asleep. She slipped over the edge of the balcony and into the apartment. Yes, Olivia smelled like sleep. Kylie'd had a slow awakening with her mother and Violet and a long early evening where she thought about little else but Olivia. What would Olivia reveal about herself tonight? Would this be the day that Kylie revealed *herself*? But after Belle left for New York, Violet had wanted to spar with her, and the exhilaration of it had taken Kylie over, blood singing, body stretched to its limits and beyond. And then it was half past midnight and she missed Olivia's monologues to her, the intimacy of her voice. That missing felt like an ache, one she could only soothe by being close to Olivia. She wanted suddenly, desperately, to touch her.

The shower she'd taken was a quick one. And now Kylie barely felt clean as she sank quietly into Olivia's bed, unable to maintain much distance between herself and the woman she had come to see. The mattress barely moved under Kylie's weight.

She regretted her haste. The sheets smelled of the dryer, and Olivia's skin like a recent bath. What had she said while she soaked in the tub, searching the ceiling for signs, perhaps, of the person she had a one-sided conversation with every night?

Yes, she had come to her too soon. The wildness of the sparring session still nipped at the edges of her consciousness. A sharp blood smell from a cut on Violet's arm rose in memory, and Kylie's mouth watered. She flinched back from Olivia on the bed, suddenly aware of the pulsing, sleeping heat and what sweetness would explode under her tongue with just one bite.

"You look like somebody's child."

Kylie stifled her hiss of surprise. Olivia's eyes stared into hers. Perfectly awake. Perfectly aware. She lay under the thin sheet with her head cradled on the pillow, a hand tucked under her cheek.

"That's because I am." Kylie sat up in the bed, pushing herself carefully away. Why the hell had she given in to the urge to sit on the bed?

Olivia followed her movements with her eyes, but that was all.

"It's you that I've been smelling." She took a quick, sipping breath. "Like lavender."

Kylie gaped at her, still not knowing what to say. She was shocked that Olivia wasn't screaming her head off and running out the front door. It was different now that Olivia could see her. Now that Olivia knew for sure she had a stalker instead of believing she had simply made one up to suit her needs. She crouched in Olivia's bed, an obvious intruder, her palms flat against the sheets, ready to fly up and away.

"Don't be frightened," Kylie said.

"I'm not. Are you?" Olivia curled up in the bed, tucking her knees into her chest. Her eyes swallowed Kylie, wonder in them.

Kylie giggled, suddenly nervous. "No. No way." It was the oddest sensation to finally talk with Olivia, instead of hearing Olivia talk *at* her. As if her world suddenly swung upside down and it was all she could do to hold on. Olivia was calm in the bed, watching.

Her steady gaze made Kylie want to confess everything.

"I'm sorry," she said. Then tripped over her tongue. "I didn't—I didn't…."

"Did you find what you were looking for when you came in that first time?" Olivia asked.

Kylie lost her words again.

Then Olivia smiled. "You're so uncertain." The smile became bittersweet. "It's like you stumbled in here with me and didn't know how to leave." She sat up in the bed, watching Kylie, a small wrinkle between her straight and thick eyebrows. "Would you like something to drink? Some tea maybe?"

Caught off guard again, Kylie could only stammer. "I don't—that is really nice of you, but—" Olivia's eyes never left her. She cleared her throat. "Tea. Yeah. Sure." She dredged up one of her granny's old lessons from childhood. "Thank you."

"You're welcome."

Olivia slid from the other side of the queen-sized bed, and Kylie swallowed in surprise at the tiny shorts and camisole she wore. Had she always worn such a small amount of clothes to bed?

On naked feet, Olivia left her, trailing her hand on the railing, looking back over her shoulder to glance at Kylie as if she couldn't quite believe she was there. The scent of her made Kylie want to follow. It was spicy with sleep, and warm.

Olivia wore a smile as she made her slow way down the steps to the main level of the apartment and the kitchen. Kylie slipped from the bed to watch her as she'd done for so many days, crouching to her favorite spot on the floor to watch Olivia empty the old water from the kettle and open the spigot to pour fresh water in with spare, elegant movements.

Soon, she finished making tea for them both and brought the steaming mugs of what smelled like ginger and lavender upstairs back to the bedroom. She set one of the mugs on the left side of the bed and put the other, the one that smelled of flowers, in Kylie's hand.

Her eyes were ravenous over Kylie's face, lingering on her neck, her body, even the way she held the mug. There was nothing sexual about it, simply Olivia digesting everything about Kylie in a way that she hadn't before.

Kylie was frozen in place, waiting for the intense gaze to fall away. She felt wholly digested, plucked over. She looked down at the tea, not quite knowing what to do with it. She hadn't put anything in her mouth except for blood and a few drops of coffee in so long. The tea smelled good, but only as something to decorate the air. She put the mug on the table beside Olivia's.

"My name is Kylie."

"Pleased to make your acquaintance, Kylie." Olivia's lips curved up in a smile. "I'm sure you already know my name plus a few other things about me." The smile faded away. "How did you get in here?"

Kylie clenched her back teeth, resisting the urge to bite her lip out of sheer nervousness. She wanted to shove back at Olivia, treat her as if she didn't have the right to ask her any questions. But she couldn't. She was the one who had intruded into Olivia's space. She was the one who had been spying.

"I climbed in through your balcony," she finally said.

"That's…that's a little creepy, don't you think?" Olivia tilted her head.

Kylie tried for a joke. "Depends on who you ask."

Olivia didn't laugh. "How long have you been here in my apartment?"

Kylie's cheeks tingled, but she forced herself not to look away. "A few days."

Olivia drew a breath of surprise. "Why?"

"I—I needed a place to hide from the sun."

"The sun?"

Kylie nodded, willing to give Olivia anything, answer any questions she needed to feel more comfortable about Kylie being in her apartment uninvited.

Olivia was silent for a while, simply sitting in the middle of the bed, eyelashes flickering delicately, like she was deep in thought. "You're different."

"Yes."

Kylie didn't know what to say about what she was. Wasn't it apparent that she was other than human? Was that the reason Olivia's gaze had lingered so long on Kylie, making her wonder for the first time in seven years what someone else saw when they looked at her.

"I'm *very* different," Kylie said.

Olivia devoured Kylie with her eyes once again. It seemed almost strange to have Olivia actually interacting with her, not drifting through her dreams of connection but being her own person and asking Kylie questions, talking to her like a real person. Despite her discomfort with having to reveal what she was to Olivia, she also felt a bit of relief.

"How different are you?" Olivia asked.

A line pressed into the smooth skin of Olivia's forehead. Kylie figured the easiest way to tell Olivia about what she was, was to show her. She moved into the middle of the bed until she was mere inches from Olivia. Olivia didn't move back, only dropped her gaze briefly to Kylie's lips. She licked her own.

"I don't want to scare you," Kylie said.

"Then don't." A smile shaped her moist lips.

Kylie shook her head. "It's not that easy."

Olivia put a hand on Kylie's thigh. "Most things are easier than we think."

"I—"

She opened her mouth and allowed the hunger to rise in her. Kylie didn't want to frighten Olivia, but she didn't know any other way to do this. She'd never revealed herself to anyone before. Her teeth flashed out. Olivia gasped and jerked away. The sudden stink of her fear flared in the room making Kylie feel ashamed and regret over opening her mouth. Her teeth snapped shut, and she slid back in the bed. But Olivia grabbed her arm. With a slight squeeze, she forced Kylie to stay on the bed.

Kylie looked down at the delicate hand on her arm, the flesh that was a few shades lighter than her own and with hints of red. Her touch was light, but Kylie could no more throw it off than she could lift the entire building where they sat.

"Does it hurt?" Olivia asked. "Being what you are."

"Yes. But not as much as in the beginning."

They seemed to be speaking on an entirely different level. Not about the impossibility of there being vampires in the world, but about this. How being what she was hurt her. How much pain she felt from being so different in a way that inspired only fear and revulsion.

"I'm glad," Olivia said. She slowly drew her hand back until she was sitting straight in the bed again. She looked away from Kylie.

"Why are you glad when you don't even know me?"

"You look so lovely, like a living doll with all that thick hair and those big, beautiful eyes." Olivia said the words with a hiccup of some strange emotion in her voice. She lifted a hand to touch Kylie's face, but Kylie flinched back. Olivia looked at her, a deliberate stare. Then she tried to touch her again.

Kylie forced herself to stay still as Olivia's fingers touched her face, fluttered down her cheeks, over her lips, down to her chin. Her hands were warm, almost hot, against her skin, and she was aware of every millimeter of skin where they touched. "You're so young," Olivia said.

Kylie felt herself trembling. Out of all the scenarios she had envisioned when Olivia found her, this was the least likely. This maternal sensuality about Olivia. The honeyed drizzle of her voice paired with the fearless way that she touched Kylie. Olivia was right; Kylie was the one who should have been afraid.

She swallowed and confronted the easiest thing. "I was eighteen when I was turned seven years ago," Kylie said defensively. "People don't consider that young anymore."

Olivia smiled. "That's young enough. You look like you have a mother somewhere who misses you."

Kylie felt her face harden. "I don't." At Olivia's curious look, she shook her head. "I mean, she's around, but she doesn't miss me. She's busy."

"We all have some sadness or other in our lives," Olivia said with a slight shrug, scraping long fingers over her short cap of black hair.

Kylie didn't know what she had expected from Olivia, but it wasn't that response. She blinked at her then smiled. "You're right. We all have something."

"You've been watching me for a few days. You probably know things about me that no one else does."

Kylie's face prickled again from the memory of the evening she walked in on her masturbating. How that sensual display had wreaked havoc with her concentration for nights afterward.

"You must know I'm sick then." Her look was direct, forcing the truth from Kylie. "Cancer."

"Yes, I do."

"Good. Then we don't have to talk about that."

A yawn stretched Olivia's jaw. "I'm going to take a shower," she said. "I need to be more awake for the rest of our conversation." She slid from the bed and took a sip of her tea from the cup getting cold on the bedside table. "Don't leave," Olivia said.

Kylie nodded, unable to fathom leaving in the midst of such a momentous evening. Olivia was awake and talking with her. She wasn't frightened. She knew what Kylie was. The only way she could leave was if someone snatched her and tossed her out. And even then, she would kick, scream, and bite every inch of the way.

The shower came on, then she heard the distant sounds of Olivia undressing, cloth lifting over her head, falling to the floor. Kylie was paralyzed by the idea of it. The reality of her. The thought of Olivia naked made her restless. It was one thing to watch other women make love, even to see Olivia masturbate; but now the Olivia she hungered for was actually speaking to her, was touching her without fear. Did that mean there was a chance she would get to do more than watch? A quiver rippled through her body.

She left the bedroom, walked out to the balcony, and sat on the edge of the sturdy brick ledge. Her hand clenched and unclenched in the red brick. Her legs dangled over the edge. She peered at the damp grass below, at the mailboxes on the lawn, a "for sale" sign advertising the availability of one of the units in the building.

"Do you realize you're endangering your human?"

Kylie jerked her head toward the low rumbling voice. Silvija.

It was a shock to see her mother's wife on Olivia's balcony, watching her with amusement in her cruel, dark eyes. Kylie flinched on the inside, but tried not to show it. The leader of their clan was in all black. Riding boots, soft pants, a black shirt that fluttered against her powerful torso in the breeze. Her hair was in four long braids wound around her head. Kylie wanted to look around to see if this was a nightmare, if someone was trying to play a trick on her.

"The only danger is from you and the rest of the clan." She stared pointedly at Silvija, wanting her to know she wouldn't stand for anyone hurting Olivia. "Otherwise, she is safe enough here.

Silvija laughed. "You're so much like your mother." She turned her back to lean against the balcony, arms crossed. In a single moment, she seemed to take in everything about where they stood, the apartment with its sounds of water hitting tile, Kylie's fingers clenched into the stone ledge of the balcony where she sat, Olivia's faint singing under her breath that they could both hear.

"You like her. That's all the more reason for you to leave her alone. What's the point of hanging around her like some sort of ghoul?" Silvija shook her head. "I was relieved when you didn't go through any of this human attachment garbage when you were just turned. But it's worse to see you like this now." Her contemptuous gaze flickered toward the curtain that hid the apartment's lone occupant. "What's the appeal? I don't understand it if you're not fucking or feeding from her."

Kylie flinched from the words that reduced what she had for Olivia to something so base. So obscene.

"I like her," she said.

"I used to like chicken, but you don't see me adopting one and keeping it in my bed."

"She's not in my bed," Kylie snapped.

"Not yet." A razor smile.

Silvija uncoiled from her lazy pose against the balcony, rising to her full height with a deadly and graceful motion. "We don't have time for you to work through your virgin issues."

Kylie hissed at the casual mockery of her chastity, something the entire clan knew of but never openly spoke about to her face.

"Deal with whatever this is you've got going on with this human in the next seven days, or I'll end it for you." Silvija raised a curved eyebrow, leaving no doubt about what she meant.

"Are you threatening me?" Kylie clenched a fist against her thigh and forced herself to stay seated on the balcony's edge. She'd never raised a hand to Silvija, had never dreamed about it until now. A scalding surge of anger and protectiveness burned through her belly, shocking her with its intensity.

"I'm telling you what's going to happen if you don't do what I recommend." Silvija looked off into the distance as if her mind had already dismissed their conversation. "Stubbornness seems to run in your family so I'm telling it to you in the most direct way I know how and that you'll understand. It seems the best way to deal with the women in your family." The corner of her mouth tilted up, but it wasn't a friendly expression. "Violet will stay at the hotel here during these seven days and return home on the eighth." She tapped her open palm briefly against the brick of the balcony, a decision made, a situation dealt with. "I'll see you back in New York."

Then she was gone. Kylie didn't even see her move. One moment, Silvija was there with her threats, and the next Kylie was sitting alone on the balcony.

"Fuck." She clenched her teeth as the challenge Silvija had thrown echoed in her ears. "Fucking bitch!"

"Kylie? Are you still here?"

Olivia's tentative footsteps sounded in the apartment.

"I'm here." She projected her voice up to the bedroom and hopped off the balcony's edge.

"I thought you left." Olivia sounded relieved.

"No. Not yet." She sank into the sofa across from the television and dismissed Silvija from her mind.

Instead, she occupied herself by trying not to imagine what Olivia was doing up there in her bedroom. She was trying not to think about Olivia's naked body, the upward curve of her breasts, and the wide nipples that she had tasted in dreams.

Without seeing it, she knew Olivia stood on the left side of her bed, naked. The golden light from the floor lamp haloed her body, highlighting its subtle curves, the graceful tilt of her neck as she looked down at her body, an automatic evaluation she always performed, checking to see what changes had happened since she last noticed.

The damp towel had already been tossed aside on the bed, a purple curl of cloth against the recently changed forest green comforter painted with lush gold stripes. Kylie knew exactly where on the bedside table Olivia kept the copper bottle of cocoa butter lotion. She could hear when Olivia pumped the thick, creamy liquid into her palm, then rubbed her palms together, smoothing the lotion in slow and deliberate movements over her arms, shoulders, her breasts.

She shivered at the thought of Olivia's breasts. Her hands moving over them, smoothing lotion into the luscious brown skin, over the nipples she liked to pinch as—

"You want to go out tonight?"

Kylie blinked, cheeks tingling with arousal and embarrassment as Olivia appeared in front of her. Olivia was already fully dressed in an ankle-length pink dress and a cropped denim jacket. She smelled of her cocoa butter and her short coils gleamed under the light. She was ready much sooner than Kylie and her decadent imagination hoped she would be.

"Come on," Olivia said. "We're going for a drive."

She didn't wait for Kylie to respond. She grabbed her bag from the coat rack by the door and her keys from the hook on the wall. She looked over her shoulder at Kylie. "Coming?"

Kylie scrambled to her feet, nearly tripping. She untangled the vivid fantasy playing in her mind from the reality of Olivia standing before her. "Where are we going?"

"You'll see."

They left the building and walked to the nearby parking lot. Olivia stopped next to a two-door, black Jeep Wrangler.

"Here we are." She jingled her keys.

Her smile was mischievous as she unlocked the doors. Inside the SUV, she leaned over to the passenger side and shoved open the door for Kylie. "Get in."

The Jeep rumbled to life and music burst from the speakers, a growling female voice and stinging electric guitars. Olivia gave a shrug of apology before turning the stereo down and changing to mellow pop music. She drove the Jeep from the parking lot and out to the small side street.

When Kylie was killed, she hadn't been able to drive. After becoming one of the clan, she'd been chauffeured around, flown to most places, or went on foot, so she never bothered to learn. For her, driving was an exotic thing. She watched Olivia handle the manual drive SUV with an expert touch. She changed gears with a sexy competence Kylie could not look away from. She watched the narrow, short-nailed fingers as they grasped the shifter, smoothly guiding the car from hill to valley then hill again. A warm tingle settled in Kylie's belly at the sight.

She cleared her throat and looked out the window.

Olivia took them into the heart of the city, through darkness and bright lights while the Jeep's tires whispered across the asphalt. Music serenaded them from the speakers, and Olivia hummed along.

"It's nice to be out of the apartment." Olivia took her eyes away from the road to glance at Kylie.

"It feels the same to me," Kylie said.

But even before her words died away, she realized the difference. The freedom of being out in a vehicle with the breeze rushing in through the windows and Olivia tapping her fingers against the steering wheel and singing beneath her breath about teenage love. Olivia seemed more relaxed, even a little happy. "It's nice," Kylie finally said.

But nice or not, the freedom of the open road couldn't allow her to forget what Silvija had said to her on the balcony. What could the clan leader do to Olivia, anyway? Kylie glanced at Olivia, thinking of her slender frailty and the way she trusted when she had no reason to. The repercussions to Olivia would be dire if she stayed. Death would be the least of Olivia's worries if Silvija followed through with her threat.

"I'm leaving for home soon," she said, unable to keep the reluctance from her voice.

"Why?" This time Olivia turned completely around to look at her. "You just got here." A hint of irony touched her mouth.

Kylie looked away from her teasing gaze. "I—there are things I need to take care of at home."

"Liar."

Olivia said the word casually and with affection. "You don't have to go anywhere." She lifted her hand from the gearshift and patted Kylie's thigh. "What would you do if I told you I won't let you go?"

"Then I won't go."

Olivia smiled faintly and put her hand back where it belonged. "Stay, my little cat burglar. I'm just starting to enjoy your company."

What if she could stay? What would that look like and how long could it last? Kylie was under no illusions that she could skirt the law of the clan—Silvija *was* the law—and get away with it. Even if she could stay, she feared very much that her clan leader would take it out on Olivia. She could not bear it if something happened to Olivia because of her.

"I have a week," Kylie finally said. "I can't stay any longer than that."

"I'm sure we can find plenty to do in that time." Olivia smiled again, her eyes warm and engaging.

Kylie almost found herself smiling back, caught in Olivia's playful enthusiasm that emerged at the oddest times from the cloak of sadness she wore.

Kylie didn't know how to frame her attraction to Olivia. Didn't know how to balance her inexplicable desire to be in her company from any selfish wish to ensure Olivia's well-being. She felt like someone had planted this need for Olivia inside her and the need had latched on to her deep down, leaving her unable to separate its insidious presence from anything that she wanted for herself. She didn't want to feel this desire for Olivia, even though it distracted her from the ocean of years that stretched out before her.

Olivia didn't have that much time. If Silvija had her way, Olivia only had a week left before being drained dry and left sprawled out in some alley in the neighborhood, another statistic of the city. She bit her lip and looked over at Olivia.

Suddenly, the car lurched from its lane, flinging Kylie against the door.

"Shit!"

Olivia gripped the steering wheel in both hands as the Jeep swerved into another lane. Tires screeched and a nearby car horn bleated in distress as the SUV narrowly missed sideswiping an oncoming car.

"Crate," Olivia muttered. "There was a damn crate in the road." Her eyes narrowed. "Who the hell does that? That's some dangerous shit."

"It's okay," Kylie said, reaching out to briefly touch Olivia's knee. "You handled it."

Olivia smiled tensely at her before turning back to the road.

Kylie could hear her accelerated heartbeat. Olivia held on so grimly to her life, not accepting in any way the possibility of her death, even with the sickness eating away at her. Belle had said she could smell the decay inside Olivia. But Kylie was blind and dumb to it. Oblivious to everything except Olivia's emotional nakedness, the need and sorrow dripping from her like fresh blood.

They drifted on into the night, the familiar sense of comfort and contentment from Olivia's presence enfolding Kylie as they seemed to float over the asphalt in the dark SUV. The roll of the tires against the road was a soothing hum.

"Where are we going?" Kylie asked.

"We are already here." Olivia gestured to the city stretched out in front of the windshield.

The smell of night drifted in through the windows, and Kylie breathed it deeply. Danger. Blood. Fear. A sweetness that reminded her of other vampires, though none of the scents she detected belonged to either her mother or Violet.

Unfamiliar vampires. She'd seen and met her fair share of beasts from other clans, but none of the scents on the air seemed familiar. Since she wasn't in the mood to make any new friends, she deliberately turned her nose away from them.

The landscape changed. No more craftsman houses or pretty Tudors lining the street. Now it was warehouses, some converted to lofts, graffitied storefronts, restaurants, music thumping from behind the walls of nightclubs. The sounds of the evening were all around them. Screams. Laughter. The staccato tap of a woman's high heels on the sidewalk as she hurried to her destination.

Up ahead, Kylie heard the sound of flesh against flesh. At first, she thought it was sex, rough and urgent, in a dark alley. But as the car drew closer, she realized it wasn't anything so friendly. On the left side of the street, separated by a steady stream of traffic, she saw it.

A fight. An unfair one. A man on his hands and knees, cowering against the wall while three boys, teenagers no older than Kylie had been when she was taken, kicking and punching. They were all dark-haired and pale-skinned, the victim and his attackers, like one big unhappy family.

Olivia drove slowly, so Kylie saw it all. The blood flying from the downed man's mouth. A hand clutching in pain at his stomach, trying in vain to protect the already damaged body.

Kylie put a hand on the door, a latent instinct rising in her despite the fact that the fighters were all human. She plucked open the door and Olivia gasped as it fell open and Kylie jumped out into the street, slamming the door of the SUV behind her.

She strode across traffic, ignoring the cars that honked their horns at her. Kylie banged her fist against the hood of a white Cadillac as it almost ran her over, the driver pressing on his horn. The three boys pounding on the man did not look up. They were focused in their ferocity. Drilling the man into the ground with their kicks and punches. They growled and panted as they did their work, sounds building fast and hard like the beating of drums.

The man on the ground grunted with each blow, shouting at them when he was able to catch his breath. He chanted the words in a long stream, so it took Kylie a few seconds to understand what he was saying. Then it became clear.

"Fuck you. Fuck you. Fuck you." Over and over again.

The smell of the blood in the alley made Kylie's tongue tingle. It took every ounce of her control not to leap into the fray and drink them all dry. Her teeth stretched with greed. She was far from hungry. She'd fed earlier that night before going to Olivia. Anything she took now would just be a snack or—she revised that estimate, taking in the potential banquet before her—a lavish second meal.

The man stopped his mindless chanting.

"Help me," he gurgled, staring up at her with blackened eyes. Blood dripped from his torn cheek. His hair hung over his face, a limp curtain gusted by each labored breath.

The boys working on him jerked their heads up to look at Kylie. "Get the fuck out of here!" one of them shouted.

The boys were thin and pale-eyed, wearing deliberately frayed T-shirts and jeans. They were college types, but savage. Maybe fraternity boys. The three boys looked at her, the bubbling acid of their anger pouring from them and threatening anything in their path.

Contrary to what Kylie expected, there was nothing smug about them. What they were doing was not a game. They were all in deadly earnest as they tended to the man at their feet.

Even with Kylie standing there, looking like a non-threatening young woman in her loose jeans and Transformers T-shirt, one of the boys kicked the man on the ground. It was a vicious and deliberate motion. But Kylie felt it was not done for her benefit, but to let the man know there was no one saving him from their punishments.

So Kylie gave them hers.

She leapt and landed on a boy's back. He screamed as she hooked her fingers in his neck, sank her fangs into his throat. Ripped. She drank deeply from him, and his screams gurgled away into the night. He dropped to his knees, already dying, blood spilling.

Before the other two could react, she jumped from him, faster than they could see, elbow stabbing at one throat, fist ramming into a soft belly. She whirled around to face the floundering boy who came at her like a toppling bowling pin. She dodged his amateurish attack to deliver a jab to his kidneys, a fist to his face.

Bones crunched under her hand. Blood splashed. There were screams, shouts for help. One was already dead. She could smell his voided bowels. Another was on his way to meet his maker. She grabbed the liveliest. The thin one who had shouted at her. She squeezed his throat.

He wheezed, trying desperately to pull air into his lungs. His breath was sharp and ripe against her face, fear-stenched, and his eyes wide with terror.

"Do you like how it feels?" Kylie crouched over him, pushing the distraction of his dying friends to the rear of her consciousness. "I see you can dish it out but can't take it."

The boy wheezed. "It was him!" he gasped.

"It was him, what?" Kylie paused the pressure of her fingers around his throat.

"He raped our sister!"

He coughed under Kylie's tight grip, his body bucking as his lungs fought for air. Her grip abruptly loosened, but did not release. She pressed him down into the ground, a hand flat against his chest, knees pinning his legs.

Kylie spun to look at the man he and his dead friends had been beating into submission. "Is this true?"

She gasped the question, already fighting a sickening feeling.

"No!" The man uncurled from a ball on the ground, scuttled backward to sag against the wall. He pressed a trembling hand to his stomach. "He's lying!"

But she had already seen the truth of it in his eyes. The boys hadn't been beating on this helpless, grown man for fun. It had been for revenge.

She released her hold on the boy, flying to her feet. He rolled his head to stare at the bleeding man who was now in better shape than he was. His look was poison, filled with rage and pain. "I wish I'd been able to bring her your dick in a paper bag!" He gasped the words, fighting for consciousness.

Kylie stared down at what she had done, horror overwhelming her.

"Kylie?"

She turned to see Olivia standing at the mouth of the alley. Olivia stared at the dead and dying men, at Kylie's bloody hands and face, a fist pressed over her own mouth.

Fuck.

"What…?" Olivia's voice trembled. "What did you do?"

"Call an ambulance," Kylie croaked. "This one is injured."

With the dead men at her feet, she felt embarrassed, the thing that she had set out to do gone horribly wrong. She turned away as Olivia reached into her pocket for her cell phone.

Kylie wanted to castrate the rapist and make sure he didn't violate another woman. But she also didn't want to be wrong. She crouched over the boys she could save, adjusted their bodies on the ground so they wouldn't choke on their own blood. She straightened and looked at the rapist, her footsteps taking her unconsciously toward him. He shrank back against the wall, whimpering.

"Kylie!" Olivia's voice stopped her. "The police will be here soon." Sirens screamed in the distance.

She straightened and backed away, watching the rapist tremble in relief with each backward step she took. Kylie wanted to rip off his dick and feed it to him.

"We should go." She felt a hand on hers. Olivia's. The warm human fingers twined around hers that were sticky with blood. "Come."

Olivia darted a look over her shoulder, tugged again at Kylie's hand. "Come," she said again.

Soon, they were in the Jeep and driving again. Kylie sagged back in the seat, her bloody hands draped over her thighs. On the radio, a song was playing, something slow and sexy, a woman singing about moonlight and leather.

Kylie closed her eyes and tried not to think of anything significant. Tried to ignore Olivia's questioning looks. The effervescent possibility of the night was over now. The only thing left of it was the blood going to waste in a dirty alley, the fearful, darting looks that Olivia threw at Kylie's hands. And that man who had been getting what he deserved before she exploded into that alley. Her mother would have never made a mistake like that. Kylie closed her eyes.

Was it over now? Was this the way she would lose the human woman? To get her to be so disgusted with her and so afraid that Kylie would have no choice but to go back to New York with her head bent in defeat.

She opened her eyes when the vehicle stopped. They were at the gas station, well lit but mostly empty at nearly midnight on a Tuesday. Olivia turned off the SUV and got out. She opened the passenger door and pulled it wide.

"Come on."

She reached into the Jeep with the hand that was already bloody from touching Kylie. Mystified, Kylie glanced between Olivia's hand and the doors of the gas station, not sure what they were doing. When she did nothing, Olivia reached in, grabbed her hand, and tugged.

Kylie allowed herself to be plucked from the Jeep and into the light of the parking lot. They walked into the gas station and up to the woman behind the register.

"Restroom?"

The woman barely looked up from her magazine, only pointed to the right, past a display of monogrammed mugs with a peach on one side and the usual collection of American names on the other. Kylie vaguely noticed Olivia's name among them.

The bathroom was empty. A small white room with cracked tiled floors, two sinks and four stalls along one wall. Olivia tugged Kylie to the first sink, turned on the water, and guided her bloody hands under the sluggish spray. She pressed the soap pump on the wall five times in quick succession then soaped Kylie's hands, rubbing them together with her own while the blood flowed off their fingers in scarlet streaks into the white basin. The suds were pink and foamy, almost like the strawberry-flavored bubble bath from Kylie's childhood.

Strangely, she felt as if she could relax again with Olivia caring for her, being tender with her in a way that no one had in a long time. She swallowed thickly and licked her lips, unknowingly bringing the flavor of the dead boy's blood to her tongue. She lifted her head and froze.

Olivia was staring at her, an intent and unreadable look on her face. All the while, her fingers moved tenderly with Kylie's under the water. She swallowed again, feeling the slow rise of curiosity in her, a need to kiss Olivia and share the flavor of the blood she had stolen, to convince her with kisses that she wasn't a bad person.

Olivia's lashes flickered, then swept down, hiding her expression. Not that Kylie was ever able to read what she was thinking. Olivia bit the corner of her lip, an act of equal parts sensuality and bashfulness that jerked a familiar ache inside Kylie.

She found that her fingers were trembling, then that Olivia felt her weakness too. She pulled her hand away.

"I can do it myself."

Olivia's hands stilled. "Okay."

She moved to the other sink and finished washing her own hands there. Kylie looked away from Olivia's face, wondering if she had imagined that flair of anger. Under the water, Kylie's hands felt cold, and she longed desperately for Olivia's touch again.

With a twist of her hand, she viciously yanked the spigot closed. She dried her hands on the back of her jeans.

"We should go," she said softly, unable to look at Olivia.

Kylie felt herself aching with the weight of her wants. Shoulders heavy, neck bent, arms burning to hold Olivia. The air moved briefly with Olivia's tiny sigh. But she didn't say anything else, only turned and walked out of the suddenly too-bright bathroom.

CHAPTER TWELVE

The ride back to Olivia's apartment was a mostly silent one, broken by the music and occasional chatter from the radio, the sound of the Jeep's tires against the road, and Olivia's quiet breaths. At the parking lot of her building, Kylie got out of the SUV and shut the door with a heavy thud even before Olivia could get out.

"Did I do something wrong?" Olivia walked around to stand next to her, frowning.

"No."

But instead of walking with her back to her apartment, Kylie lightly touched Olivia's arm and wished her a good night.

"Wait! You said nothing was wrong. Why are you leaving?"

She gave her the simplest answer. "I need to feed."

Instead of waiting for Olivia's response, she walked away. She left behind the tempting dark comfort of Olivia's apartment to find and keep her own company. Olivia didn't say so, but she must have been disgusted by what Kylie had done. It was one thing to show her teeth to Olivia as a demonstration of what she was. But it was quite another thing to actually use those teeth in front of her.

She shoved her hands in the pockets of her jacket and hunched her shoulders. Kylie didn't know she was heading for the airport until she was in a cab and opening her mouth to give the driver her destination.

The driver put on the meter and Kylie pulled her phone from her pocket and dialed the number to the private jet company the clan used. By the time she got to the airport, a plane was ready and waiting for her. Less than three hours later, she was locking the doors of the penthouse behind her and stepping into the wide and empty foyer.

The house was quiet. Kylie's sneakered footsteps were loud against the tile floor. There were familiar smells in the house, hints of lime and nutmeg, but they were faint; most of the other vampires had gone off for a night of play.

She walked ahead through the house not knowing why she had even come home. Home. This place with memories of blood splashed on the white tile, sparring or horseplay gone wrong. Julia lying on the piano in nothing but a corset and high heels, humming along while Rufus played one of his songs. Her mother walking down the stairs, an elegant beauty the likes of which she'd never seen before. Silvija challenging her with an icy look.

Home. So complicated, and not always welcoming.

Kylie headed for her room, determined to put the events of the night behind her. It hurt, that possibility that Olivia would turn her aside now because she had seen what she was. Yes, Olivia had tended to her after the fight and after the mistake she'd made, but that meant nothing. She shook the thoughts away, deciding at the last second to head to the pool instead of her room.

She suddenly craved that feeling of her real home in Friendship, Jamaica. Water against her skin, the starry sky above her, wind in the trees like music itself. Yes, that was what she needed. She had to go outside to the terrace then back downstairs to access the second floor pool. But as she drew closer to the water, low voices reached her. The smell of cloves and the sea. Her footsteps faltered and she didn't know what to do.

She tightened her jaw and headed down the stairs. The pool was Olympic-sized and mostly hidden from outside view by large planters filled with tall rosemary bushes. Stairs led down to the sparkling turquoise water that was like a large piece of art on the entire right side of the second floor.

Kylie walked outside where she took a long and deliberate breath of the night air. It was so different from Atlanta. The air was crisp with the smells of the sewer and of money, of animal gratification and despair. Fall was a deeper bite on the flesh. The sky like a stormy sea. She closed her eyes and clutched the railing leading down to the pool.

Their words were soft. Love words. Intimate, so Kylie barely heard them. Still, the meaning of the words was unmistakable. She stepped out onto the wide metal stairs, sneakers banging gently on the steps.

Kylie was hardly quiet, but they didn't care. Her mother and Silvija lay face to face on white furs near the pool, their bodies, two shades of dark, glistening under the stars. Her mother wore her hair loose, a magnificent halo of dark around her face while Silvija's was still braided and wound around her head like a crown. They were both naked. Lionesses after the hunt. Their voices whispered and wove like a magical incantation in the night, creating a spell around them that made them seem apart from everything but each other. Silvija touched her mother's face. Her mother tucked her cheek even more into that large palm like a kitten being stroked.

She heard laughter. The sound of the Jacuzzi jets on the circular part of the otherwise electric blue rectangle of water, each rush of water seemed to say "you wish, you wish, you wish." Kylie widened her eyes, trying to push back the sudden prick of tears.

From her perch on the stairs, she'd never felt more alone. The mother she'd dreamed of reuniting with had no time for her. The love she thought she would receive was denied her at every turn. Always it was Silvija who received that love. Never Kylie. Always it was Silvija's name on her mother's lips. Kylie wished. She wished that one day, some of this love would trickle her way.

She stumbled to her feet, her knee clanging against the metal railing, and turned to leave them alone.

But even in the twisted coils of emotion that overtook her while watching her mother and Silvija, there was something that had become clear. She did not hate them. She did not despise their love because it was shared between two women. She was simply jealous.

Yes, she wanted her mother to pay more attention to her. Yes, she wished Silvija wasn't so important to Belle. But even more than that, she wanted something like what they had for her very own. Something that burned and blessed and made her existence about more than blood and survival. She wanted love.

The realization stunned her. She grabbed the railing that led away from them, went up the stairs, and to the thick, steel door leading inside. Kylie stepped in and closed the door behind her. Stood in the hallway and thought about going to her empty room.

Love. That was something she was bred to deny herself. Even when her grandmother had talked about finding "the one" and waiting to have babies with them, she always made it sound as if it were a far way away. That Kylie would do well to dismiss any thoughts of that from her mind.

"You all right, little one?"

She jumped at the unexpected voice. Too many seconds later, her brain processed the sound as Rufus. He looked stage-ready with his long and beautiful dreadlocks twisted in a braid down his back. He wore combat boots, black skinny jeans, a white T-shirt that showed off his muscular arms and wide shoulders. A smile twitched on Kylie's face, quickly coming and going. She was happy to see him.

"Yes, I'm good." She shoved her hands in her jacket pockets, glad for the distraction of his presence.

"I thought you were still in Atlanta." Rufus plucked his cell phone from his back pocket and looked briefly down at it before giving his attention back to Kylie. "You finish whatever secret mission was keeping you and Violet down there?"

Secret mission? Did that mean Silvija and the others never told the rest of the clan what she was doing away from home? That surprised her.

"I'm not sure." She shrugged. "It's confusing."

Rufus was the only one she would ever admit such uncertainty to. He was more than a little clairvoyant so she figured he would know what she was feeling anyway. Plus, she liked him.

"Feel like talking about it?"

"Not really."

"Cool." He hitched a shoulder. "Heading downstairs?"

She wasn't but decided to go. "Sure." Kylie started walking.

Rufus fell in step beside her, lips tilted up slightly in amusement. "If you ever decide to say what you have to say, just remember that the conversation doesn't need to belong to everyone. I'll respect your privacy."

Kylie nodded even though she knew that already. "I'll remember that."

She ended up in the common room where he dropped down on the bearskin rug near the fireplace, tossing his bag to the floor beside him and stretching out in front of the grated and crackling fire. "It's good to be home," he said, then glanced at her. "It doesn't look like you feel the same way." The flickering yellow flames created shadows and hollows in his already haunting face, highlighting the grave dark eyes, his cheekbones.

Kylie sat beside him, wrapping her arms around raised knees. The fire felt pleasantly warm on her side. "What is this, an interview?"

He laughed. "That wasn't even a question. What's going on with you?"

She was tightly wound. She couldn't help it. The realization that her jealousy was linked to something else that she'd never had in her life and never even knew she wanted had her turned a bit upside down. But it wasn't like she had come to Rufus for tea and sympathy. He was simply there and it was good to sit with him and allow what she was to fall into the background of things.

Outside in the city, the hungers and dangers of the world were rampant, beautiful with their savagery, but it was moments like this one when she didn't necessarily need to take part in it, that she loved. And those moments were what she'd often experienced with Rufus and at times with the twins. And always with Olivia.

At the thought of Olivia, she almost smiled.

"Atlanta is what's going on with me," she said in response to his earlier question. "There's someone there. A woman."

His eyebrow ticked up. "A woman?"

The entire clan knew she wasn't into sex, and had probably assumed that she was only into men. Well, perhaps not exactly an assumption since she'd said as much whenever anyone made even the most remote suggestion that she take a female lover or do more than feed at the neck of a human woman. She nodded. "Yes."

"Ah, that's the confusion." He nodded with another of his mysterious smiles. The shadows created by the fire moved languidly over his face.

"Yes," she said again.

"I assume it's with a human?"

She looked at him. "How did you know?"

"Because if it was with another one of us, the situation would be dangerous, or at least more dangerous than this. Silvija would be talking about an alliance with another clan, you leaving us, or the clan taking in someone else. We'd have a meeting to discuss the possibility that your lover's clan might try to destroy ours and claim our territory for itself."

After their forced relocation from Alaska where they'd owned practically an entire town, the clan didn't have much physical territory. Not here in New York. What they had was largely financial. Billions of dollars. Priceless assets. Worldwide influence.

Kylie stared at Rufus in disbelief. "All this just because I wanted to have sex with another vampire?"

"Women are emotional creatures. Chances are if you hooked up with another bloodsucker, it would be more than a casual thing."

"I think I should be offended!" But she laughed.

"I think you shouldn't be." He crossed his booted feet and smiled back at her, his teeth bright in the firelight.

Kylie laughed again and dropped to lie beside him on the furs. She poked him in the ribs. He chuckled and flinched back. "Watch it, little one. My fangs are bigger than yours."

"Size isn't everything."

"That's what the little ones always say." He grinned wolfishly and snapped his teeth at her.

Kylie rolled onto her back and smiled up at the ceiling, enjoying the quiet with him. *Home* was moments like this.

"So what are you planning to do about your human?" Rufus asked.

Wasn't that the ultimate question?

"I'm going to stop seeing her." A heaviness descended on her chest at the thought. Yes, Silvija had told her to leave Olivia alone. And truth be told, it was probably safer for Olivia.

"Why?" Rufus propped himself up on one elbow and watched her. "Do you think that's the best thing to do?"

Yes. Kylie kept the word trapped in her mouth. "I want her."

"Then take her." He smiled. "Although we are supposed to live until the end of days, nothing is promised. Someone could take your head and your entire world tomorrow." His gaze darkened as memories moved behind his eyes. Or maybe he was seeing the future to come.

Kylie fell silent. Thoughtful. This was about more than just Silvija's ultimatum. She had nothing to offer Olivia except blood-filled nights and dark days.

"You could always turn her, if that's your concern." He said it so casually that it almost fooled her.

Kill someone. Take responsibility for them. Live with their hatred of you until one or both of you turned to dust. She saw how her mother hated Julia. And she knew how she felt about her own maker, that natural born loathing that sprung between a maker and a child. She shuddered at the thought of Olivia feeling like that about her. And somehow too, she balked at the thought of killing Olivia. Yes, she was dying now, but even her abbreviated life with cancer was better than what Kylie suffered through every night.

"No," she said softly. "I could never do that to her."

Rufus shrugged and smiled at her. Kylie got the feeling that he knew something. Something important that he wasn't telling her. He sat up on the furs.

"I'm getting hungry. You want to head out for a bite?"

"Sure." The alternative was to lie around the house and run the risk of encountering her mother and Silvija caught in their haze of love. "I'm ready whenever you are."

Their hunt was fruitful. They didn't have to go far before they found an evening meal. A pair of lovers walking through the park under the streetlight, holding hands and laughing about something only lovers cared about.

The man was a pretty toffee shade with a brutal boxer's face, but with the boring walk and bearing of a gentleman. He wore a leather jacket over a black cashmere sweater and slacks. His woman was equally gorgeous. She had waist length black hair, skin like the lead in Kylie's favorite pencil, and beautiful cream-colored teeth. Her gray sheath dress came down to her calves and met the shaft of sumptuous black leather boots. Very stylish.

Rufus never killed the humans he fed from. She had learned that early on. Instead, he preferred to take them, give them tiny bites of pleasure that made them forget themselves, made them give themselves over to him with small sighs of delight.

"Any one of us can kill," he told her once. "But it takes a special skill and patience to leave them alive, wanting more, wanting you."

He liked to take at least two per night, snacks that amounted to a meal and left them as alive as when he'd found them, only with bites in inconspicuous places and barely a coherent memory of how they got there. Kylie decided to do the same.

They walked toward the humans with the penthouse at their backs, moving in silence through the night and toward the cooing couple. Rufus took the man without asking which one she'd prefer, bumping her shoulder and pushing her toward the woman.

They parted just enough to allow the pair to walk between them. The couple barely noticed them, they were so caught up in each other. They smelled delicious as they passed, like garlic and fine red wine. She and Rufus came back together then turned as one to look at the humans, to move lightning-quick and grab them. One after the other. The woman gave a sharp scream before Kylie slapped a hand over her mouth and dragged her into the trees. She wanted privacy.

Rufus's man only struggled briefly before falling under the spell of Rufus's hypnotic eyes. Kylie didn't have persuasion in her arsenal. Humans were drawn to her kind, she knew, but it usually took seduction—honeyed words or an adept tongue. She had neither of those things so she simply dragged the woman down into the leaves scattered on the hard ground and slipped a hand under her skirt, to her hip.

"Shh," she said. "I won't hurt you."

It was a lie, but she was a big believer that intentions lessened the sting of a misdeed. She didn't want to hurt the woman; she only wanted to feed and give the human a little joy to erase any memory of pain.

"I just want a little something from you. Okay?" The woman's eyes were dilated and terrified. She nodded, her head moving jerkily under the prison of Kylie's palm.

Her fear was delicious. It lent a lovely complexity to the garlic and grape flavor already caught in her skin. Kylie held the woman down, buried her nose in her throat, and inhaled. She shivered.

Pinning the woman's body with her own, a hand still caught over her mouth, she grabbed the woman's arm and lifted it, baring her artery. Her entire body pulsed with fear. A lush and seductive perfume.

"Shh," Kylie whispered again, the thudding drum of the woman's pulse pulling her mouth closer. The woman whimpered under her hand at the press of teeth, a delicate touch that Kylie had perfected over the years, canines denting the hot flesh but not piercing it. Not yet, not until that moment. The perfect moment.

"Oh." The woman grew still under Kylie, her body slack, thighs falling open in luscious invitation. An even sweeter fragrance began to seep from between her thighs, a hot and sticky nectar that made Kylie's mouth water.

It was because of Kylie's own natural perfume. She'd never smelled herself before, but others had remarked on it. Other vampires. The humans that had fallen beneath its spell. As delicious as the smell of fear was, acrid and complex, it was the scent of surrender that she enjoyed the most. She sank her teeth into the woman's willing flesh and nearly wept from the joy of it.

Chapter Thirteen

Kylie never planned on being a twenty-five-year-old virgin. It was simply something that happened.

As a child, as a human really, she constantly battled against being the odd one. The one on the outside of things. Back in Friendship, Jamaica, where she was born and spent most of her life, she had been the only one with a missing mother. If it had been an absent father, things would have been different; she would have been normal. But the missing mother abomination left her always on the outside of things, watching others, knowing their secrets but never being part of them.

She walked down Bleecker Street, hands in the pockets of her jacket, the flavor of the woman's blood still bubbling like champagne on her tongue. Rufus was long gone, tired of the hectic lights of the city. He pled exhaustion and went back to the penthouse, but Kylie was too keyed up for rest. It was night. They were night beasts. It didn't make sense not to be out in the savage beauty of the evening.

Kylie ambled down the sidewalk, shoulder to shoulder with what felt like thousands of humans. She had long ago perfected the New York way of walking through a crush without slamming into anyone coming or going, a graceful dance she had been in awe of when she'd first seen it in action.

New York in the fall smelled like the sewers and dead leaves, a thousand perfumes, and the aroma of millions of deliciously blood-rich humans. It was a crisp and heady bouquet she enjoyed holding in her nose for as long as possible before releasing it in a slow and blissful exhale.

Lights were on in every building she passed. Yellow cabs rumbled past. Beautiful people paraded by her with their particular city strut. The city was alive and blazing with sound, a lovely cacophony that was uniquely New York. Beautiful. Though sometimes, she longed for something quieter. A thought of Olivia floated into her mind. Her smile faded.

She dipped into a quiet side street that had red brick buildings hung with black metal fire escapes. The street had fewer people, a cleaner smell. High up on an eighth-floor escape, a woman sat smoking a cigarette, her legs bared in shorts although she wore a jacket and a thin, blue-patterned scarf.

"I can't believe you took me to that party."

She looked away from the smoking woman at the sound of the low, feminine voice near her on the street. The tone was teasing and intimate, not meant for her ears.

"Don't act like you didn't enjoy it." The person who answered was a surprise. Another female voice. This one lighter, higher, as if she were singing. But singing only for the woman who had spoken first. "I saw the way you were staring at Izolda's chicken Kiev."

"Marie, I'm trying to stay on my diet," the first woman whined prettily while the second laughed.

"You don't need to be on any kind of diet. You should eat everything I put in front of you. To hell with counting calories."

"The only thing you put in front of me that I should eat is pussy."

Kylie drew in a breath of surprise as the other woman laughed again. She could see them now. They were walking toward her, fingers linked, their heads tilted together as they exchanged the quiet intimacy of their words. The first one who had spoken had a soft, rounded body. There was nothing anorexic about her and she looked lovely. Long, red hair in curls draped over her shoulders and breasts. She wore a green sweater and tight black jeans. Pretty little flats. She was as luscious as a cherry tart with her red hair and scarlet lips.

Her companion was taller and thin and had something of the hungry wolf about her. She had narrow features, a sleek, shoulder length bob, and skin like an oak in winter. She wore a sheer, long-sleeved blouse, tight jeans, and boots.

They were both attractive. Not young, maybe already in their forties, and the way they held and teased each other spoke of an experience with love, lovemaking, and life that made them even more delightful. The couple smelled like food. Fattening and rich food that Kylie would have found delicious in her human life. Buttery rice. Meats simmering in hot spices and olive oil. Melted cheeses.

"You eat my pussy so well I want to see you eat other things," the wolf said.

Another laugh. The wolf's fingers sank into the lush hip of her lover. They stopped in the middle of the sidewalk to exchange lingering kisses. The wet sound of their mouths meeting, their tongues sliding together, disturbed Kylie, made her uncomfortable in a way she liked. She kept walking past the couple who reluctantly pulled apart and continued on their way down the street. Half a block away, she turned around and followed them.

They weren't going very far. Only to a building near the end of the street. Kylie quickly examined the building, the locks, deciding finally to let them carry on with their evening. Still, she stood on the street under the barely there moon, looking at the door they'd disappeared through. She didn't know how long she stood there staring, but it must have been too long, long enough for the women to make their way upstairs and to a fourth floor apartment. She heard them inside amid the noise and chatter of the other people at home, their love talk, their laughter.

Why was it that women together always drew her? Did she want to touch them? No, that was something her mother and others in the pack did. But the gentleness in them called her, even when it was a thin layer to mask the savagery lying in wait. Yes, Kylie enjoyed the illusion of sweetness that women had. It had nothing to do with what *she* wanted to do sexually.

She blinked up at the window, saw the dim light there from the women being in another room. Her body made the decision for her. She climbed, digging her fingers into the rough brick of the building to quickly scale the four floors, wrench the bars off the narrow window, push the window open, and slip inside. There was no one else in the apartment except for the two lovers.

A living room. The evening's darkness surrounded the clutter of couch, chairs, knickknacks on the tables, and IKEA prints hanging on the walls. She quietly navigated the room and slipped through it to a narrow hallway, following the sounds of kissing, of whispers, of clothes falling away. They were too caught up in each other to notice her shadowy figure in the hallway. She stood just beyond the open bedroom door to watch the wolf devour her cherry tart.

They made love with the lights on.

The wolf, still fully clothed, dragged her lover across the bed and into her lap, then finished undressing her with tender skill. She whispered soft words in her tart's ear, telling her how beautiful she was, how delicious she smelled, how she couldn't wait to taste her hot pussy. In the hall, Kylie bit her lip, feeling a rush of arousal that came out of nowhere. She was familiar with the sensation but caught off guard by it every time.

Naked now, the redhead lay back against the sheets while her lover pressed a jean-clad thigh against her pussy. The cherry tart made soft, needful noises, hands gripping her lover's ass. Her red hair slid across her bare shoulders, the white sheets.

"You're teasing me," she gasped. "Stop teasing."

The wolf only laughed and continued what she was doing, kissing her lover's throat, squeezing the plump breast, her thigh pressing and teasing. Her laughter was a low rumble in the room. The tart's eyes were closed and she looked undone by what her lover was doing to her. The wolf kissed her mouth one last time and pulled back to rest on her knees, watching her squirming lover on the bed, paying close attention to the pussy that was bare and open to her, a pussy that Kylie imagined leaked its ambrosia on the sheets as she lay there spread out for her lover to take and taste.

The tart squirmed against the sheets, touched her breasts, squeezing her nipples, tugging them to get some of the satisfaction that her lover denied her. The wolf laughed again and slid her leather belt from her jeans. With quick efficiency, she lashed her lover's hands together behind her back, tightening the leather around plump wrists until the tart cried out. But her cry seemed like play, an exaggerated noise of lust that made Kylie squirm in her jeans. She moved in the hallway to see more. She bit her lip again.

The woman was pressed into the sheets, spread open and gorgeous in her lust. She bit her lip and pleaded for her lover's touch. But the wolf knelt between her spread legs, watching her pussy drip, waiting.

"Touch me," she begged. "Touch me, please."

The wolf didn't take pity on her. Instead, she drew back to unbutton her blouse and pull it from her shoulders, revealing surprisingly lush breasts pushed up in a black lace bra, a gold crucifix dangling between the plump and mouth-watering flesh. Kylie's teeth ached at the sight of the woman's breasts, the press of her hard nipples through the cloth. The wolf stood up to pull off her jeans. Everything matched. Lace black thong panties. A beautifully rounded ass to complement breasts that Kylie imagined another vampire, Ivy, biting into, sucking the blood that would well up, as the engorged nipple poked into her cheek, begging her to pull it into her mouth.

She gasped softly as the image overwhelmed her; Ivy stepping in to rip the wolf from her lover, pressing into her on the hardwoods, sliding her thigh between those strong legs to make the wolf cry out. Kylie tightened her jaw to stifle any noise that might alert the women to her presence. But she realized that not even a bomb going off next to their bed would stop the women from finishing what they'd started.

The cherry tart watched her lover undress, grinding back into the bed to find relief from her desire. The scent of her sweat mixed with the leather of the belt keeping her captive.

Kylie felt caught up in the drama taking place in front of her. In the naked longing of the woman on the bed, in the seductive control the wolf had over her lover. The slender woman strode around the bed, taking the time to admire her handiwork, the lust she stirred in her partner.

Kylie pressed her thighs together, wanting something, but she wasn't sure what it was. Did she want to touch herself? Did she want to join the two women in their bed? Did she just want to drain them both dry and taste on her tongue the rich life that they enjoyed and the love they shared for each other?

But it didn't matter what she wanted. Or *that* she wanted. The wolf, standing on the side of the bed, grabbed the belt that imprisoned her lover and used it to drag her down to the middle of the bed then slung her across the width of the mattress until her head hung down the other side. Her thick, red hair tumbled down to the floor, and she gasped. Her legs pressed wide open, each thigh touching the mattress as she made herself completely open for her lover.

It was as if they knew Kylie was watching and wanted to give her the best view. With a growling smile, the wolf reached out and touched her lover's pussy. The tart panted with relief when her lover touched her, stroked her heated wetness with a lush and sensual sound that nearly brought Kylie to her knees.

Fuck her.

Kylie's hand fisted at her side. She didn't know what it felt like to experience the act herself, but she wanted to see it up close as she had done so many times before. And though she longed to see it, she was also afraid of it. That kind of lust, that kind of strength of feeling, stripped away everything. Every control, every humanity.

She'd seen it with Belle and Silvija. How they sometimes knew nothing but each other in certain instances, so far gone in lust that all they could do was mumble incoherent words to whoever was listening before rushing off to fuck behind locked doors. But the wolf and her tart weren't behind locked doors. Kylie could watch them. She could observe that stripping away that happened with lust and love and still remain apart from it. But even she had to admit that it touched her deeply to watch these women please each other.

The wolf pulled her hand back, licked her fingers one by one.

"You're so wet, I bet I could use the big girl on you." Her voice was low and deep.

The tart's eyelashes fluttered. Her breath sped up.

"Is that what you want? You want me to fuck you with the big dick? You want me to make you scream?"

The tart squirmed even more on the bed. "Yes," she panted with big, bright eyes. "Yes. That's what I want!"

The wolf's eyes gleamed. "Maybe another time."

She climbed into the bed then, full of mischief and purpose. "I *am* going to fuck you, baby. But not like you want." She smiled. "And you'll love every minute of it."

The wolf's teeth flashed in the light, and Kylie felt her body tighten in response to the commanding tone, the low and growling voice. The woman climbed back into the bed and pounced on her lover. She bit her bare nipples, licking the dark peaks until a low moan began in the tart's throat. Then gasps from what Kylie assumed were the wolf's teeth, sinking into delicate flesh, turning the softness into hard as the woman undulated even more on the bed, her pussy dripping so much that it seemed like she had come. But the wolf was just getting started.

She had her ass in the air as she licked and kissed her woman's breasts, treating Kylie to the sight of her rounded ass, the lips of her wet pussy open around the lace thong panties, dampening the fabric. She was as aroused as the tart, but she didn't touch herself. All her satisfaction came from making her woman moan and cry out. Kylie imagined another woman walking up behind the wolf. Pulling aside the wet string of the thongs and pressing her mouth to that needy flesh.

Would she cry out in alarm, or merely look over her shoulder in surprise before sinking back into the warm flesh of her lover, pleased by the attention she was getting but not at all distracted from her task? Kylie could imagine many women she'd watched do that. Violet. Julia. Even the woman she'd just taken blood from in the park. But she couldn't imagine herself doing it. Her imagination wasn't that strong.

Slowly, the wolf kissed her way down her lover's body, kissing her belly, her hipbones. Then she dropped between the tart's thighs, crouching lower and giving Kylie an even better view of her luscious rear and pussy, the steady trickle of arousal down her thighs and around the string of the thongs. Her mouth touched the tart's pussy. They both moaned, a joyous sound that made Kylie feel like she was a part of something miraculous and beautiful. A pleasure she could not only see but hear, even feel in the delicate wakening between her own thighs, the pressing of her nipples against her shirt and jacket. She swallowed.

They were beyond beautiful. The wolf crouching between her partner's thighs, fingers slipping neatly into her pussy as her mouth continued to lick and suck at her clit. The tart moaned and panted as the fingers moved in her wetness. Three fingers and she gasped. Four and she moaned softly, her lashes fanning open and closed, chest heaving.

"Phoebe!"

The wolf lifted her head, still fucking her steadily with her fingers. "Yes, baby?"

"Don't stop!"

She dropped her head and went back to pulling the thick clit into her mouth. The tart's thighs pressed wider into the mattress as Phoebe tucked her thumb in with the other fingers sliding into the soaking pussy. She sighed. Moaned. Whispered. Prayed.

"I can feel you!" she gasped. "I can feel you."

Phoebe slipped wrist-deep into her lover. Kylie stared. She'd never seen anything like that before. Hadn't even known it was possible. The tart gasped, her chest heaving, sweat pouring off her in lust-scented waves. Phoebe slowly started to fuck her with her hand. A delicate buildup. A wet tightness.

The three of them were caught in a triangle of lust, experiencing what should have been impossible, the dripping pussy swallowing the wolf to the wrist while she used the thumb of her other hand to agitate her lover's clit in time to the strokes of her fist. Smooth and firm. Slow and tender. Sweat covered the wolf's muscled body, her teeth skinned back in concentrated intensity. The muscles in her arm jumped as she fucked her woman.

"Fuck me, baby!" The tart moaned. "Fuck me! Don't stop." The sound of her pleasure stretched out like hot caramel. "I need you."

Kylie watched the wolf's face, saw a trace of discomfort there, her hand cramping. But she didn't slow her movements. She didn't stop what she was doing, only pushed into her lover's welcoming body, both of them gasping and crying out, the tart's moans rising higher and higher in the room.

"Come for me, baby," the wolf whispered. "Come."

The tart screamed, waves of sound rolling in the room as her pussy pulsed around her lover's wrist, dripping its cum. The wolf pressed a hand between her own legs. It only took seconds before she was gasping from her release.

The wolf was still for an instant before she slowly raised her head, kissed the soft flesh of her lover's belly, and then tenderly, carefully, withdrew her fist. Kylie's thighs trembled. She didn't realize how stiffly she'd held herself against the wall, her legs pressed together as the two lovers shared their passion. Would she ever find lust and tenderness like that for herself? She pressed her teeth into her bottom lip and slowly backed away from the sight of them.

While the women cooed together, lying in the bed with their legs tangled, foreheads lightly touching as they talked softly, the end of their lovemaking, a gentle denouement, Kylie slipped quietly out of the apartment.

She clambered down the side of the building, shielded in darkness, keeping as quiet as possible. Her feet hit the sidewalk, then seconds later, she smelled jasmine, a perfume mixed with the tang of blood.

"Did you see anything up there you like?"

Kylie only just stopped herself from whirling around in surprise. How the hell did Julia know where she was? "Are you following me?"

"Yes."

Her honesty never failed to surprise Kylie. Julia stood on the sidewalk in six-inch heels and a couture cat suit, all in black. A tiny creature made average sized by the towering heels and even bigger attitude. She put her hands on her hips and fell in step with Kylie.

"Why?" Kylie asked, irritated at Julia's presence and its threat to her afterglow.

"Because I wanted to. And because I think this behavior of yours is a little risky. What if the humans saw you?"

"But they didn't see me. They never do." Kylie looked at Julia. "When did you start worrying about humans?"

Julia scoffed, a laughing sound that swept her head back to show off the slender length of her throat, the strong jawbones. "I'm hardly worried about humans, little one." She smiled widely then. "But it does pay to be careful around any creature. Especially when you're trespassing on their territory. Anything on this earth can become vicious."

"But not everything is dangerous," Kylie said. "Besides, it's harmless. Watching is just something I do every once in a while when I'm bored." She'd rather cut out her own tongue than confess to Julia how often she spied on humans without actually stalking or killing them.

"Watch yourself, little Belle," Julia said with an intent look. "You don't know quite everything in this big world of ours."

"Don't call me that!" Kylie snapped. But she knew she was wasting her breath.

"Fine, *Kylie*." Julia drew out her name, exaggerating each syllable. "Take care of yourself. Your mother would be very displeased if anything happened to you." An unreadable look crossed her face. "And she'd probably blame me."

"I don't think you have anything to worry about. She doesn't care about me as much as you think."

"Oh really?" Julia made that laughing noise again, only this time there was no amusement in it. "She loves you more than everyone in this clan. God help us if it ever came down to her choosing you over us, Silvija included. You would win every time."

Kylie made a dismissive noise and kept walking, deciding to ignore Julia and her nonsense for the rest of the night. It was, after all, what her mother would do.

CHAPTER FOURTEEN

Kylie decided to go back to Atlanta.

It wasn't even a conscious decision on her part. She spent that day in her bed, pressed between Liam and Violet, marinating in their warmth and the combined scent of their bodies that drew her down into sleep like a gentle lasso. But she fought its pull, thinking for far too long about her night both in Atlanta and in New York. About Olivia. The threats Silvija had made. The short nature of human life.

Olivia would die soon. Kylie could see that as clearly as the first flush of sunrise. She wanted to save her, to keep her in the world for as long as possible, but she would never damn Olivia to an existence like the one she had. Never.

So, in the heat of her daytime bed, she made the decision to defy Silvija. But did not have the heart to tell her mother.

Kylie stepped out of the cab from the airport well after ten o' clock. With butterflies dancing in her belly, she stood looking up at Olivia's window and wondering what she could say after how they left things the last time. The hurt look on Olivia's face had made her ache in return. She clenched her fists tight in her jacket pockets and crossed the street, heading for Olivia's apartment and the easy climb to the balcony.

Within moments, she was inside the apartment, smelling that sweet and bitter scent that had seduced her that first morning. Olivia slept. As usual, she slept only on one half of the big bed, her slender body on top of the sheets tonight, sprawled on her belly and wearing a thin black camisole that rode up her thighs, the lace edge resting on the gentle curve of her bottom. She hugged a pillow to her chest, leaving the other half of the bed to the three pillows stacked end to end in the shape of another body.

Music played from the iPod and small speakers on the bookshelf, the same song, like the soundtrack to a merry-go-round. Like a memory.

Kylie sat on the bench in Olivia's bedroom listening to the music, a song by Lizz Wright, lulling Olivia through sleep. Her childhood. Kylie thought of her childhood in Friendship. Playing basketball with Tracy-Anne and Kenya on the playground with her socks drooping around her ankles and the smell of the orange Popsicle she'd eaten at lunch still clinging to her hands, making the ball sticky when it was her turn to grab it and try for a basket.

Tracy-Anne and Kenya laughed, wild like seahorses, tossing their short tufts of hair while Kylie missed her shot. They laughed when she made the shot, too. The rubber ball slammed into the backboard, rattling the chains of the net.

In Olivia's bedroom, Kylie stirred. Her childhood in Jamaica was different from any Olivia might have had. No PTA. No minivans rumbled down the dirt road near her school to signal a homemaker mom's arrival. No, they had nothing in common in their pasts. But the smell of amaretto from Olivia's evening drink still lingered in the room, so strong that Kylie could almost taste it, a small thing anchoring them together in the present.

A soft noise pulled her from her thoughts. Olivia waking. She opened her eyes, the long lashes blinking once, twice. The corners of her mouth curved up.

"I'm glad you're back," Olivia said.

Kylie bit her lip to reel in her smile. "Yeah?"

"Yes." Olivia closed her eyes and smiled again. She pushed the covers aside and swung her legs over the side of the bed. Sleep scent clung to her, warm and tempting, creating an illusion of softness around her that tugged Kylie from her seat on the bench to crouch at the bed's edge.

"Do you want to come out with me tonight?"

The invitation sprang from Kylie's lips whole and unplanned. But with it given, she realized how much she wanted to share the night with Olivia. It was barely ten thirty. And from the smell of her skin, she had been asleep for at least four hours.

"Do I?" Olivia repeated.

"Come with me." Kylie moved closer toward her on the bed.

The days and nights of being in Olivia's small apartment had been pleasant, creating an intimacy between them that the night had the potential to shatter. She reluctantly remembered the only time they had been in the night together, the blood in the alley, Olivia's frightened eyes. But after being in New York and talking with Rufus, Kylie wanted to do more with Olivia. Damn the risks.

"Okay."

They left the apartment at Kylie's suggestion, but once they stepped out into the night, Olivia took the lead.

She took Kylie to a sex club.

Kylie's eyes widened as she and Olivia walked together into the club. It was a large, converted warehouse space with brick walls and a maze of rooms. There were windows and mirrors everywhere. All the better to see the sex on display.

There were couples, triples, quads, and more of every conceivable mutation. Male and female and everyone in between, their bodies prettily presented, their hunger and pain for everyone to see. Kylie wanted to grab Olivia and bring her closer, protect her from the brutality and naked sexuality around them. But she had brought Kylie here. Was this the type of lovemaking she liked? Was she like Belle and Silvija?

"My mother comes to places like this sometimes," Kylie said.

Olivia looked around, her face calm, although Kylie could almost taste the shock and surprise on her skin.

"Does she bring you with her?" Olivia asked.

"No." Kylie quickly shook her head, disconcerted by the thought of coming to a place like this with Belle. "She doesn't."

Olivia looked at her. "But she brings someone else with her?"

"Yes. Her lover. Well, her wife." It wasn't that Kylie wanted Belle to bring her to places like this. Places that she didn't care for, but sometimes she wished that they would do something together. She cleared her throat. "She and Silvija got married years ago."

They walked through a narrow hallway with glassed-in rooms on either side. In one room, a pale woman was tied up and hung upside down, naked, with her legs spread and tied to the wall on either side of her. A thick, wooden beam in the center of the room held her body steady for whatever was to come. Rope twined around the beam and around her throat, her ribs, and hips. Her hands were tied behind her back. Her pussy was completely shaved and dripping wet, the orifice slightly open and reddened as if she'd just gotten fucked. Her long black hair brushed the floor, and her eyes were wide with bliss. A latex-clad woman, dark-skinned and short-haired, sat on a nearby wooden chair, reading out loud from a paperback. She wore latex from throat to ankle, her feet clad in six-inch black heels. A big, green dick was strapped to her hips. It glistened with a mixture of pussy juices, spit, and lube.

"That's nice." A smile ghosted across Olivia's lips. "I imagine marriage to be this wonderful state of constant happiness and sex." She laughed softly. "I know it doesn't make any sense, but it looks beautiful from the outside."

She didn't seem at all impressed by or interested in what was happening between the two women. Following her lead, Kylie pulled her own attention away to focus on what Olivia was talking about. Right.

Marriage: The greeting card.

Sometimes, it *did* seem like Belle and Silvija's life together was like that. Their front was a united one. And even when they fought, it was almost like teasing, one of them invariably wearing a smile, even if there was blood involved.

Kylie opened her mouth. "It does seem nice enough. But does a marriage like that make room for anyone else?"

"What do you mean?"

As they walked through the house of sex, she found herself telling Olivia the beginning of everything. How her mother had disappeared when she was a child. The rumors of Belle abandoning her for sex with a dangerous stranger. Kylie skimmed over how she was turned, but found her mouth curling down as she talked about her existence now with her mother and how everything seemed to be about Silvija.

"You should tell her how you feel," Olivia said, her voice low and soothing. A delicate counterpoint to the harder sounds around them, of sex and effort and pain. "She won't know there's something wrong unless you tell her."

Talk to Belle? That happening was about as likely as either of them becoming human again. She pressed her lips together and said nothing.

Olivia pursed her lips. "Oh, you're one of those."

"What do you mean?"

"Oh, *now* you've got something to say." Olivia lightly tapped Kylie on the shoulder with a finger. "I mean you're not a talker, but you expect everyone else to know exactly what's wrong with you and know how to fix it. If they don't, then they're the bad guy."

"That's not true," Kylie said with a quick shake of her head. At least she hoped it wasn't.

Olivia looked at her in silence, her lashes low over dark eyes. "I wish it wasn't true, because a quality like that will lead to a very lonely life."

"I don't need anybody anyway." Kylie shrugged.

Olivia rolled her eyes. "Oh, brother."

They walked in silence past a room with a doctor's examination table. A man was spread out on the table on his back, naked and panting, his arms tied above his head by thick rope and held in a masked woman's fierce grip. His legs were spread and a woman dressed in a white rubber nurse's uniform stretched his anus open with a speculum. The man released a trembling moan, begging the women for more of what they were already giving him.

Olivia raised an eyebrow. "Who knew Pap smears were for men too?"

Kylie didn't bother asking her what a Pap smear was. If it had anything to do with the wicked-looking chrome instrument holding the man's ass open, she didn't want to know. She startled when Olivia took her hand. Olivia led her away from the scene to gawk at something else. If she hadn't heard Olivia's hiss of surprise, she would have thought Olivia had seen this sort of thing a hundred times before and was simply bored by it.

"Is this the kind of sex you want?" Olivia asked.

With their fingers still intertwined, Olivia tugged Kylie through the seemingly endless club. So much sex. So much decadence. But Kylie felt utterly removed from it all.

"I—I," Kylie stuttered. "I don't know."

Her feet stumbled to a halt outside a room where a woman, angelically beautiful with curly black hair and artificially long lashes, was tied up and gagged on an X-cross. Her naked brown body already wore several long, sluggishly bleeding slashes. There were surface wounds along her ribs, her arms, and between her breasts. A woman who was dressed as a lumberjack, complete with massive and tattooed forearms, held a sharp knife between the angel's spread legs. The angel whimpered in fear, but her pussy was swollen and wet.

There was a fierceness to this sort of lust that seemed perfect for the way of the pack, of vampires. Slaps meant love. Blood was devotion. Manacles were a symbol of forever. But despite her dependence on blood, despite the fact that she was her mother's daughter, Kylie didn't know if these hard things were for her.

Olivia's touch soothed her. "You don't have to know. I just wondered." She paused. "I'm sorry if this makes you uncomfortable, I just thought with the, you know, the fangs, the blood"—she gestured to the sexual decadence and domination around them—"that this would be your kind of thing."

Kylie shook her head even as embarrassment touched her cheeks. "I've never done any of this." And she could not imagine herself in such positions, open and vulnerable.

They walked through the dungeon, Olivia leading her by the hand. The bodies and sounds settled into the background—the lash of leather against human flesh, moans and gasps of pain, the wailing music of pleasures Kylie had never allowed herself to imagine. It was all a background to the light of surprise in Olivia's face, the way the skin around her eyes tightened just the tiniest bit when she saw something she didn't like. The slim grace of her back in the black halter dress as she pulled Kylie along through a narrow corridor packed with the night's revelers.

Soon, they were through the hall then walking past the woman at the door who once again gave Kylie a suspicious look. *Are you old enough to be in here?* Kylie bared her teeth and allowed Olivia to pull her out into the cool night. They left behind the pounding bass and the barely visible front door for the lamp-lit streets. Olivia drew a deep breath of air, then another. She didn't release Kylie's hand.

Olivia took her barely a half mile away to a hill with a house—tall, white, and stately. For sale and empty. It reminded Kylie of the house where she and her mother had found the photographer and his pretty model. She abruptly remembered the feel of the chase, blood in her mouth, the girl's unfocused eyes staring up at the dark sky.

She and Olivia sat in the creaking front porch swing and looked toward Midtown, the slender tower of the Bank of America building rising up from Ponce de Leon Avenue.

"I love it here," Olivia said.

She tucked her feet under her and sighed softly, her scented weight swaying toward Kylie. "I was born here, you know," she said glancing briefly at Kylie before looking back out into the night. "But even though I went to California for both my degrees and loved it there, I couldn't imagine living any place but Atlanta." She smiled. "It's the perfect city."

Kylie smoothed fingers over the knee of her jeans, hyper-aware of Olivia's breath and honeyed scent. They'd stopped holding hands long ago, but she could still feel the imprint of Olivia's fingers on hers. She cleared her throat. "I've never been here before," she said. "I only came because of something I saw on the news. A museum opening."

Olivia tilted her head back in the swing to look at her. "I didn't know you were into art."

Kylie thought of the ruby necklace she'd taken, the cold fire of it in her hand, how the human men had chased her to get it back. "I'm not. Not really. I like how certain things make me feel."

"That's the point of art. It makes you feel things."

"I like to steal," Kylie confessed abruptly. "That feeling is the closest to being human that I know."

Silence whispered between them. The porch swing creaked. The night breeze toyed with Kylie's heavy hair.

"Being human isn't a bed of roses you know," Olivia said finally. There was something dark in her voice, an ache. "Look at me. I'm human. I'm dying."

The chains of the porch swing creaked rhythmically as they rocked.

"I have a tumor inside me," Olivia continued. "I'd rather be undead, like you, than face a painful death at the mercy of some disease that I can't control." Her voice was low and rough, pain tearing through her words. "I would give up my humanity at any time to be free of this disease."

Olivia's words filled Kylie with a quiet horror. "You don't understand what it's like to be like this." Kylie shook her head. "But I guess it's impossible for you to really know." She looked away from her. "It's hell."

Olivia put a hand on Kylie's thigh. Warm and firm, it forced Kylie's gaze back to her face. "Hell is waking up one morning and finding out that I have cancer. Hell is never having a broken bone in my whole life, living in what I thought was a healthy way, treating other people how I like to be treated, only to find out that I'll be dying soon anyway. I'd kill for a hell that involved me living forever."

Kylie sank her fingers into her knee through the jeans. She bit her lip and said the one thing she thought would dissuade her. "You would have to kill."

"Yes," Olivia said. "I would."

She stared meaningfully at Kylie, her gaze steady and bright in the darkness. Although Kylie didn't think Olivia could properly see her face, she looked unerringly into her eyes, passion and desperation blazing from her.

"You…" She paused, taking a deep breath that expanded her chest and lifted her shoulders. "You could turn me into what you are."

Kylie flinched as if Olivia had slapped her. "No!" She jerked back from Olivia in the swing and the warm hand on her thigh fell away. "I could never do that to you."

She shook her head, unable to believe what Olivia had just asked her. She stared out into the darkness, at the glittering brightness of the city, the long streets, the humans rushing through the late night, savoring the precious time they had to live.

Light. Blood. Darkness. All these things were easy for Kylie to find with her eyes closed. With the change, she'd been transformed into a squirming mass of wants. Desire with teeth. Only these things mattered. Love. Darkness. Blood. Blood. She hated what she'd become. And because of that, she'd never give Olivia what she asked for. She would never curse her with the kind of existence that made nearly every second an agony.

"No," Kylie said again. "This is a curse." She couldn't imagine anyone wanting to exist like this. She had lost her mother. She had lost her life. She had become a killer and, most days, she actually enjoyed it. She was a monster.

Olivia breathed deeply again. Kylie could hear the agitation in her blood, the heavy beat of her pulse. But her face remained calm.

"I've always known that vampires existed out there in the dark," Olivia said. "I know the terrible things that they—that *you*—can do. But I don't care about that. I only want for myself the light that darkness brings."

"Trust me, you don't want that."

"I want more things than you know, Kylie."

Kylie's hands clenched into fists on her thighs. Olivia was actually *asking* to be turned. Imagine if she had asked the one who had made her into this beast. How would that conversation have gone? Would she have rushed headlong into an undead existence just for the chance to walk at her mother's side again?

Kylie stood and the swing squeaked suddenly, a pained groan in the night. "Are you ready to go?"

Olivia looked up at her through the darkness. Silent. "Since you're ready, we'll go."

Kylie ignored the deliberate snap in Olivia's voice and walked away from the swing and toward the porch steps. Soon, the swing creaked again as Olivia got up to follow her.

They walked back to the Jeep in silence. They drove to Olivia's apartment in the same quiet. In the parking lot, Kylie closed the door of the Jeep and turned to Olivia, opening her mouth to wish her a good night even though sunset was still at least a couple of hours away.

"No." Olivia came around to her side of the SUV, the keys jingling in her hand. "Spend the day with me."

Kylie hesitated, knowing that she should refuse. Their night had turned out so differently than she ever could have predicted. She needed time alone to think about it. She needed to consider what it meant that Olivia wanted to be like her.

"Please." Olivia lightly touched her skin left bare by the V of her T-shirt. That warm hand burned. "Don't leave me tonight," Olivia said. The pain in her voice stopped any protest Kylie would have made.

"Okay," she said, sighing. "I'll stay."

CHAPTER FIFTEEN

Kylie dreamed about being bitten. She remembered everything about that terrifying night. Her fragile human self trembling with fear, her hands lashed together as the smell of death grew stronger around her.

It was carnage. The small vampire, Shaye, had lied to her mother and the others in the clan, had been the poison in the apple all along.

Kylie remembered fear. Terror. Thinking that she would die that night when the girl who looked even younger than her eighteen-year-old self slipped close to her with a smile, fiendishly kind. And Kylie had trusted that smile despite the gleam of malice in Shaye's eyes. She had trusted despite being taken by force from her grandmother's home, tied and blindfolded, thrown down in the basement, crying out for mercy. Kidnapped in retaliation for what her mother was and who she loved.

"What are you doing?" she had screamed, her voice scraping raw against her throat.

She rocked in panic, jerking against the chains that shackled her wrists and suspended them high above her head. They rattled from their bolt in the ceiling.

But now, the little beast was trying to appear kind. She touched Kylie's face after an eternity of staring at the chaos around her. Staring at Kylie with the fire and tenderness in her eyes.

"Your bitch mother loves you," she said. "That's why I have to kill you."

And Kylie screamed. A piercing wail that made her want to clap her hands over her own ears. Shaye laughed merrily, flashing white teeth, her nose crinkling in her mirth.

Then a slender blade was in her hand. She grinned and rammed it into Kylie's chest. A sharp, quick pain stole her breath and dropped her mouth open in astonishment. What did Shaye just do?

Kylie's heart pounded in her chest as if trying to fly away from the terrible room, from the blade. Her breath heaved. Her hands tingled from lack of circulation and scraped in the shackles above her head.

Her screams died away. Frightened breath rattled in her throat, and a cold sweat washed her palms. She couldn't think; she could only feel the absolute horror of her life about to end. And all without ever seeing her mother again. Tears scalded her face, and she shuddered even more against the hard cement floor. Her chin dropped as her entire body suddenly became too heavy.

Then she became aware of a scent, strong and new, very near her. Then a hand touched her shoulder. The beginnings of kindness.

"Things will be better soon," a soft voice crooned.

Then razor-sharp teeth sank into her throat.

Kylie screamed.

"Wake up!" A voice was calling her from far off. "It's only a dream. Wake up." Hands touched her face.

Kylie's eyes flew open. Instantly, she was aware of being in bed. With Olivia. She was trembling with remembered terror, and they were both naked. Olivia was pressed against her belly, the warmth of her skin heating Kylie in a way she'd never experienced before. It was almost too hot. Too much. Her hands framed Kylie's face, stroking her cheeks.

"I'm awake," Kylie whispered, her voice hoarse from screaming.

She cleared her throat and slowly sat up in the sheets. Olivia moved slightly back, giving her some space, but not too much. Kylie gasped, noticing that Olivia was startlingly naked. Her small breasts with their succulent nipples were bared to her and the furred temptation of her cunt on display. She breathed quickly, concern in her face. Kylie backed away and found herself pressed against the headboard. How had she ended up here?

Then she remembered. The night before, Olivia had asked her to stay, spend the day in her bed and take some of her warmth while she slept. She had hesitated, but seduced by the mixture of flirtation and plea in Olivia's eyes, she relented. They had slipped into the sheets together, both wearing clothes in the early morning. But Kylie remembered vaguely, waking up to rip the T-shirt from her body, tug off the thin camisole and panties Olivia wore to get at her intoxicatingly human warmth.

Then the nightmare happened.

The memory of being human and having it taken away from her in one savage moment. The confusion. The pain. Her fear.

"Are you okay?"

It took a few beats of Olivia's heart before Kylie could respond. The nightmare memory tugged her down into terror still, teeth sinking deeply into her, holding her under the surface of complete awareness.

"Kylie!" Olivia called her name again, reaching out for her.

"I'm fine," she said quickly, unable to stop her eyes from devouring the naked Olivia. Olivia's flesh and breath and her concern distracted her from the memories of the nightmare, but brought their own set of troubles.

"Where are your clothes?"

Stupid question. She remembered well enough in the night, taking them from Olivia's body, that feeling of satisfaction that had come when there was no longer any barrier between their bodies, in that half-dream half-awake state, only heat mattered. There was no such thing as desire, no such thing as a tempted virgin.

Olivia looked confused. She frowned. "What?"

"Never mind." Kylie was losing her focus, tempted by the sight of what she'd wanted for days.

"Are you okay?" Olivia asked her again.

Kylie could only nod. She stared again at Olivia's nudity. She felt itchy and hot and out of her element. Then Olivia seemed to understand.

"Do you want me to put my clothes back on?"

"No," Kylie said. "Yes." She bit the inside of her cheek as the confusion and want distracted her from completing a real sentence.

"It's okay that I'm naked, Kylie." Olivia said the words softly. "It doesn't have to mean anything."

She sat up straighter in the bed, giving Kylie a long and thorough look at her body. At her whole self. Her black, black hair, a short and elegant helmet of kinks framing her beautiful mahogany face. Her long neck with the small, coffee bean shaped scar at the base of her throat. The small and tempting breasts.

Kylie dropped her gaze lower, distantly aware that she had started to breathe, the sound loud and unnecessary in the room.

Olivia's belly was flat and moving easily with her slow and deep breaths. Her hips were narrow and boyish, slender where Kylie's were rounded and noticeable in her jeans. It occurred to her that she'd never seen Olivia in jeans, only dresses that flowed over her graceful shape, skirts that showed off the tempting curve of her ass.

And she was aware too, that she was mentally rambling, anything to distract herself from the V at the top of Olivia's thighs. But the noise stopped when her eyes fell those last few inches, tumbling into the neatly trimmed black bush, the hint of Olivia's sex peeking out.

Kylie swallowed thickly. A voluptuous ache bloomed between her thighs. A familiar agitation. She pressed her flattened palms into the mattress, the adrenaline pulsing through her body. Fuck or flight. All the sexual things she'd ever seen, all the longings that had ever flooded her inexperienced body came back in one overwhelming rush.

She jerked forward, a puppet at the hands of an amateur, and smashed her lips to Olivia's. Olivia froze. Trapped by an inexperienced girl's unwelcome lust, Kylie thought. She jerked back, embarrassed that she had allowed her appetites to rule her, but Olivia grabbed her, pulled her back, lips soft on Kylie's. A hot kiss.

She was so warm. Her hands slid up Kylie's back, under her arms, pulling her closer, the lips parting to taste. A flick of tongue against her lips. Surprised, Kylie tried to pull back again, but Olivia followed, still kissing, still warm, an insistent temptation that held Kylie prisoner in the bed.

Her body was singing. It was burning. It was dying all over again.

She opened her mouth to Olivia's tongue and gasped at the feel of it, the instant rush of wetness between her legs. Her fingers curled into the sheets. Her head was swimming and she was frightened and excited by the delicate and slow movement of Olivia's tongue licking the cool interior of her mouth. She gasped again, sexual need overwhelming her, the feeling only familiar because of what she'd felt from watching other women touch each other.

She lifted her hands, not sure if it was to push Olivia away or pull her closer. Her senses spun wildly, her pussy wet and aching for a knowing touch. Kylie moaned and pressed a hand against herself, a sound of confusion and agitation. She yanked her mouth from Olivia's, her breath coming heavily.

Olivia's eyes were nearly black in the dim light, her lips wet and parted. She looked hungry. Ravenous. Her gaze dropped to Kylie's mouth, but instead of kissing her again, she reached out and covered the hand between Kylie's legs, pressing Kylie's hand into her own pussy.

Kylie gasped, her breath coming harder, faster. A smile flashed across Olivia's face, then she darted in again, covering Kylie's mouth with her own, kissing, licking, sucking until they were both gasping, the sound of their lust building the flames of desire even higher between Kylie's legs. Her fingers tore into the sheets. She gasped at the sensation of her own fingers pressing into her cool wetness and against her clit, guided by Olivia's warm hand on top of hers. A hand touched her breast, then squeezed her nipple, a light touch. Then firmer. Then a sharp pain.

Kylie's eyes flew wide open. She stared at Olivia's closed eyes. Olivia was caught up in their kiss as she ruined and saved Kylie's world with one touch. Fingers tugged at her bare nipple again. Kylie shuddered and came apart, her world exploding again and again with the crack of fireworks in her evening sky. She panted, frightened of the shudders in her own body, the sensation ripping her apart under the press of their joined hands. Her back slammed against the headboard.

"I—I—what did you do to me?"

But she knew exactly what it was. She'd seen it happen enough to other women, the look on their faces like they were dying. Had she looked like them? With her body still fluttering, she slid abruptly from the bed, away from Olivia.

Olivia reached for her. "Where are you going?"

"Away. I—just, I—I need to be away for a minute." She stumbled back, grabbing her clothes from the floor.

"But the sun!" Olivia sat up in the bed, her face tight with concern. "It's still daylight. The sun won't set for another hour."

No. Kylie wouldn't allow herself to be trapped. She couldn't stay here with Olivia. It was impossible. She grabbed a hooded sweatshirt from Olivia's closet, a scarf, and gloves. A pair of sunglasses from the rack by the door. She unlocked the front door and ran out into the hallway and down the stairs. At the door of the apartment complex leading into the sun, she lost her courage. Instead, she crouched under the stairs in the small shadows she found there. It wasn't long before Olivia's footsteps pounded down the stairs after her. She appeared in her robe and bare feet, the smell of sex surrounding her like perfume.

"What are you doing?" she demanded. "Come back upstairs."

"No. I can't. I just can't."

"There's nothing wrong with what just happened, Kylie. It's perfectly normal—"

"No!" she cried. "I don't want to talk about it."

Olivia frowned, stepping closer. "Did I hurt you?"

"You can't hurt me."

Olivia stiffened, but didn't back away. "Is there anything I can do for you? Anything?"

"I. Do. Not. Want. To. Talk." She bit off each word, her teeth snapping sharply together. "Leave me alone."

The emotions were too confusing. She didn't want to deal with the sudden sexual energy between them, the idea that she was like her mother and could get caught up, swept away. Taken. It was comforting to watch; she had convinced herself that was all she needed. She did not need to participate in the mess of sex that left the body trembling with raw want, thoughts and actions out of control.

What they had done together made the nightmare she had woken from even more real. It made her remember again what it was like to be human. It made roughness of Olivia's plea to be turned. Everything was confusion and pain and a cyclone of destruction to the last shreds of her well-being and peace of mind.

"Please," she said softly. "Not now."

"Okay." Olivia made a placating gesture.

Her robe gapped open. Kylie caught the flash of a bare breast, the darker nipple. She groaned then turned and rushed out into the sun.

Even through her thick clothes—socks, shoes, jeans, shirt, jacket, hooded sweatshirt—it burned. But the pain was bearable. She ran from Olivia's building and out onto the sidewalk, into the crush of humans and their smells. They stared, but she didn't care. She ran through them, her sneakered feet pounding on the sidewalk, in gutters, through alleys, in search of protective shadows. She didn't stop until she reached the hotel. She slipped into the room with her keycard and into the bed next to a sleeping Violet. A human lay next to her, also asleep, her face pressed into Violet's breasts.

Violet stirred, turned, and was instantly alert, sitting up to stare at Kylie with narrowed eyes. "What's wrong?"

"Nothing," she whispered. "Go back to sleep."

But as she lay there in the dark next to Violet and her human, the smell on her fingers rose up to choke her. It was her own intimate scent, the trace of the shea butter lotion Olivia smoothed into her skin before bed. It was her damnation. She rolled away from Violet, pressing her back to her, and shoved her lust-smeared fingers in her mouth.

CHAPTER SIXTEEN

Kylie was running. The events of the night with Olivia, the touches and the avalanche of feeling that had her sprinting into the sun rolled through her brain again and again in an unending loop. She tried to outrun them, flying from Atlanta back to New York to escape the feelings, all the lust and anxiety and fear that Olivia stirred in her.

Then she was in the penthouse, walking through its pregnant silence while listening only to the chaos careening inside her. Sex and desire and pandemonium were things she associated with Belle, not herself. This was her mother's territory. Only she could help Kylie sort through the mess and settle her into something resembling normalcy.

In the penthouse, she allowed her nose to lead her to Belle, her scent of the sea, of home. Kylie didn't pay attention to where she was going; she only knew she was searching for her mother, the one who would have any answers she needed. That particular scent led her to the hotbox.

The hotbox was a room that was rarely used. It was a place any of the clan could escape to when they wanted to be truly alone. A rare enough occasion. The box was soundproof and tucked away from the rest of the penthouse's rooms.

It was an architectural quirk of the building, a glass box leading nowhere and attached to the rest of the house by polished steel girders, arching out from the main building and gripping the top and bottom of the box. Steel stairs and a railing led from the box to the rest of the penthouse. Like a Rubik's cube attached to the larger rectangle of the house. The entire room, only about thirty square feet, was made of tempered bulletproof glass and steel. There was a thick bearskin rug on the floor, a black sleeping mat wide enough for three, glass on all four sides. The room gave anyone in it the sensation of being suspended in the air over New York City.

Belle and Silvija were in the hot box. The room smelled like them. Their individual vampire scents, their sex. The noises they made rushed at Kylie. Harsh groans. Silvija's grunts. The heavy, wet sound of Silvija fucking Belle with a thick, red dick.

They were naked and on their knees; Belle's arms cuffed behind her back with wide leather straps, Silvija behind her, gripping her upper arms to keep her from falling forward as she pounded her pussy with the lipstick-red dick strapped to her hips. Belle groaned, begging for harder and more. Silvija grunted with each thrust of her hips, the white bands of the dildo's straps bright against her brown skin. She gripped Belle's arms, jerking her back into the dick as they made painful love.

Idiot. Idiot!

She stared at them, unable to look away. With the sight and sound of their sex, she was immediately yanked back to the room where, with a simple touch of her hand, Olivia had Kylie completely under her control. Kylie's teeth snapped shut on her tongue. She turned, and she ran. She didn't stop running until she was back in Atlanta, back at the hotel with Violet and her human blanket. That night, she hunted with a particular viciousness. When daylight dreams came, they were only of Olivia.

Chapter Seventeen

I can smell you."

Olivia unwrapped the plaid scarf from around her neck, draped it and the thick jacket on the hanger, and closeted them. The little knit cap, she left on. She walked down the hallway and deeper into the apartment without turning on a light. It had been an unexpectedly cold fall day in Atlanta. Humans scurried from place to place, building to car, in search of escape from the brisk wind and evening temperatures in the forties. Olivia's cheeks had a touch of deeper color, but she seemed otherwise untouched by the chill.

Kylie stood up from the couch, ignoring the tremor in her fingers, the fear that Olivia wouldn't want to talk to her again, but Olivia acted as though they hadn't argued. As if they hadn't…touched.

"I saw them fucking," Kylie said.

Olivia stopped and wrinkled her nose. She didn't look in Kylie's direction or ask her to repeat what she said.

"Who? My neighbors?" She continued through the living room and into the kitchen.

Olivia was a slender wraith in her bright yellow knit cap, the hem of her denim skirt brushing the floor with each step. Kylie followed her to the kitchen. Teakettle. Water. The flare of the gas stove. Olivia blew the flame off the match.

Impatience and irritation rippled across Kylie's skin.

"No." She didn't keep the sharpness from her voice. "My mother. Her lover."

"Her wife." Olivia turned, bracing her palms behind her against the stove, her body's incline dangerously close to the orange kettle sitting on top of the blue flame. "Did it excite you?"

The breath exploded from Kylie's lungs powerfully. Once. Then she froze. "Shut up!"

Even to her own ears, her words sounded childish, tinny and small in Olivia's kitchen. They strangely reminded her of what *had* excited her: being with Olivia in her small bed, kissing and being kissed, falling outside her own body.

"Were you spying on them?"

The gentleness of her gaze rubbed Kylie raw. "No!"

But she couldn't explain the reason she had been there, the need to spill her honest self into her mother's ear and create something sweet of this bitterness that lay between them. The fear of what she and Olivia had done, what that made her. What she was really afraid of.

Although Olivia wasn't saying anything, something about her coolness, her almost dismissive manner, made Kylie think she was pissed about how things ended last between them. She read Olivia again, not judging by her own standards or perceptions but what she had learned over the last few days of watching her. Yes, she was definitely pissed.

Kylie turned and left her alone in the kitchen, stomping back to the living room where she had waited for Olivia to get back home, rehearsing what to say to the woman who was not her lover but her…friend? Even in her agitation, she was very aware of Olivia's movements. Getting the brown sugar and box of tea from the cupboard. A mug. Her back was turned to Kylie, her body straight and unyielding in its pretty fall clothes.

It was time for Kylie to pull her head out of her ass. "I'm sorry," she finally said.

Olivia turned from the cupboard to look at her. "Are you just saying that because you want me to engage with you about this foolishness you have against your mother?"

"No!" She shoved her hands in her jacket pockets.

"Honey, I don't know the woman, but I do know everyone has a right to happiness. This existence can be lonely. Why are you unhappy because she's found someone to share her darkness with?"

"Why do you assume that it's me?" Kylie muttered the question from the couch.

"Because sex frightens you. And, as an only child, I get the idea that you don't share very well."

Olivia sat on the couch with her mug of tea. Steam rose from the large red mug, drifting up to her serious face. "I'd offer you something to drink, but I know you wouldn't take it."

Kylie crossed her arms in her lap, feeling combative. "There's something you could offer me that I'd accept any time." She eyed Olivia's throat where the pulse beat steadily.

Olivia slid her a wicked look, the corner of her mouth tilting up. "Unless you're talking about putting those lips of yours on these lips"—she pointed between her legs— "then no deal."

Kylie's mouth slammed shut. All her antagonism wilted away as she stared at Olivia in astonishment. Olivia's smile blossomed even more.

"Calm down. I'm not going to rape you."

Kylie stuttered. "I didn't think you would." Although if Olivia made any advances toward her, anything that happened between them afterward would definitely not be rape. She squirmed on the sofa.

"So," Olivia said. "Tell me what's on your mind. Why did you run out of here so quickly the other evening?" She brought her mug of tea to her nose and inhaled deeply the scent of bergamot rising from it. "Or shouldn't I even ask?"

The teasing smile had fallen away from her face, leaving her once more serious, distant. Kylie wanted that playful warmth back again. Her hand curled into a loose fist next to her thigh. "What is it that you think about me, anyway?"

Olivia looked at her, examining Kylie and obviously trying to decide whether to tell her the truth. "I think you're scared and angry. I think that you love your mother but you hate that she left you for another woman. Whether that means you hate lesbians, hate your mother for abandoning you, or are just confused, I don't know." She sipped her tea. "Even after what happened between us yesterday."

Yesterday. Had it only been so short of a time since those head-swimming few minutes between them? A few minutes where Kylie felt like her life was changed forever. She couldn't hate her mother with the same intensity anymore. Could she even hate her at all? But the other, she wasn't sure about. Just like Olivia wasn't sure about what Kylie hated and wanted to run away from.

"I'm not like my mother," she said.

"Okay." Olivia sipped her tea.

"I would never abandon my family and everything important just for sex."

"Why would you ever say that's what she did? It sounds like she loved you as a human and loves you now. She didn't have to bring you into the clan. She could have killed you or let you die all those years ago."

Would it have been better if Kylie had died? What would it have been like if she'd never heard that low voice at her ear, felt the sharp pierce in her throat that both saved and damned her? That voice hadn't been her mother. And no matter how many things Kylie accused her of in her mind, she knew that Belle would never have let her die in that blood-splattered basement.

"It sounds like you wanted her to just dump her wife and the rest of them just because you were back on the scene." Olivia put the red mug in her lap. "That's not fair."

"Nothing's fair," Kylie muttered. "She abandoned her family to sleep with another woman. A stranger she didn't even care about." *Julia.* She leaned back in the sofa, arms crossed, mouth tight. "That wasn't fair to me and Grannie."

"I don't think she'd have left you if it crossed her mind that she wouldn't see you again," Olivia said. "From what I've seen, mothers are mostly selfless. They'd sacrifice sexual happiness in a heartbeat to be with their children, to keep them safe and to stay in their lives." Olivia's mouth twisted into another of those smiles that Kylie didn't quite know what to make of. "Most mothers though, not all."

Kylie fell silent, having nothing to say about mothers and their sexual happiness.

Olivia sighed. "There's nothing wrong with wanting sex, Kylie. And there's certainly nothing wrong with wanting it from another woman. If our pussies stopped working after we gave birth, it would be another thing, but your mother is still a woman. So am I. And so are you."

Her lashes left shadows against her sharp cheeks as she looked down into her mug. "I won't mention what happened yesterday if it makes you uncomfortable. But—" A ripe smile touched her mouth. "I want you to know I very much enjoyed touching you. I'd like to do it again."

Agitation squirmed in Kylie's belly, and she found herself turning away, unable to look at her. *I'd like to do it again.* The words bounced around in her brain, distracting her from anything else. And her imagination swept her away, put her and Olivia in the countless scenarios she had witnessed in bedrooms, parked cars, and back alleys as a voyeur. She wet her lips and shifted on the sofa as arousal pinched between her thighs.

After a tense silence, Olivia made a determinedly cheerful noise, putting aside her mug on the coffee table with a dull tap. "Anyway, there's a Stephen King marathon on TV tonight. You want to watch it with me?"

Caught off guard, Kylie could only say, "Okay."

"Great. Our first date night." Olivia grinned.

Kylie stared at her.

"I'm just kidding!" She bounced up from the couch and brushed a palm under Kylie's chin, leaving her with the scent of her salty sweat, brown sugar, and bergamot. Her skirt swayed with the movement of her hips as she walked toward the kitchen. She looked at Kylie over her shoulder. "If this was date night, I'd take you someplace much nicer than this."

CHAPTER EIGHTEEN

Date night came much sooner than Kylie expected.

Only two nights of the seven that Silvija gave her were left. She arrived at Olivia's after an early feeding and climbed over the balcony and into the small apartment to see Olivia waiting for her in the living room. Olivia stood, hands on her hips. She wore a floor-length, diamond-patterned black and white dress with long sleeves and an attached hood that draped from her shoulders. She looked like a sorceress. She looked...curious.

"Tell me, what is this?" She held up her hand. In her palm glimmered the ruby necklace that Kylie had forgotten all about. The thing that had brought her to Atlanta what seemed a lifetime ago.

Kylie's face prickled with embarrassment at Olivia's intent look. How had she found the necklace? Kylie was sure she'd hidden it deep in the back of the closet.

"It's a necklace," Kylie finally said. She clasped her hands behind her back, not sure how else to proceed.

"Did you steal it?"

"Yes."

A smile touched Olivia's lips. "I saw something about it on TV the other day. The cops are still looking for the necklace, and the thief."

"Are you going to turn me in?"

"I thought about it," Olivia said. She closed her hand around the rubies and diamonds, caressing them with her fingers.

Kylie felt something cramp in her stomach. Disappointment. Because it certainly wasn't fear of any human police.

"But then I realized that, like you, I don't like to share." Olivia held up the necklace in her palm again then turned her back.

"Put it on me."

Kylie froze, then jerked into motion, the words of the command automatically moving her feet the scant inches across the hardwood floors. She took the necklace and it slithered into her palm, the rubies flashing fire in the small apartment. She undid the clasp, moved closer to Olivia, and smelled her skin that was fresh from the shower with a hint of the coconut mint soap she used. Olivia bent her neck.

Kylie put the necklace around her throat. The flashing rubies and diamonds were like kisses of light on her perfect skin. The V of the necklace pointed down to her modest cleavage bared in Olivia's dress. But it was her neck with its throb of hot and rushing blood that distracted Kylie. She'd eaten before she came over, had sated that always ravenous hunger. But the thought of biting Olivia rose readily to her surface.

And it would be easy. And delicious. Already she could imagine the slow thrust of her fangs in heated flesh. The moan of surrender Olivia would give, that they always gave. Slender neck falling to the side, she allowed Kylie to settle her cool mouth on hot flesh, and suck until they were both satisfied.

She trembled and finished fastening the necklace. The jewels had barely settled on her flesh before Kylie stepped back, biting the inside of her cheek as temptation flooded through her in a way that was disturbingly like arousal.

Olivia turned around.

If Kylie had breath, it would have left her. Olivia stood across from her as regal as a lifelong queen, standing tall and still under her awed regard. Her mouth tilted slightly at the corners; her chest moved with easy breaths.

"You look delicious." The unbidden words spilled from Kylie's lips.

Olivia arched an eyebrow. "Would you like to eat me?"

Kylie clamped her mouth shut; otherwise she would have stuttered and made herself look like a fool in front of this woman she wanted to what? Impress? Eat?

She swallowed. "How would *you* like to eat?" Kylie got the words out in one go, an idea taking shape in her lust-fogged brain. "A picnic in the park?"

Olivia looked amused. "Okay." She put her hands on her hips, looking at Kylie with a light dancing in her dark eyes. "I would love that."

It didn't take Kylie long to wrangle some of Olivia's favorite foods from the fridge and into a shopping bag. Then she grabbed a blanket from the hall closet, Olivia from the middle of the living room, and then the car keys.

She guided Olivia to a park she had seen often on her wandering hunts through the city. It was mostly isolated, with a scattering of golden and orange leaves on the ground from the fall season, an area of undulating hills and valleys under strewn ginkgo and oak leaves with the occasional stray cat or dog making its way past.

Kylie spread the blanket over the ground, set down the picnic supplies, and waved Olivia to sit down.

She had thought it through enough to bring Olivia a jacket, but the night was apparently warm enough for her to shrug it off almost immediately. She sat on the blanket, her legs curled demurely under her, the necklace shimmering against her skin and under the piercing moonlight.

"You look beautiful," Kylie said.

Olivia smoothed the dress over her thighs, her slender fingers making a hypnotic motion over the black and white fabric. "What's gotten into you?" she asked Kylie.

"Nothing."

But that wasn't quite true. There was something, and that thing was desire.

The thing she always condemned her mother for being victim to. But with that desire singing through her own veins, desire for a woman, she felt much of her animosity toward her mother drain away.

"I want to make love with you," Kylie said, then clamped her teeth on her tongue until she tasted blood, surprised at her own daring in asking for what she was suddenly aware that she wanted, and wanted very much.

Olivia sat on the blanket, watching her with calm eyes. The necklace and the moon and the short drive had mellowed her into something manageable, a nymph resting on the blankets beneath swaying trees instead of a sorceress with overwhelming power.

"I would very much like to make love with you."

Kylie swallowed the taste of her own blood. *Now what?*

She did not know what sex truly was, at least not from her own experience. She heard it in the whispers between Silvija and her mother and saw it between the women she spied on, from the vampires whose passion resounded through the house they all shared.

When she was alive, her grandmother had kept her from sex, sheltered her from anything resembling male attention so she remained trapped in ignorance, even a little frightened, of physical intimacy. And later, even though she watched people have sex and sometimes enjoyed the uneasy feelings the act stirred in her, she had still preferred to observe instead of participate.

But Kylie didn't want to dwell on the past. She had this moment to experience.

"I don't know how to start," she confessed.

A smile touched Olivia's mouth before she uncurled from her lotus position on the blanket and got to her knees to lift the dress up and over her head. She swept off the thin material and dropped it in the grass beside the blanket. Then she sat again, tugged off her panties, and put them with the discarded dress. She didn't wear a bra.

Kylie stared at Olivia, her slender frame, the bones delicately carved under her gorgeous mahogany skin, breasts the size of antique teacups. The ruby necklace was a bright red lasso around her slender throat. Her eyes looked up at her through lushly dark lashes, her mouth pink and damp. She licked her lips, lashes fluttering down. Her human body breathed and exhaled its delicious scents. Fear. Longing. Indecision.

Finally, Olivia made her choice.

"I want you to touch me," she said.

Olivia stretched out against the blanket, propped up on her elbows while the moonlight washed over her brown body. Her nipples were already hard with her want; her breath was quick. The rubies and diamonds of the necklace were restrained fire against her skin. She seemed wholly calm as she contemplated Kylie over her, watching with implacable eyes that from the very beginning, once she'd actually seen Kylie, noticed everything. But it was her hands that gave her away.

They flexed minutely against the blanket, a light tremor in the delicate fingers that made Kylie want to soothe her, comfort her. These were alien feelings to her for seven long years. She barely knew what to do with those emotions. What was it to soothe a woman like this? What did it mean to comfort her? What would it mean to touch her?

Kylie must have waited too long.

"Take off your clothes," Olivia said.

Kylie quivered again at the soft authority in her voice, and automatically started to do what Olivia demanded. In seconds, she was naked. Socks and shoes, shirt and jeans discarded on the grass. Bra and panties on top of them. No preliminaries. No seduction of a strip tease. She knelt beside Olivia again, slowly easing into the blanket until her butt rested on the heels of her feet. Grass poked at her legs through the blanket.

She didn't know what to do with her hands. Drape them in her lap? Put them on her thighs? On Olivia?

"Damn...." The word passed from Olivia's mouth like a sigh. "You're exquisite."

She sat up. Kylie couldn't help but notice her breasts again, the delicate weight of them that moved as she moved. The firm dark nipples that her mouth watered to taste. Kylie licked her lips.

The ruby and diamond necklace hung below her collarbones; the lowest cluster of rubies and diamonds dipped between her breasts. The gold and jewels would be warm from Olivia's body, and the heat of the stones would be intoxicating beneath her fingertips if she touched them in prelude to caressing Olivia. A hunger surged in her.

She wished she had been curious enough before to ask, to experiment. When all those boys and men had approached her as a child, wanting to lead her to some quiet away place. When the visiting lecturer at her college, a sly girl with lazy-lidded eyes and a suggestive smile, had blown in her ear and invited Kylie to her rooms off campus, even when, in the beginning, Julia had shown an interest in initiating her into the intricacies of sex, she had refused. Now Kylie wished she had said yes. Her inexperience paralyzed her.

"I—" Kylie stammered. "I don't know what to do."

She bit savagely into her lower lip as the beast inside her battled the inexperienced virgin, simultaneously wanting to ravish and savor, to devour and learn.

Olivia laughed softly in wonder. She touched Kylie's face, swept a finger along her jawline and trembling lower lip. Kylie felt her hands clench. She wanted to be better at this. She wanted so badly that it ached.

"You are so very lovely, Kylie. A part of me can't even believe this is happening."

Under the moonlight, Olivia was a goddess, the jewels gleaming against her throat, the silver light falling over her short black hair. Lashes long and luxurious, created beguiling shadows on her cheeks. Her mouth was lush. Perfectly shaped. The most perfect rose in any garden. Kylie stared at Olivia's mouth, the top and lower lips that were perfect complements to each other that she wanted so very much to feel beneath her own. But couldn't. She was frozen.

Then Olivia kissed her. Thawed her. A light brush of mouth against mouth that left Kylie trembling even more. Her hands jerked up to grasp Olivia's arms, the beast taking its due, to clutch and drag her abruptly closer. Warmth to coolness. Olivia's divine breasts against hers. Olivia's fragile breath in her chest, the beating heart that thumped wildly. Kylie wanted it all. Totally. Completely.

She opened her mouth and accepted, no *demanded*, more of the kiss, going by instinct and from the bits and pieces of what she'd seen of kissing, of intimate touching. She shuddered under Olivia's touch.

Kylie got to her knees on the blanket and pulled Olivia closer. Olivia came to her with a joyous cry, her body exhaling its delicious feminine scent, the nectar between her legs making Kylie's mouth water. They knelt together on the blanket, kissing while Kylie thought she would die from the feelings rocketing through her body. Olivia touched Kylie's skin, her ass, her thighs, while her mouth devoured.

Kylie wanted to yield to the experience of Olivia, but the beast inside would not let her. She lifted Olivia abruptly into her arms, dangling her over the blanket before she dropped her onto the thick cotton and fell on her, her hips falling between Olivia's parted thighs. She pinned Olivia's hands to the ground. Growling, she licked the small breasts, marveling at their salt taste and silken texture, ran her tongue along the scarred tissue of her left breast. Her ribs, the delicate cage that held her heart and other organs, her belly that trembled beneath Kylie's touch. The lower Kylie went, the stronger the scent between Olivia's legs became. Her head swam with it. Her mouth longed to taste. Her teeth flashed out, and she heard Olivia gasp in fear. Or was it excitement?

Olivia's hands tangled in her hair, urging her lower. The devil inside Kylie stopped her descent. She slowly licked her way back up Olivia's stomach to tease her breasts again, licking the firm nipples, biting gently on the delicate flesh as she'd seen other women do. Olivia's slender body writhed against the blanket. Her pussy, slick and hot, pressed to Kylie's stomach. She instinctively moved on top of Olivia as she suckled the delectable breasts, pulling at the fat nipples and drawing soft cries from her open mouth. Kylie's stomach muscles gliding over the hard button that was the source of Olivia's pleasure.

"Touch me." Olivia's nails bit into her shoulder. "Please."

Feeling truly impish now, Kylie grazed a nipple with her fang. "Where should I touch you?"

Breath hiccupped in Olivia's throat. She gasped. Her hips circled on the blanket, pressed up into Kylie's belly. "Touch my—"

"Do you mean here?"

Olivia released a trembling groan as Kylie touched her cunt, floating her fingers delicately along the damp flesh. She ignored the immediate urge to engulf her sensitive fingers into Olivia's viscous warmth. Kylie knew even more delight waited there for her.

"So good." Olivia moaned. "So good." She grabbed her own knees and pulled them wide to give Kylie the fullest access to her wet pussy.

The sensitive pads of her fingers felt every twitch and movement of Olivia's intimate flesh, felt the rise of arousal, the rush of moisture, the writhing need in her. Kylie pressed her palm hard against her pussy, agitating the fevered flesh while Olivia moaned and begged for more. She lifted her head to watch Olivia's face.

Olivia clutched at Kylie's shoulder, her nails sinking deeply into flesh. She gasped and bucked against the blanket. "Are—are you sure you've never—ah!—done this before?"

"You're the only one." Kylie watched the pleasure transform and soften her features. Beads of sweat popped to the surface of her skin. Her tongue flicked out to dampen the already glistening lips. Her eyelashes fluttered down to shield her eyes from Kylie's gaze.

"Look at me," Kylie said.

A single breath. Then two. Olivia's lashes lifted with difficulty, unshading the passion-dark eyes as Kylie lavished her wet flesh with alternating firm and delicate strokes of her hand.

"Oh." Olivia licked her lips again and latched the lower lip between her teeth. She stared down at Kylie.

She felt powerful. More than when she had some human on his knees pleading for his life. There was nothing like being the key to a woman's pleasure. Because in that moment, she felt that she was the only one who could bring Olivia the sensations that were transforming her face, that made her lose her breath and call out her name.

Kylie slowly slid her middle finger into the dripping opening. She hissed in reaction. The hot and wet canal slid millimeter by millimeter up her finger, encasing her cool flesh in heat. Her own pussy slid wet and swollen between her thighs, begging to be touched. But now was about Olivia. Kylie touched, caressed, stroked until Olivia was whimpering from her lust, body dripping with sweat. She shuddered again and again as Kylie stroked her clitoris.

For a moment, sharply, Kylie felt alive again. Blood rushing, cunt streaming, tears rushing down her face, pulse racing out of control. Then she realized it was Olivia whom she felt, Olivia and her vivid emotions pressing in at her from all sides.

The realization startled her, lurched what felt like a pulse in her throat, made her dive into Olivia even deeper to get more of the wild storm of sensation. She slipped down Olivia's body, latched on to the juicy clit and suckled it, slid her tongue under the hood to stroke the deliciously sensitive flesh. Olivia's hands dug even more into her shoulders, drawing blood. She quivered, calling Kylie's name.

Kylie fumbled up for the slight breasts, the hard nipples above her, stroking them the way she wished for hers to be stroked. She twisted the hard points, tugging on them, rolling the eager nubs between her fingers. A gush of wetness dripped down her chin.

"Oh God!" Olivia surged up on the blanket. "Oh my God!"

Her voice rose up in the night like music, threatening to reveal their secret tryst to anyone who would listen. But Kylie didn't care. She only continued pleasing the woman who writhed and gasped beneath her. The woman who raked her fingers over her naked shoulders, hissing her bliss, undulating her dripping wet center against Kylie's mouth.

Her nectar was like blood. Nourishing and necessary. The delicate flesh pulsed against her mouth like a little heartbeat, and Kylie opened her mouth wider for it, gulping down the hot flood. In sudden inspiration, she beat her tongue against Olivia's clit, fast and faster, moaning her lust into the damp flesh.

Olivia screamed her name, her body arching up into a bow. Her pussy fluttered against Kylie's mouth, dripping. Kylie drank more.

"Yes." Olivia pulled her hair. "That's—so good—yes!" Another moan left her throat as Kylie pressed her mouth even more into the dripping pussy, licking lower, then slid her tongue into the heated wetness.

Oh, heavens above! So good.

She touched Olivia's clit, stroked it, pinched it. Kylie trembled. She was nearly split in two from her pleasure. Waves of sensation rippled through her.

She gripped Olivia's waist, holding her fast as she drank from the source, plunging her tongue deeply into the wet center. She tasted so good, a hint of blood deep inside her body. Hunger flashed higher inside Kylie's body, a desperation to possess what she'd only known from bloodlust. It was almost Olivia's time of the month. She shoved her tongue deeper, faster, lapping at the vaginal walls, harder, more, as if she could call the blood up. It smelled so close.

Kylie shoved her hips into the blanket-covered ground, pushing her swollen and wet clit against the hardness beneath her, searching for any form of stimulation she could get. She pinched the clit again, gentler this time, milking the exquisite, slippery length between her thumb and forefinger.

Olivia bucked against her face. Gasping.

Kylie moaned with relief. Glorying in the river of lust running between her legs, the whimpering sounds that Olivia made as she shoved her pussy again and again into her face. The organ between her fingers swelled even more. Olivia screamed again, a long and luxurious sound, her pussy clutching tight around Kylie's tongue, a muscular pulsing that set off Kylie's own explosive reaction.

"Oh! Fu—!"

It was even better than the first time with just Olivia's hand on her. It felt incredible. As if her entire body was engulfed in healing flames, as if she were human again and every fiber of her was alive and wanting and giving and pulsing with possibility and sensation. Her entire body went immobile with the shock of it, an overwhelming feeling that stopped time. Blocked out all sound. Everything was sweetness pouring out from her pulsating center.

Then her surroundings came rushing back. Olivia's gasping breath. The crickets chirping nearby. The prick of the grass through the blanket. The soft pussy throbbed once, then twice beneath her mouth. Hands clutched and released in her hair.

Kylie licked her lips and slowly raised her eyes. Her head felt heavy, her body slack. Like she was waking from a long dream. She blinked up at Olivia, her lashes like great wings laboring through thick air. Olivia laughed, and it was the loveliest sound.

"My poor baby," she crooned and propped herself up on her elbows, watching Kylie with her eyes swimming with the remnants of her bliss.

The wind moved through the trees, whispering a soft seduction while Olivia seemed to sway to the same rhythm as the branches overhead. Out in the woods, away from the cell of her apartment, she seemed to grow into her power, a strength that Kylie had no idea she possessed. Olivia almost seemed like a different person. Her eyes were large and luminous in the light of the moon, long-lashed and wicked under the distantly winking stars.

She swept her thumb along the sensitive line of Kylie's lips still smeared with her juices. She put the thumb in her mouth and, with her eyes locked with Kylie's, sucked off the nectar she found there. Kylie's belly clenched fiercely at the sight of Olivia's tongue and the sly and dangerous smile.

The heat of it, the humanness of it, was almost too much for Kylie to bear. But she withstood the touch, her body weighed down by the aftermath of release.

"I think you just took me to heaven," Kylie murmured with wonder.

Olivia's smile widened. "Not yet, baby." She sat up completely on the blanket, all luscious flesh, intoxicating scent, and more beautiful than Kylie deserved. "But I will."

Chapter Nineteen

Olivia was in the shower when Kylie climbed the balcony the next night. She heard the hypnotic sound from the street, water falling on flesh, on tile, and underneath, quiet sobs.

She froze between the whisper of night at her back and the sadness pouring from the apartment. Did it have something to do with what she and Olivia had done together the night before? Did Olivia regret making love with her? The thought made Kylie pause longer, made her stomach ache.

Their night of sexual discovery had ended at dawn when, chased from the park and their comfortable blanket by the shadowy bruise of morning, they had raced back to Olivia's apartment. Kylie, afraid that her sexual craving would turn to bloodlust, kissed Olivia good morning then dashed off to the hotel where Violet was already asleep.

She had one more day until Silvija's time clock for her stay in Atlanta ran out.

A night breeze rippled the curtains, stirring the deep orange fabric that concealed Olivia's apartment from the street. Kylie stood clasped between the window and the curtains, listening to the water and the tears. Finally, she moved deeper into the apartment, deliberately making noise, bumping into the edge of the sofa before sitting in it. She didn't have to wait long.

"You're late." Olivia came out smelling like coconut and mint soap. A thick orange robe nearly swallowed her body, and the collar of a gray T-shirt peeked from beneath the terrycloth. Olivia drew a towel carefully over her short hair, drying it.

"I didn't know we had an appointment," Kylie said. But they did.

She'd gotten distracted talking with Violet about what Silvija would do if Kylie didn't come back home by the end of the seven-day grace period. Violet was worried for her.

Olivia sat beside her on the sofa and reached for the remote to turn on the stereo mounted on the wall like a piece of art. She turned it to National Public Radio and turned the volume low.

"You normally come just before dinner," she said matter-of-factly. "It's already time for the late news."

"Will you make me dinner then and pretend that I'm on time?"

Olivia's mouth briefly held a smile. She shook her head. "No pretending tonight."

She rubbed the towel through her hair again then brought the white cotton close to her face. "I'm already losing my hair," she said, peering at the small curls scattered across the towel.

Kylie had noticed the rain of black follicles, more plentiful than usual, at the collar of her dress a couple of days before.

"It's only hair. It will grow back."

Olivia looked at her. "Why do people say such stupid and obvious things like that and ignore the larger meaning of what I'm trying to say? Even you." Something like contempt flickered across her face.

Kylie felt it like a lash. "Your life won't ever be the same again. Your cancer changed you in ways that you probably don't even know yet. But you already know that." She looked carefully at Olivia. "Do you want me to state the obvious?"

"I want you to care about my hair!"

The towel hit Kylie in the face. She flinched although she'd seen it coming. She gripped the towel in a fist and dropped it on the couch between her and Olivia. "I thought you said no pretending tonight."

Olivia turned away in disgust but not before Kylie saw the tears hovering at the downward sweep of her eyelashes. She felt a flicker of alarm, of helplessness. What had happened in the last few hours to transform her smiling, seductive lover from last night into this?

"If I asked you to kill me tonight, would you do it?"

"No." An unexpected spasm jolted through Kylie's chest. She could never do that.

"Why not?" Olivia jerked her eyes back to Kylie. "What have I ever done for you to drag out my suffering like this and not give me this *one* thing that I asked you for? It's nothing to someone like you. I'm sure you kill all the time."

"Yes," Kylie muttered with a wry twist of her mouth. "I even kill in my sleep."

"Don't dismiss me. Don't bullshit me." Olivia stood in a flurry of terrycloth. The robe's sash loosened showing the shirt she wore underneath, the long, bare legs. "God! I'm so tired of everything."

Fear gripped Kylie's stomach. "You don't mean that."

"Don't tell me what I mean. You're not the one dealing with cancer right now."

"You're right; I'm not. But that's no reason to let it consume your life."

"What the hell do you know about life anyway?" Olivia's eyes became poisonous and grim. "You're nothing but a bloodsucking parasite who forgot what life is all about." She crept close to Kylie, bending to meet her eyes. "Aren't you?" Her hand whipped out and smacked Kylie hard across the face. When she lifted her hand again, Kylie grabbed it and grabbed Olivia, forcing down her own anger.

"Kill me," Olivia begged, falling into Kylie. She weighed less than nothing in Kylie's lap, a delicate misery. "I don't want this anymore." Her tears finally fell, splashing on Kylie's wrist. "Make me like you."

"Your life is not over yet," Kylie said. "You don't want this."

Olivia jerked in her grasp. "Don't fucking tell me what I want!" She tried to twist from Kylie's grasp, but Kylie held her bird-like frame, firmly but carefully. Olivia abruptly collapsed into her, her anger disappearing as quickly as it had come. She trembled against Kylie, trembled and sobbed.

"I'm not telling you what you want, but you can't want this." Kylie's hands tightened around Olivia's arms. "This is worse than death."

"I'll take anything before death." Olivia's breath brushed against Kylie's throat.

Kylie closed her eyes, rubbed Olivia's back, and made impotent soothing noises that even she didn't believe in.

"Oh, God!" Olivia cried into her neck, her hot tears falling on Kylie's cool skin. "I don't want to die."

She held Olivia for a long time, through the wild bout of tears, the hiccupping of her breath, then the calm that left her lying limply in Kylie's arms. She raked her fingers through Olivia's short hair, saw again the tiny coils of hair floating to defeated shoulders. Finally, Olivia sat up and drew in a deep breath. She wiped the tears from her face with the edge of the T-shirt under her robe.

The shirt, Kylie noticed, was tattered and gray and had the words "Bertram Family Reunion Smackdown" in faded block letters. Olivia twisted the hem of the shirt in her hands and sighed. She pushed away from Kylie to lean back in the couch. Her anger seemed to have passed, leaving only resignation. Wiping her eyes again, she looked down at the shirt as if it represented more than just something to wear.

"Where is your family?" Kylie asked. "Shouldn't they be helping you through this?" She couldn't imagine going through something as devastating as cancer on her own as a human. Kylie guessed that even Belle would have come back to Friendship if something like that happened to Kylie.

"I—I have no family." Olivia's hands dropped away from the T-shirt.

"That's ridiculous. Everyone has a family." *Even me.*

"Not everyone." Olivia stood then looked aimlessly around the apartment as if she had been about to do something but forgot what it was.

Despite Olivia's words, it didn't seem like she was truly alone in the world. She didn't wear that air of grief people did when death had stolen their family.

"Did they do something? Is that why you abandoned them?" Kylie asked softly.

Olivia spun to her. "How dare you assume I abandoned them? Family is forever. They were the ones who abandoned me." She turned abruptly away, pressing her lips together.

That didn't make any sense. "Why?" Kylie asked.

Long lashes flickered up, revealing the pain in her eyes. "They didn't want a vampire loving dyke in their family," Olivia said.

Vampire loving—?

"What do you mean?"

"They know I want to be turned. They know we've been—together. They know I've asked you." Olivia watched her face, unapologetic.

For the first time in her life, Kylie's jaw literally dropped.

"How—? I—?" Kylie broke off, not sure what to say.

She remembered Olivia mentioning once that she had known about the existence of vampires. But there had been other things going on during that conversation that Kylie had latched on to. Olivia had known about vampires before Kylie came to her balcony. And her family did too. Kylie stood and turned away from Olivia.

If Olivia's family had abandoned her, how could they know about Kylie? She'd only been with Olivia a few days. She thought about the sensation she'd had of being watched, of Ivy's warning.

"How does your family know about vampires? And about me?" Kylie asked. "Are they watching?"

Olivia's lashes flickered in the lamplight as she glanced away. "The Bertrams have known about vampires for a long time." She sat on the edge of the couch, crossing her thin arms over her chest. "My great-grandmother was seduced by a vampire. That vampire kept coming to her night after night and pulling her deeper under his spell until she ended up in a nuthouse." Olivia's voice was low and resonant, as if reciting events from legend or the family bible. "My great-grandfather saw them together. He gathered members of the family to track and kill the vampire, but they never caught him."

Thank God for that!

Kylie's mind spun. She knew some vampires had humans they regularly fed from. Even the twins had a man in the city whom they liked to share. But she never considered the families of these humans and what they would do if they found out about the vampires in their midst.

"What about me?" Kylie asked. "How do they know about me?"

"They watch my apartment and they listen." Olivia said it matter-of-factly, like she was used to being under surveillance by her own family. "But they never talk to me." Sadness echoed in her voice.

Kylie resisted the urge to go to Olivia and comfort her. Instead, she focused on the image her brain readily supplied, of a ragtag bunch of overambitious humans bursting into Olivia's apartment to attack her, make her pay for the seductions of a vampire she didn't even know. They would fail, of course, but the attempt would be annoying.

She should leave, and soon.

"Are you going to abandon me too?" Olivia read her easily, her face a cheap flyer advertising her emotions for all the world to see.

"No," Kylie said, but that wasn't quite true.

And Olivia seemed to see it. She sighed. "I'm tired." She turned away from Kylie, the open robe and T-shirt swaying around her narrow form as she walked toward the stairs for her bedroom. "Let yourself out when you're ready."

But Kylie wasn't ready to go. Her mind swirled with questions. And, truth be told, her body was already mildly addicted to the pleasure that Olivia so effortlessly stirred. She spent enough time running away from the difficult situations in her life, she wasn't going to run from this one. Not when so very much depended on it.

Instead of following Olivia to her bedroom, she went to the kitchen, put on hot water for tea, and waited while the water boiled, all the while listening for the sounds Olivia made in the bedroom above. She heard the mattress sigh with the weight of her body, the whisper of sheets, her slow breaths.

Kylie finished making the tea, added the one teaspoon of brown sugar that Olivia preferred, slid two shortbread cookies on the mug's saucer, and walked carefully up the short flight of stairs.

Olivia was in bed, lying on her back with her robe hanging off a shoulder, T-shirt rucked up around her thighs, her body in a pose of dejection. She was facing the wall. For a moment, Kylie thought she was faking it. The look was too perfect: mouth turned down at the corners, body sprawled on top of the sheets, the large robe pooled around her small frame and making her seem even smaller, more fragile. She turned to face Kylie.

One look from her devastating eyes and Kylie dismissed the idea of pretense.

"Have some tea." She set her offering on the bedside table and moved back to sit on the bench at the end of the bed.

"Why didn't you leave?" Olivia's voice was tired. Heavy.

"Because I'm not ready to." Kylie felt separated from Olivia by too much, the stretch of sheets and landscape of pillows, their different experiences, their longings. She broached the one that was the easiest.

The mattress sank with her weight as she sat near Olivia's feet.

"What if I want you to leave?" Olivia watched her, unblinking.

"Do you?"

Olivia sighed, turned her head away, and looked at the tea and cookies on the bedside table. Fabric whispered when she stood and left the bed. She grabbed the mug and saucer and took them back to the kitchen. Kylie waited a beat before following. She got to the kitchen in time to see her pour the tea down the drain and sail the two shortbread cookies into the silver garbage can under the sink.

"There's only one thing I want from you right now, and it's sure as hell not tea and cookies!" Olivia slammed the saucer into the sink. The red ceramic cracked as it met the mug, shattering into pieces.

She cried out and jumped back from the sink. "Shit!"

"Stop acting so spoiled," Kylie shouted, suddenly tired of it all. "I'm not going to kill you, so it doesn't matter what else you break in this damn kitchen."

"Doesn't it?" She growled the question at Kylie.

The robe drooped off her shoulder, fully revealing the T-shirt that came almost to her knees. *Bertram Family Reunion Smackdown*

"How about me?" Olivia stepped closer to her. "Do you want to break me?"

Her breath brushed against Kylie's face. She grabbed the front of Kylie's shirt, fingers grazing her skin. She tried to shake Kylie but wasn't strong enough. Kylie grasped her arms.

"You're going to hurt yourself," she hissed. "Stop it!"

"You can stop this," she moaned. "You can stop everything that's wrong right now."

The pain of Olivia's words gushed from her mouth and washed over them both until Kylie felt like she was drowning in it. Olivia's body was overheated against hers, strangely wrong and right at the same time. The familiar desire crawled from between her thighs. Heat licked over Kylie's skin from Olivia's touch, sinking its claws into her skin, shredding her self-control. She didn't have enough strength in her to fight it.

Kylie kissed Olivia.

Olivia gasped and tried to pull back, but Kylie didn't let her. She held her close, held her tighter in the tender prison of her arms, not hurting her, but definitely not letting her go. She sucked Olivia's pain into her open mouth, drawing it in, licking the wounds she could find with her tongue. Olivia pressed her hands against Kylie's chest, at first like she was going to shove her away, but her fingers curled in Kylie's shirt. Then they were kissing each other, sharing the sweetness and pain on each other's tongues.

Olivia grunted when her back slammed against the wall. Kylie muttered against her mouth in apology, but that didn't stop her hands from touching Olivia's breasts tentatively, then more firmly, seeking the tight nipples through the shirt. Olivia shoved off Kylie's jacket, fumbled for her zipper, but Kylie pushed her hand away and yanked up Olivia's long shirt. She moaned deep in her throat when she found that Olivia wasn't wearing anything underneath it. And she was wet. Astonishingly swimmingly wet, her pussy slick and hot to the touch.

She gasped. Olivia felt so warm. So vibrantly alive that Kylie wanted to dive inside her body and never leave it.

Kylie dropped to her knees, shoving Olivia back even more against the wall.

She was ravenous, and Olivia had everything between her thighs that she ever needed. Kylie jerked the shirt out of the way, tipped her head into the steaming pussy, and died all over again. The heat. The wetness. Olivia's gasp from the coolness of her mouth. Delicate fingers digging into her scalp. A brief second of pain, then she forgot everything but the salty sweet on her tongue, the moans above her head, the relief, the agitation in her belly. She licked Olivia's pussy, swirling her tongue around the clit that grew larger and thicker with each swipe of her tongue.

"Kylie…." The word trailed off into low moans as Kylie made her inexperienced way around her pussy, light licks, deep swirls of her tongue, not worrying about Olivia's satisfaction but sating her own hunger. There was no blood between her thighs, but the liquid dripping down her chin was just as good to her, nourishing her in ways she never imagined.

She gripped Olivia's thighs, shoving them apart, diving between them. The shirt floated down around her head, shrouding her in darkness, but it didn't matter. She could make her way around this miraculous pussy in the dark, blind and with no sense but taste.

Kylie wanted to connect with Olivia, tell her with her tongue and touch alone that she wouldn't abandon her, that she would never leave her. She wanted to take her pain away. Olivia bucked against Kylie's mouth and Kylie gasped, careful with her teeth that throbbed in her mouth, aching to burst out, suckle from her thigh, drink up the heat of her blood. But she held herself back, gorging instead on the swimming, hot pussy. On the noises Olivia made. Olivia's fingers sank into Kylie's hair, her thighs pressing back and widening even more against the wall.

"I want to see you!" Olivia gasped.

Kylie felt her reach for the shirt, try to pull it up. Kylie shoved the shirt up, but when it fell back over her head, she gripped it in her fists and ripped it in two, and reached up to shove it and the robe from Olivia's shoulders. Olivia grunted and sighed under Kylie's mouth.

Even after last night, she didn't quite know what she was doing, but she knew what she wanted. Olivia's pain gone. Her need to satisfy satisfied. Kylie closed her eyes and licked her, sucked the seductively salty juices from the soft and hot pussy. Kylie groaned and dropped a hand between her own legs. She yanked down the zipper on her jeans and shoved her hand into her panties.

"Fuck!"

She was nearly shocked at her own wetness, the flood between her legs, her hips bucking as she touched her own clit, rubbed it, and slid fingers into her cunt to fill the aching emptiness. Slick and cool. Wet and slippery. Their moans rose in the kitchen together, a chorus of sex and joy.

"Kylie!"

Olivia's fingers clawed the back of her neck. She screamed out her cum, shuddering, caught between the wall and Kylie's mouth. Her pussy danced against Kylie's mouth, squeezing out the last sensations. Kylie sighed with satisfaction, although she was far from satisfied herself. She blinked and stood up, yanking the robe and pieces of the torn T-shirt from Olivia's shoulders. She dropped the superfluous cloth to the floor.

Olivia looked stunned, lips red and wet, eyes glazed over with lust. Kylie grabbed her and lifted her slight weight to sit on the kitchen counter, thighs sprawled open. She dove back into the pussy.

"No!" Olivia gasped, trying to slam her thighs together. "I can't. It's too soon…."

Kylie shoved her thighs wider, her tongue already spearing apart the swollen and salty lips to dip into the slippery cunt and drink her up. Olivia grunted, hips sliding back away from Kylie who grabbed her, held her captive to the coolness of her mouth, still mindful of her grip and trying not to hurt her. She slid a hand between them, fingers on Olivia's clit, circling, pressing. A hiccup of sound. Olivia's hips pressed toward Kylie's mouth, her palms flat against the counter, shoving her pussy into Kylie's mouth.

"Fuck!" she cried out. "Your mouth…." she panted, hips moving faster, her clit getting bigger under Kylie's fingers. "It feels…it feels…." Then her coherence fell away, leaving just her breath and her gasps and the wet sounds of Kylie's mouth licking her dripping pussy.

Kylie deepened her cunt kisses, her hand working between her own legs, bringing herself closer and closer as Olivia rose toward the peak with her, Olivia's voice singing out above her head, a beautiful solo of impending fulfillment.

Olivia wailed and jerked against Kylie's face, shoving her pussy hard against Kylie's mouth, screaming out, hips tipping off the counter, bare heels thumping the wooden floors as she fell. Kylie caught the twitching pussy with her mouth, hands gripping the trembling thighs around her face, shoving Olivia back against the counter. Olivia screamed as the cum rushed through her.

Kylie didn't stop. She slid her fingers deep into the weeping pussy and latched her tongue to the fat clit.

Olivia pushed at her head. Frantic. "No! No! I'm too—ah!"

Despite Olivia's protest, her pussy greedily swallowed Kylie's fingers, sucking them deep. The sensation of the slick cunt around her fingers made Kylie's pussy twitch and throb, the lust easily reawakening and rushing through her. The blushing wetness of Olivia's pussy was an aphrodisiac that made her want to endlessly eat her up, fuck her, drink her, take her to the point of fulfillment and beyond.

Kylie felt Olivia's thighs trembling, threatening to buckle. She held her up with one hand while the other steadily fucked her, curving her fingers up the way she'd seen a woman do once, the pads of her fingers touching a soft sponginess. Olivia cried out, her fingernails shredding the back of Kylie's neck and her shoulders. She sucked her clit, stroked her deeply, fingers curling and stroking, relentless, tireless. A hot fluid gushed from Olivia's pussy, splashing Kylie's face, rushing over her hand, down to her wrist, down her chin, gushing over the kitchen floor.

"Kylie!"

Her cunt clutched around Kylie's fingers as she came again. Kylie's knees slid in the wetness on the floor, but she didn't stop. She kept eating and licking and sucking and fucking, following Olivia on her knees across the kitchen when she tried to escape the press of Kylie's fingers, the lash of her tongue. Kylie wanted to give her more of that, let her know without a doubt that Kylie wasn't going anywhere, and it was only if she pushed her away was she going to go and even then she would have a hard as fuck time getting rid of her.

Olivia's hips jerked again in orgasm, her knees completely giving out as she collapsed on Kylie's face. Kylie caught her, gave her delicious pussy one last lick before she swept her up into her arms, and took her back to her bed.

Olivia was delirious, her thighs painted wet with her cum, head hanging limply from her neck. Kylie let her slide from her arms into the sheets and started to move away. But Olivia gripped her with a surprisingly strong hand. "Don't go."

"I...are you sure?" Kylie asked. Olivia had been so angry at her earlier.

"I want you here." Her voice was hoarse from her passionate screams.

After a brief hesitation, Kylie shrugged out of her clothes and slid into the bed beside Olivia. Instead of falling immediately asleep, Olivia rolled over until she was lying on top of Kylie, heavy-lidded and satisfied.

She lifted Kylie's hand and put it to her breast. "Can you feel it?"

"Your breast? Yes." She gently squeezed the soft mound, the miraculous, feminine flesh.

"No. The tumor." Olivia curled her fingers around Kylie's. "It's going to kill me."

A flash of fear made Kylie twitch. "No. It won't."

Olivia looked at her with serious, dark eyes. "Then what's going to happen? Will you make me what you are?"

Kylie couldn't answer.

"Unless you give me what I need, I *will* die."

"You won't," Kylie insisted.

She grabbed Olivia's waist and pulled her closer. If her will was all that kept Olivia from being cancer-free, she'd be cured. But it wasn't, and Olivia was dying. Kylie squeezed her eyes shut and held on to her.

Olivia didn't want to be held; she wanted to be changed. And since Kylie couldn't give her that, she left. She left the small apartment and slid from the balcony, intent on finding food and some way to bury her unease.

CHAPTER TWENTY

Outside, she was vaguely aware of shapes around her, humans, who smelled faintly metallic. But they were humans, so she dismissed them almost immediately from her mind. Olivia was the only human she needed to concern herself with. Her pain. Her wish to be made into a monster.

The sickness was slowly ravaging her body. Kylie could feel it and Olivia could too. And although she didn't know anything about cancer and its various treatments, she had the sick feeling that Olivia was putting off any normal human medical treatment on the off chance that Kylie would exchange blood with her.

But she couldn't.

Kylie wanted to save Olivia. She wanted her to live as long as possible so they could spend more time together. She wanted something like what her mother and Silvija had. But each time she even contemplated giving in to what Olivia asked for, she remembered the terror of her own change. She remembered how miserable her existence in the clan was. Before Olivia.

She bit her lip, barely paying attention to where she was going. The smell of easy prey was to the west and she followed it, putting her body on automatic pilot as her thoughts spun around the problem, although each revolution brought her back to the inevitable conclusion. She had to give Olivia what she wanted. No, what she *needed*.

As Kylie's feet sank once more into the grass of the building's front lawn, she heard a "click!" then felt a sudden sting in her shoulder, a shock, an electric pulse that dropped her to the ground, jerking uncontrollably. Grass at her back, her body seized tightly, going completely rigid. She felt nothing but pain.

She screamed behind clenched teeth.

The seven days Silvija had given her were up, she thought wildly. "It won't last long! Go!"

She heard the words, heard the humans, but could only lie there staring at the night sky unable to do more than twitch. Another stinging shock and another. Then male figures shadowed by the clouds obscuring the moon. One man. Then three. A woman. They swarmed over her, rolled her down the slight hill. The world spun and wet grass clung to her jacket and jeans, swiping across her face. Then she stopped with a jolt. A van door slid open. Then she was abruptly lifted and thrown into the van on the floor. She jolted from the impact, head slamming against the metal floor, teeth snapping together.

"Go! Go!"

It was only one voice that had spoken. Everyone else was quiet, moving in a way she could only describe as efficient as she shuddered on the floor from what she realized then was the effect of an extraordinarily powerful Taser.

"Knock it out. I don't want it getting ideas about where we're going."

The words were barely gone from the speaker's lips before she felt a hard blow at the base of her skull. A sharp pain that made her want to rip someone's head off. Then darkness.

❖

She emerged from the darkness minutes or seconds later, uncertain about how much time had passed.

Kylie blinked but could not penetrate the darkness. She closed her eyes again, this time tightly, then she realized they had blindfolded her. They had chained her. Humans. The pain was gone, but she was shackled tight, her ankles and wrists bound together. A piece of thick tape trapped her mouth shut. Whoever it was had taped an opaque cloth bag around her head to keep her from seeing her surroundings.

What the fuck?

"You have no idea who you're fucking with!" she growled from behind the tape.

But whatever it was they were up to, they had done their research or at least prepared to bring down a lion. Or a small vampire. Chains clanged when she tried to move her arms from behind her back. They were on loosely, but not so loose that she could maneuver very well in them. The chains were hard. Damn near unbreakable. What kind of material were they made of?

"She's trying to break the chains." A new voice attached to a body that smelled of chemical enhancements, steroids.

"Good. I was hoping she'd do something stupid like that."

Kylie heard a slight pop. Then something sharp pricked her arm. A needle. She hissed as something medicinal, something unusually strong, rushed into her body from the needle. What were they trying to do? Before she could think through whatever it was that was happening to her, darkness reached up and dragged her down once again.

She woke up in a cage. She lay in the dark provided by her own closed eyes, trying to get her bearings. Her body felt weak, arms lying heavily at her sides, the blood moving sluggishly through her, telling her it was almost time for her to feed again. Kylie lay still, listening to the sounds around her, the ticks, hum, and pulsing of a vast place. Electricity humming through lines. Water rushing through pipes. Refrigerators. Humans.

Kylie heard their voices, their breaths, conversation that seemed to be about nothing. Some sort of game. A winning side. The loser that was about to be obliterated off the field. She counted. Twenty-three of them. Maybe twenty-four. Most of them scattered throughout the complex, at least eight gathered at a point nearly thirty feet away. The ticks and hums were concentrated there. Some sort of monitoring station probably watching her while she twitched and woke from her artificial sleep.

She'd been captured. Drugged.

Fear began to pulse to life deep in her chest. But Kylie fought for calm. Fought and lost. This was too much like the night she had been taken and turned. The terror of that night in Jamaica still burned at the back of her throat even after all these years.

The memory of those terrified mornings, of that night her life had ended, shot her upright on the cold and unforgiving floor. Her eyes snapped open and chains rattled. Her hands and feet were still imprisoned, and this time the chains were attached to a thick pylon that ran from the ceiling to the cement floor of her cell. She was naked. Her jacket, her jeans, her tennis shoes, her cell phone were all gone. A harsh, bright light flooded down at her from the ceiling.

In a panic, she swore she heard her long forgotten heartbeat, the sound of blood pounding in her ears. Her calm dropped away from her.

"Where the *fuck* am I?" she shouted, rattling the chains.

Across from her was a row of cages, all empty but with signs of recent occupation. Bloody handprints on the bars. Clothes strewn on the hay-lined floor. Hay?

She shouted again and again. But no one came. The floors in front of the cages were cement, leading away from her in both directions. She struggled to her knees and crawled as close to the bars as she could while her chains rattled. There was no one in sight. No humans and certainly no vampires. The smell of gun oil, old blood, metal, and pain assaulted her.

What the fuck?

She yanked at her chains again, but they were stronger than any she'd encountered as a vampire. Meant to hold someone like her prisoner. A deeper alarm stabbed at her. She twisted her neck to see more of her prison. Her captors had planned well. She saw nothing that gave her hope for escape, only signs of her absolute imprisonment. Other cages. The hard cement floor that looked like it had been recently hosed down, flickering shadows of the humans who were close but did not come toward her. Anger and dread burned in Kylie's chest.

"Fuck you!" she screamed.

The shadows beyond her cell moved. She heard the sound of footsteps, calm breathing, smelled a male scent.

"No, fuck *you*, little bitch."

A tall human stood in front of her cage. He looked down at her with cold indifference, although it seemed that a deep anger burned in him. He wore fatigues and combat boots, like he was in the middle of a war. He had khaki skin, pale blue eyes, and a muscled body under the long-sleeved shirt and pants. There was a patch over his right breast pocket, a bright yellow sun with arrows flying from it. Something about him tugged at her memory.

"What am I doing here?" she growled.

"You're here to suffer and die." He said the words almost tenderly as he put his hands in his pants pockets. "But I'll give you the courtesy you never gave to your victims. You won't have to scream as we drain the life out of you and we won't toy with you. Much. We want to give you vampires a taste of your own bitter medicine." His eyes narrowed with malice, the mask of indifference falling away. "You'll see how it feels to be hunted and exterminated." He grinned now, his hatred completely out in the open. "I have some toys especially made in the lab for you leeches. You won't enjoy them, but I know I will."

Despite the fear rising up to choke her, Kylie snapped at him in anger. "What the fuck are you talking about?"

"Don't bother with the innocent act, leech. It's much too late for that." He smiled again, baring teeth that were almost too sharp and white to be human.

"I'm not acting, blood bag!" A growl rumbled in her chest. "I don't know what you're talking about."

Shit. What the hell had she gotten herself into? She suddenly longed for home with an intensity that made tears burn the backs of her eyes. Fuck! If only she'd stayed there and not wandered back to Georgia like Silvija had warned her. She squeezed her eyes shut, then opened them again. But it was too late now for that.

The man grinned again. With his hands still shoved in his pockets, he walked away. She yanked at her chains, trying to get free. But her body felt sluggish and heavy, almost human in its limitations. Kylie sagged in her bonds, sinking to the floor in a defeated crouch.

Time passed, but she didn't know exactly how much. No one else came to bother her, but she heard their sounds in the rest of the vast complex, their obviously coded language, people arguing, others laughing. Then a familiar smell jerked her from her stupor. A woman. She twitched in her chains, looked around in confusion.

"No!" the woman shouted. "Why are you doing this to her?"

"Get in there and shut up." The sounds of a struggle, hands on flesh, feet dragging across the floor. "If it wasn't for you, the leech wouldn't even be here."

Kylie stared at the empty place in front of her cell in disbelief. The woman appeared seconds later.

Olivia.

She gasped when she saw Kylie, her face a mask of horror and guilt. Only hours before, Kylie had left her in bed, naked and melancholy, her body lushly scented from their sex. Now Olivia was wearing sneakers, jeans, and a long-sleeved black shirt. Kylie had never seen her in anything but long dresses or skirts.

The man had his hand clenched around her lower arm. He bared his teeth at Kylie, a triumphant smile.

"Do you know what I'm talking about now?" he asked.

She breathed Olivia's name. "What the fuck is going on?"

But even as she asked the question, she felt there was some connection between Olivia and the man. She knew this was no coincidence. There was something planned about this.

Olivia stared at Kylie in the cell, looking everywhere but in her face. The concrete floor. The chains around Kylie's wrists and ankles. Her naked body. Then she looked back at the man with his hand gripped around her arm. "Let her go."

The man shook his head, like a dog suddenly finding himself in water. "You know I can't do that."

"I told you to leave things alone, Max!" Olivia yanked her arm from the man's and crossed both arms over her chest. "I made my choices and you did too."

"The family would never abandon you to some bloodsucker, Olivia. We'd rather kill her first." He matched her stance, arms crossed, legs planted wide. "Or you."

Kylie jerked in her chains.

Family?

She stared between the man—Max—who held her captive and the woman she had been growing to love. He was pale and she was dark. But looking beyond that, Kylie could easily see the similarities. The shape of the eyes. The sharp cheekbones. There was even an identical curve to their lips. Then she remembered his face from Olivia's photo album. And from the street in front of the apartment.

What the fuck?

Olivia glanced at Kylie and flinched. "I need to talk with her, Max."

He tightened his arms crossed over his burly chest. "Go ahead."

"Alone. I want to see her alone."

For a moment, Max looked like he would refuse, his jaw bunching and releasing as he stared at Olivia. Then he shrugged. "Fine. But don't do anything stupid." After a cold look at Kylie, he walked away and left them together.

Kylie shifted against the cement floor, the chains around her wrists and ankles rattling as she tried to find a comfortable position. The metal pylon was hard and cool against her back. "What's going on, Olivia?" A tremor ran through her body, anticipation of news she didn't want to hear. "What are you doing here?"

Olivia hesitated. "You've been taken."

"No shit. Tell me something I don't know." She swallowed to stop herself from shouting. "What's this place? Who are these people? What are you to them?"

The questions tumbled from her one after the other, unstoppable. Any firm foundation she thought she had before just crumbled to the ground. Humans had aggressively and successfully taken her. Olivia was among them. Kylie couldn't break free.

"I'm sorry, Kylie. I really am." Olivia hugged herself as if she were cold. A frown marred her normally smooth forehead, and her mouth was pinched with tension. "I never thought they would do this."

"Who is *they*?"

"My brother, Max. The rest of my family."

The family that had abandoned her for being gay and still not come around even after her cancer diagnosis?

"You're joking."

But Olivia wasn't laughing.

"So what the hell are they? Why do they have me here? Is fucking you punishable by death?"

Olivia drew a deep breath. "They're vampire hunters."

Kylie wasn't sure she'd heard right. "What?"

"They hunt vampires," she said quietly.

Kylie shrank back against the pole in disbelief, feeling her foundations crash down even more. The trembling in her body grew worse. She felt encased in ice. "And you...you're one of them?"

"No. No, I'm not." Olivia gripped the bars of Kylie's cell. "I promise you."

"I don't think I'm up to believing your promises right now." She jerked her wrists in the chains. "Get me out of here, Olivia." She heard sounds from down the hall, the brother returning.

"I'm working on it."

"Then work harder!" Kylie still couldn't believe what was going on.

Olivia looked like a stranger standing on the other side of the cage with guilt riding her face, her body covered in clothes that belonged on another person. Kylie squeezed her eyes shut, then opened them again.

"I think your alone time is up." Max ambled in front of Kylie's cell like he was out for a stroll through the park. His eyes narrowed as he dissected Olivia and Kylie. "Did you get in a quick fuck while I was gone?"

"Don't try to play me, Max. I know there're cameras everywhere." Olivia dropped her hands away from the bars of Kylie's cell. "Nothing happens in this place without you knowing. Don't forget I know this place."

"If you're so damn knowledgeable, then you know I'm not going to let this little bloodsucker go." He lanced Kylie with his gaze. "I'll kill you first." He looked completely serious.

But Olivia was unfazed. "Don't threaten me, Max. Bertram won't like it."

"Bertram?" he sneered. "Either you have the family's protection and live by its rules or you do what you want. You can't have it both ways."

Olivia's lips thinned. "I wasn't the one who started this." Her face was cold. Colder than Kylie had ever seen it. Unreadable and detached, as if the person she had known over the last few days had gone, leaving a stranger behind.

Her brother stabbed a finger in front of her nose. "How many times do we have to tell you? No dykes allowed. And definitely no dykes with vampire pets."

Kylie flinched. *Vampire pets?* Anger began to simmer along her nerve endings, replacing the fear and disorientation. She felt almost hot with it.

"You're deluded if you think none of the women who fight for Bertram don't love pussy as much as I do." She made a noise, like he was a fool she was trying to educate.

"As long as they fuck me or some other guy's real dick, they're not dykes, and that's all I care about."

"Oh, okay," Olivia muttered. "That makes so much sense."

They snapped at each other like true siblings, growling and spitting at each other like the human children Kylie had grown up with when they were fighting over marbles.

"Don't give me any shit!" Max shouted. "Or I'll make you wish you were the one behind these bars." He jerked his head toward the cage.

A growl rose up in Kylie's throat. This human didn't get to talk to Olivia like that. When Kylie got out of this prison, she would kill Olivia, make her regret with her screams every betrayal she'd ever served up on her luscious body, on that lying tongue.

She wanted to growl and scream and yank the chains from her wrists, break everything in the place, anger like boiling lava bubbling inside her until she felt choked, humiliated by her helplessness.

Never again, she promised herself. Never.

Kylie made the vow to herself as she stared at Olivia. The power of her stare forced Olivia to turn around. Their eyes met, and Kylie growled louder, the frustration like thunder in her throat. Olivia took a jerking step back even though she was on the other side of the bars.

"Afraid of your little fuck toy?" Max mocked her. "You should be. Bertram told you not to do whatever stupid thing you were thinking of." His gaze found Kylie. "What you tried to do was beyond stupid."

Olivia turned away. "I don't want to talk about that here." Her voice shook.

"Does it matter? These freaks can hear us from all the way above ground if they want."

So they were underground. The logical part of Kylie, the part that wasn't snapping and furious like a wild dog, processed and tucked away that piece of information.

"It doesn't matter what she can hear. I'd rather talk about this someplace else." She shot a look at Kylie. One full of apology and something else Kylie didn't want to see. Every muscle in her body twitched with anger.

"Fuck you." She aimed the words directly at Olivia.

Olivia jerked her gaze away. "Let's go, Max."

"You don't fucking tell me what to do," he said. But he walked away from Kylie's cell, following Olivia's swift and purposeful steps.

The sight of them together, walking and talking like companions, like the siblings they were, made Kylie snap her teeth. She followed the sound of their footsteps, counted them to ten before she started plucking at her chains behind her back, trying to hook her fingers in the rings of the chain to snap them apart.

She heard the sound of a sharp zap! Then felt pain. A burning current through her fingers and the manacles on her wrists. She screamed in agony, then rage.

"You bitch!" she screamed. "You fucking bitch! I'll rip your heart out for this! I won't stop until I have your guts hanging from the rafters like confetti."

She fell over. Her head thudding against the floor. For wild seconds, she saw stars behind her tightly clenched eyelids. Her stomach heaved. Then the stars cleared and she was only captive again, not flung adrift in a bright and alien universe. Still twitching. Humiliated.

"I'm going to kill you," she whimpered with her cheek pressed into the hard and gritty floor. "You're already dead. You just don't know it."

CHAPTER TWENTY-ONE

It felt like an eternity before Olivia came back. Lying on the floor with grit and old bloodstains under her naked body, Kylie heard every footstep, nearly every breath as Olivia approached.

The fury caught fire inside her again, and she wanted to fly up and fling herself against the bars of her prison. Show Olivia the full force of her anger. Olivia stood in front of her cell. She looked small and helpless in her loose jeans and a large gray hoodie with University of Georgia scrawled across the chest. She must have gotten cold and borrowed the sweatshirt from one of the men. It looked too big to be hers.

Kylie still couldn't get past the clothes, Olivia wearing pants. That small thing felt like another betrayal. Was anything Kylie had seen of her real?

"I'm sorry about this, Kylie." Olivia drew a deep breath that smelled of a recent meal. Miso soup and kale.

Kylie lifted her head. "I don't give a shit about your sorry. That won't get me out of here."

Was it her imagination or did Olivia flinch from her words? Not that it mattered. Olivia had gotten her into this. There was no going back from a betrayal like this. No. Fucking. Way.

"I know it's useless for me to say this now, but I want you to know I never thought the plan would end up like this. I didn't know you'd be the one to come." She clenched and unclenched her fingers, shoving them in the pockets of her jeans then pulling them out again.

Kylie had no idea what she was talking about and didn't give a damn enough to ask.

"I'll do whatever I can to get you out of this," Olivia said. "I promise."

"You can shove your promises the same place as your sorrys, *human*. I was so damn stupid to trust you."

Another flinch crossed Olivia's face. She licked her lips and took a step back, then another. Then she was walking away from the cell and down the hall where a hint of darkness waited to embrace her. Kylie watched her leave, biting her lip at the regret burning in her belly.

And don't come back!

She wanted to shout the words, but they wouldn't leave her lips. She groaned softly, turned her head, and pressed her forehead into the gritty floor.

It scalded her to think that she had been played for a fool. Even now, she wanted to call out to Olivia and ask her if it had all been an act. Had there been any time at all during their days together that her feelings for Kylie had been genuine?

Fuck.

"She's such a bitch, isn't she?"

She'd heard the man approach but paid him little attention. Kylie didn't bother looking up at him.

"Olivia is such a self-righteous little bitch." Max's boots sounded against the floor as he came closer. "She's been part of this family from birth. She knew what we've been doing and have done for generations. We kill vampires, not fuck them. Just because she never got into the family business doesn't mean she gets to spread her legs for any of you leeches."

Kylie heard him put his hands around the iron bars, felt him lean closer. "I'm not gonna lie. I've been tempted to see what it's like. That cold skin. The way you heal up real nice from a knife cut." He bared his teeth at her. "Is your pussy cold too?"

She felt his eyes on her, examining her naked body as if eager to violate and hurt her. She shuddered with revulsion. "One of the last vamps we had in here said you get warm when you fuck. Would you get warm for me if I stick my dick in your ass?"

Kylie's hands clenched into fists behind her back, but she said nothing.

He laughed then and leaned in to press his forehead against the bars. "Maybe one day I'll find out and make Olivia watch."

"Fuck you."

He chuckled again. The sound of his laughter merry and amused. "No, honey. Fuck *you*. And when I do, I'm going to enjoy every second of it. Cold pussy or not." His hands flexed around the bars of the cell. "I'm sure I'll figure out a way to warm you up."

Kylie's teeth flashed out, sharp and long, eager to taste his blood. "I'd rather die than let you touch me."

"Really? You want to throw down that challenge?" He grinned. "I don't think you know who you're fucking with. When I play chicken, guess who blinks first?" He looked over her body with an insolent stare that made her feel immediately unclean. "When I'm done fucking your cold little cunt and ass, you'll be begging me to kill you."

"You'll be the one begging before I'm done with you." She stared at him, unblinking, her teeth elongated and dripping with saliva.

Kylie felt humiliated and helpless. But even with no power over her situation, speaking the fearless words gave her some spark of rebellion, something to get her through until a plan for escape came to her.

"Just you watch me, bitch." He nodded once in her direction then shoved away from the bars. The human walked down the hallway without a second glance.

Kylie pushed herself to her knees after he left, straightening her body the best she could while the chains clanged and pressed cold and hard into her skin. The manacles scraped her wrists bloody.

She hissed with pain and sighed as the hurt disappeared almost instantly, the cuts healing on her skin even though she didn't have to look to know it was happening. She looked around her, noticing again the small but chilling details of where she was being kept. The tiny cameras high on the ceiling outside her cage, the small, quarter-sized holes in the stone walls of her cell, eight of them at shoulder height if she had been able to stand. She had no idea what they were for, but she didn't want to find out.

The floor was concrete, cold and unyielding under her naked body while the ceiling soared at least twenty feet over her head. They had covered every possible base, it seemed, having learned, she guessed from trial and error, what would keep a vampire captive in a cell for as long as they wished.

She heard the continuous chatter of the humans down the bright hallway, beyond her sight. But they only spoke in that coded language of theirs, in metaphors, with no specifics she could use to fight her way out of her cell. She snapped her teeth, pissed at herself again for being caught so easily.

She rattled the chain around her wrists, yanked at it. The metal didn't even strain under her efforts.

Shit. Shit. Shit.

Kylie sank back to her haunches and deliberately slammed her head against the steel pylon at her back. A brief pain, then nothing. She wanted to bang her head against the pylon hard and harder until someone came, until something happened. But the rational part of her, tiny as it was, warned her that any efforts in that direction would be completely useless. She would just hurt herself, heal, and be in the exact same position as before only with her blood splattered everywhere.

At the thought of blood, her teeth ached with hunger. The light inside her cage and out in the hallway was unrelenting. It hadn't dimmed at all since she'd been captive so she had no idea how long it had been since she was taken. But her body sensed the coming of the sun. It squirmed with discomfort. With hunger and a longing for home.

She closed her eyes, giving in to her body's exhaustion, relaxing into the cold pylon. She wished it were another body. Violet. Rufus. Even Julia. She wanted the comfort of another. Ached for it. Prickles of need rushed over her skin. Her fingers twitched to twine around an arm, touch a hip, anything.

The last time she had slept with her kind, it had been with Violet. The presence of Violet's flesh pressed to hers had been a narcotic, pulling her down into a day's rest. But even with Violet near, it had been Olivia she wanted. It was Olivia she dreamed about pulling down into simple cotton sheets with her, kissing her, stroking her lean body, pushing open her thighs to press against her wetness, sigh into her mouth as they shared good morning kisses and the desire that flowed like thick honey between them. Olivia would be wet against her thigh, then on her fingers, on her tongue, her cunt fisting under Kylie's mouth in orgasm.

Kylie swooned into sleep with the thought of fucking Olivia, then shuddered seconds later when she woke again. Her lashes fluttered as she stared up into the bright light of the cell.

It happened to her again and again and again. So many times that she lost count. Her body grew more and more distressed, her nerves jangling with need each time she jolted awake.

Fuck this shit.

She wanted to stay awake and fight the desire that always led to the disappointment of sleep interrupted. But she couldn't stop that cycle any more than she could stop wanting blood. Or stop being Belle's daughter. She opened her eyes again to the harsh lights and sounds of footsteps coming down the hall toward her. Two people and someone being dragged. Kylie smelled death.

She heavily lifted her head in time to see two men in fatigues. Max and another human with long dreadlocks, someone she remembered seeing near Olivia's apartment. They carried a naked body between them, its feet dragging on the floor. The body didn't have a head. Congealed blood had dried in streaks down the ragged, meaty stump of a neck, down its bare, male chest. The fading scent of eucalyptus clung to the dead vampire.

"Hey, leech." Max grinned at her. "We notice you're having some trouble sleeping. This might help you out." His teeth flashed sharp and wicked in his pale face. He turned to nod at someone beyond Kylie's sight. There was the sound of an electronic click then the doors of the cell slid open.

"Enjoy."

They threw the body into the cell with her. It landed against her thighs with a wet thud. She flinched back in revulsion. The smell of death and accelerated decay exploded against her face.

"Why don't you cuddle up with that?" Max snorted as he laughed. "Sweet dreams."

Kylie stared down at the dead beast. It wasn't anyone she knew. This one was pale, the color of over-cooked rice, his penis uncircumcised and stubby between his legs. It was just his sprawled body, his arms flopped out at his sides, palms up, as if in supplication. But it was too late for anyone or anything to help him.

The other man walked away after a quick, almost shamed, look at Kylie's nude body. But Max stayed to watch her, his eyes moving with relish between her and the dead vampire. "He lost the game," Max said, then turned and walked away.

Kylie was disgusted. Not by the body, since she had seen death before and had been the cause of it on many occasions. She was disgusted by her response to the body. The instant pulse of need inside her. She slid to the ground, burrowing against the cold flesh to find warmth that she knew was long gone.

The stench was overwhelming. Old blood. Quickly putrefying flesh. The dead vampire's natural eucalyptus scent that was fading fast. She fought back a spasm of nausea, her body simultaneously moving into and away from the dead creature, seeking rest but also aware of and repulsed by its permanent death.

She pushed into its chest and sighed. The dead vampire was sticky with old blood. She bathed herself in the wasted nourishment, staining her skin, her face. She felt like an animal. But she needed the comfort. Her cheek touched the body's cold chest. Cold on cold. The vampire had been dead for at least a full night. There wasn't much warmth to find in it. And all the blood was gone. Spoiled. But her flesh needed what it needed, and in seconds, she was asleep.

"You see what a fucking disgusting animal it is?" She heard the question from far off, but did not wake. Did nothing to acknowledge it even though she knew the voice, knew it was Max, and knew he was talking to Olivia.

She shut out the noise and remained beneath the soothing balm of sleep, only vaguely aware of her twitching limbs, the smell of the dead body, and her own desperation.

"Get it the fuck out of the cage. I'm not providing a tuck-in service here."

Olivia's scent retreated.

Kylie's lashes fluttered as the warmth she had found in sleep slipped away from her, the balm she clung to abruptly yanked from her grasp.

"I'm not here to do you any favors, bloodsucker."

Her eyes flew open and she snarled, rushing up from her sleep in a snap of teeth and clinking chains for the blood-rich throats she smelled nearby. Max and another man.

"Christ! That bitch is fast!" The dreadlocked man skittered back and away from her, his hazel eyes wide. He nearly dropped the legs of the dead vampire he stole from Kylie. His pulse thudded hard in his neck, the adrenaline and fear creating an intoxicating cocktail of scent in the air.

The chains yanked Kylie back before she could get very far. She tumbled to the floor in a crash of limbs, her back smashing into the steel pylon hard enough to make her feel it. Her eyes felt gritty, her body sluggish from its need for blood.

She registered the man's heady scent, imagined biting into his neck and spilling all that blood down her throat. Kylie swallowed with hunger, even as she knew it couldn't have been true hunger. It hadn't been that long since she fed.

Normally, she could go at least three days without drinking before she started to lose it. And she knew that only because she had tried in the very beginning of her vampiric existence to not be what they had made her. Now, she embraced her need and fed as often as she liked.

"Yeah, she's fast but not faster than those chains," Max said. He kicked the dead vampire's arms all the way outside Kylie's cell.

But she heard the tremor in his voice, had heard the abrupt slide of his boots across the floor. "Door!" The echoes of his shout barely died away before the electronic doors slammed shut.

Kylie stared at them, her throat vibrating with her anger. With her hunger. Her body trembled. She must not have been asleep for very long before they pulled the body out of the cage. It wouldn't do to provide her any kind of comfort, would it? She sank back onto her haunches, leaned into the steel at her back, and tried to stay awake.

❖

She lost track of the hours. Or had it been days? It was constant wakefulness and bared teeth and aching fangs and the cramp of hunger in her belly that started to move through the rest of her body. Her veins felt as if they were drawing tight, drying up. Her limbs twitched without pause, her mouth too dry for her to call out for help or even scream in anger. But who would even hear her? Who would help?

Kylie felt terrorized by her aloneness. By the fear.

One day or evening or night while her body was in shock from its lack of sleep and food, the doors of the cage shuddered and flew open. She smelled Olivia's scent, heard her voice from far away quietly chanting Kylie's name.

"Kylie, get up. Kylie. Kylie! Get ready to run."

But where could she go? She could do nothing while chained and weaker than a newborn cub. Olivia chanted her name again, a sound she couldn't ignore. Kylie blinked away her confusion and latched on to the sound of her name on Olivia's lips.

Run. Yes, she had to run.

Kylie yanked at her chains as she got to her feet in a crouch, unable to do much more than that. Frantic footsteps pounded down the hall. Olivia's. Like an apparition, she appeared in front of Kylie's cage with something that looked like a remote control in her hands, a black rectangle covered in buttons. She rushed into the cage, frantically pressing buttons on the device, pointing it at the shackles around Kylie's wrists. With Olivia's scent so close, Kylie shivered, already on her knees and weakened, the smell of her blood and fear and the frantic sweat waking up every one of her senses.

She smelled everything about Olivia and could hear the pounding inside her narrow chest, the impotent slide of her sweaty fingers across the rubber buttons on the remote control. Even more than when they had thrown the vampire corpse in with her, Kylie felt gutted by her hunger.

Olivia cursed under her breath and shook the device at the shackles.

"What…what—are you…doing?" Kylie fought to get the words past her dry lips and heavy tongue. She felt as if razor blades were slicing through her throat with each syllable. But it was a welcome distraction from her hunger that yanked hard at her belly, seizing her every breath in its talons.

But Olivia didn't answer, only continued pressing the buttons, pointing the device at the shackles. A zap of electric current rushed through the shackles, knocking Kylie from her shaky crouch. She tumbled back into the hard ground, groaning more from the torture of having Olivia close than any other pain.

"I'm sorry! I'm so sorry!" Olivia panted and cursed. She slammed the remote against the chains. "This worked yesterday when I tried it."

Suddenly, the doors to Kylie's cage shivered. Her head jerked up just as they slammed shut, trapping Olivia in with her. Olivia looked up, startled, fear widening her eyes and perfuming her skin.

"Fuck!"

Kylie trembled, cringing back from her and the hunger tearing her control to ribbons. She dug her fingers into the concrete under her, crawling back as much as the chains would let her. They rattled, mocking her weakness.

Olivia's brother appeared on the other side of the cage, his boots thudding against the concrete floor. "I told them you'd try something stupid."

Olivia flew to her feet. She was trembling as fiercely as Kylie. "Let me out of here!" Her voice shook.

"You want to be with your little fuck toy so bad, enjoy." He pulled a remote identical to the one she had from his pocket. "This one," he said, holding up the device, "actually works." He pressed a series of buttons on the remote, and Kylie's shackles snapped open. Silence descended in the small cage as the cuffs dropped to the floor with a metallic clang. First the ones on her wrists, then the ones around her ankles.

Olivia's heart thudded harder. She flew to the bars of the cage and gripped them hard. "Get me out of here, Max! Bertram will be so pissed when she finds out about this." Her voice was sharp with rising hysteria.

"Pissed about what? Your vampire-loving ways? Finding out that her daughter is a traitor to the family?" He made a disgusted sound. "The best thing I can do for you is not tell Bertram what a dirty little vampire fucker you are."

"Let me out, dammit!" Olivia screamed. "This is not a game!"

Kylie was lost in her terror. Her hunger. With her hands and wrists no longer in chains, she was free for the first time in hours, maybe even days. There was food for her to eat. She could touch as much as she wanted. But even as the wonder of her situation hit her—food, sweet God, food!—she recoiled.

This was Olivia. Not some blood sack waiting to be drained. She couldn't do this. She just couldn't. But the more she held herself back, the stronger her hunger became. It throbbed inside her throat like a frantic pulse. Her teeth ached in her jaws. In a hot rush, they pushed out of her mouth elongated and ready to feed.

No. No. No. She couldn't do this. She couldn't.

But the more she mentally resisted, the stronger the hunger held her in its grasp. A growl reverberated throughout her entire body. Her fingers curled into talons at her sides. The hunger pounded hard at her, drumming through her brain, overwhelming all her senses.

Olivia was only a few feet away, her back stiff with fear. She shook the bars of the cage and screamed at her brother who only stared at her with a look of satisfaction.

"Let me out, Max!" The fear sang out through her voice, more potent than any aphrodisiac, any ambrosial scent. "Damn you!"

Kylie's tenuous control snapped. With a growl, she sprang to her feet, grabbed Olivia by the waist, sinking claws into her skin through her thick sweatshirt, and pulled her back into her. Olivia screamed, her sweat-slick fingers losing their grip on the cell's bars. Her blood scent rose in the air.

"Kylie, no!"

Olivia closed her eyes, screaming, refusing to look at Kylie. But Kylie didn't want her to look. She only wanted to drink her up and not see into the eyes of the woman she had made love to what seemed like only a few hours before. The woman who had betrayed her.

She pulled her back, Olivia's fingernails tearing at her hands as she fought the grip on her waist. But Kylie didn't care about that minor, inconvenient pain. She yanked Olivia's head to the side to get access to her slender throat. Kylie sank her fangs into Olivia's neck. They both moaned at the same time.

She was sweet. And Kylie was ravenous.

It was beyond pleasure. Beyond the simple satisfaction of hunger. Within seconds of the penetration of her teeth into the butter-soft flesh, Olivia went limp, her body accepting the delectation Kylie brought even while was being drained of every drop of her lifeblood.

The flood of ambrosia rushed into Kylie's mouth. She groaned with the bliss of it, feeling her own body sway with the weight of Olivia's. They fell to their knees, Kylie behind Olivia, Olivia with her head hanging limply as Kylie drank from her with fangs buried at their deepest depth inside her throat.

Olivia had stopped clawing at her hands and now held on to them, gripping Kylie with a surprising strength.

With the gush of blood into her mouth, reason and perspective reasserted themselves. She knew suddenly that it had been four days since she had been taken by the humans. That Olivia had tried to help her. That Olivia was dying, and dying at her fangs.

But she couldn't stop herself from drinking. She had been starved for too long. Her control was no longer hers. And the blood was filling her up, plumping so many parts of her. Even with her hunger, she was aware that this was not an ordinary meal. She couldn't stop feasting.

"Stop!" The breath heaved in Olivia's throat. "Stop. Please." But the words contradicted the way she bent her neck for Kylie, how she pushed her hips back into her, the kittenish sounds in the back of her throat that were so much like the ones she uttered when they made love.

Kylie was undone. She was confused. Lust and right and wrong and control had all melted away into the same thing: Olivia under her fangs where she belonged. No one else mattered. Nothing else in the world deserved her attention but the woman in her arms.

She released her grip on Olivia's waist to rip away the sweatshirt and the shirt underneath it, exposing her bare skin. Olivia flinched into her, moaned her name.

"Touch me," Olivia gasped.

It wasn't what she wanted. It couldn't be. Not to be taken on the cement floor while her brother watched and the surveillance system recorded it all.

But she was as much a prisoner of Kylie's hunger as Kylie was. Kylie knew it and fought against it. But not hard enough. Her fingers found Olivia's nipples, caressed and squeezed them, tugged at the points that were hard with arousal. She wanted to suckle her breasts, take her nipples one after the other on her tongue. But she could only do one thing at a time with her mouth, and the crimson fountain was much more important.

Olivia groaned as Kylie slid her hands down her jeans, between her thin panties and her hot flesh. She was wet. Slick with a different kind of hunger, eagerly welcoming Kylie's fingers into her pussy. She dipped her fingers in for a taste, delving as deeply as the position would allow then came for her clit, caressing the hard nub of feminine flesh. She sucked harder on her neck.

"Baby...."

The faintest sound of protest fell from Olivia's lips although her hips moved with Kylie's fingers, encouraging the erotic caresses, the float and feather on her clitoris that brought Kylie to life. This was a moment to live for. A woman giving in to her passion. She sucked harder at Olivia's throat, drinking deeply at the gift she knew could only be given once.

Kylie was only vaguely aware of the audience around them. Olivia's brother. The cameras. Others who had come to stare. Others who were shouting at Max to pull Olivia out of the cage.

Kylie wasn't aware of the words, but they didn't matter. The only thing that mattered was feeding her hunger. The blood. Olivia's whimpers. A mixture of arousal and fear. The frantic tremor of her pulse that gushed blood harder and faster into Kylie's mouth.

Her skin tingled. She felt that Olivia was emptying, felt her life rushing out along with the blood and then, it wasn't about feeding anymore but about the sensuality of the experience, the life under her, rushing toward her with open arms that all she had to do was take. Pleasure exploded in her mouth, under her skin, between her legs.

Because of what she was, she could not stop being aware of her surroundings. She knew that once she started feeding, Max stared at her and Olivia with a look of satisfaction, malice bright in his pale eyes. Kylie knew that his men had come running to stare in horror and tell him to stop this thing and let Olivia out in the name of their god! But even he had to know it was too late for that.

Kylie was loose and rabid with hunger. If anyone opened the cage, she wouldn't stop with the prey she already had in her grasp. She wouldn't stop until they were all dead.

She was distantly aware of a new scent, someone powerful who the others reacted to with fear. A cold-voiced command instantly quieted the room. Then the smell of medicine. A spit of sound. Dart guns. She twisted so the darts wouldn't hit Olivia, protecting her with her body while the darts rained down on her shoulders, back, and thighs. The pain stung her.

She snarled when the first few tranquilizer darts hit her, but did not release her hold on Olivia. She felt five shots. Eight. Then fifteen before she lost count and began to feel their effects.

No! A part of her screamed out when the first wave of unconsciousness hit. But it barely lasted a second. *Not yet! Don't take her away from me.*

She tightened her hold on Olivia, sucking harder, her fangs wetly tearing more of the blood-splashed flesh to allow more nourishment to flow into her mouth. She sucked harder. Hunger and pain twisting her body as more darts poured down at her. She fought the effects of the tranquilizers but could not win the battle. Her body sagged with weakness. Her eyes dropped closed.

"Now. Get Olivia now." The cold and controlled voice sliced into Kylie's awareness.

The doors of the cage slid open. Freedom! She shoved at Olivia's limp body and leapt up. Or at least she tried to. She could only manage a weak flick of her hand before she felt Olivia being pulled away from her. Human hands grabbing her wrists and ankles to shackle them once again and wrap chains tightly around her middle, binding her to the metal post in the center of the cell.

The humans rushed out of the cell with their burden. The gate slammed shut. It all took only seconds. Kylie knew because she counted them while waiting for the tranquilizers' effect to wear off as she lay on the hard floor, her muscles limp and useless.

Nineteen seconds after the last concentrated burst of darts and she felt like herself again. No body-aching hunger. No tunnel vision.

Just her with the stolen blood leaping through her veins and scarlet nourishment dripping from her face.

She came fully to herself to see the humans carrying away Olivia's body down the hallway, a barrage of emergency activity. Boot steps pounding against the concrete, shouts for a stretcher, a blood transfusion, a doctor.

Kylie could still taste Olivia on her tongue. Her body was healing and getting stronger with each breath the humans drew while Olivia was only getting weaker. Her life was in Kylie's mouth. She swallowed the lightly spicy flavor of her. The blood slid down her throat in a delicious slither that made her tremble with satisfaction.

Her body was replete, satisfied for the first time in days. But inside, she felt flayed alive. It was like killing her grandmother all over again, draining someone she loved simply for her own survival.

She cringed back against the thick metal at her back, sending the manacles on her wrists and ankles clanging. Kylie stared at the woman on the other side of the cage, but all her attention was focused on Max. Kylie noticed then that the woman, despite her combat boots, jungle fatigues, and black tank top that showed off lean and effective-looking muscles, was elegantly made. She had queenly features, skin the color of blond oak, and she wore her hair in thick cornrows down to her waist. She looked ageless. And familiar. Ah, yes. Another face from Olivia's photo album.

"She better survive this," the woman said to Max. "Or not even God can help you."

The temperature in the room seemed to drop at least ten degrees with each word she uttered, words so cutting and deliberate that Kylie felt their effect. But she didn't feel sorry for Max. Not at all. She wanted to tear him apart with her fangs and claws then spit out every ounce of his poisonous blood that ended up in her mouth. Kylie trembled with anger and fear.

Olivia.

It didn't matter that she had been thinking of destroying her a few hours before. It didn't matter that she'd gotten the chance to do just what she had threatened. None of that mattered now that Olivia's human life was hanging by a frayed thread just a few yards away.

The woman in fatigues turned away from Max after a charged instant to look past him and down the hallway where Olivia had disappeared. "Volt it," she said.

"With pleasure, Bertram." Max flicked a glance at Kylie. "For how long?" His voice held a note of relief, as if he were glad the human woman was focused on something else besides him.

"Until I say stop." Bertram looked at Kylie.

Kylie felt as if the woman was mentally dissecting her, assessing each of her parts in order to properly break her down later. Strangely enough, Max was looking at Bertram the same way.

"The highest voltage available," Bertram said.

At the word "voltage" Kylie jerked to attention. Her body stiffened at the thought of what Bertram could mean. The woman walked away from the cell without a backward glance. Seconds later, Kylie began to scream.

CHAPTER TWENTY-TWO

Agony.

Every second passed in a haze of agony for Kylie.

She felt intense pain and the scrape of her screams against her throat. Electricity surged through her body in an unending stream, frying her nerves and synapses over and over again as they healed. Her skin twitched and burned and jerked against the concrete slab, her body shuddering and bucking into the hard cement, scraping her skin, bruising her bones, knocking her into merciful unconsciousness for precious seconds at a time. Her back jerked in an excruciating arch off the metal pylon that only heightened the electricity's effect on her flesh. The shackles around her bare wrists and ankles burned into her skin with each burst of current.

The smell of her flesh and hair burning filled her nose. The blood boiled in her veins. Her fingers and toes and arms and legs twitched. Minutes passed. Hours. Maybe even days. Then the electric current stopped its assault on her body. The respite caught her in mid-tremor, and her knees slammed once more against the hard concrete. Kylie panted in fear and relief, reverting back to the human habit of breathing in the midst of her pain. Her skin hummed. Her heart felt like it was still beating.

"You've taken my daughter away from me." The woman in fatigues appeared in front of her cell. Her face was cold in its anger. There were dried tears on her cheeks, but sadness had already given way to fury. "So I'm going to take everything away from you."

Kylie panted against the floor, head hung low and heavy, unable to process what the woman was saying, only knowing that Olivia was dead. She wanted to scream at the unfairness of it all. She regretted her decision to come to Atlanta. She regretted seeing the ruby necklace on the television. She regretted the chase, the sun that drove her into Olivia's apartment. She wanted to tell the woman that she was sorry. But because apologies would change nothing, Kylie kept the words to herself.

"Where is she?" she croaked.

"It doesn't matter where she is. That's none of your business."

She looked up at the woman through the heavy fall of her thick hair, the kinks and curls falling into her eyes. "You started this," she said. "If you had left me alone, she'd still be alive."

"Would she?" The woman came closer to the cage. She had a much more fearsome presence than Max, her eyes burning with a killing fire that promised to lay waste to everything in her path. "She drew you to her. This wasn't a result that either of us put into motion."

What did the woman mean? Kylie couldn't bother to hide her confusion.

"I guess you didn't know that, did you?" The woman looked at her with contempt. "Olivia had cancer and she wanted to survive at any cost. She wanted to be turned into one of you." Her lips twisted with distaste. "I banished her from the family thinking that once she'd seen what she lost, she'd give up on that stupid idea." Her fingers curled into fists at her sides. "Then you stumbled into her trap, stupid little vampire. We should have killed you that first morning."

Kylie stared at the woman in horror. *That first morning?*

Olivia had been plotting to get Kylie to bite her the whole time? Her head spun with the revelation.

The woman's eyes raked Kylie. "She may have set this up, but you're the one who killed her. You're the one who took her away from me."

"No," Kylie said, finally finding her voice. "No." She refused to take any responsibility for what Olivia had done. Now that the current had stopped burning through her body, she clearly felt the anger surface. The rage building higher and higher until she was gasping with it. Olivia had used her. Led them to capture her. Taken the trust Kylie had given to no one else and twisted it for her own use.

"Fuck you," Kylie growled.

The human woman snarled, sounding like a beast herself. "You don't want to go there with me—"

A sudden noise, barely audible, jerked Kylie's attention away from the woman. There was something familiar in the noise, an agony she remembered from not too long ago. When the noise came again, a scream, she knew what it was. Seconds later, a flash of movement down the hallway, a creature moving inhumanly fast. Then darkness abruptly fell in the underground complex, the screech of metal, the spark of electrical wires.

"Kill it!" someone screamed.

"No!" A hysterical wail.

But then a steady stream of automatic gunfire rang out. A shout of rage and fear from the same vampiric throat. The sound of a blade slicing through flesh and striking stone. Silence.

The noises told a story that struck a cold lance of fear through Kylie's chest. What the hell had they done? She spun to ask the woman what was going on, but she was already running down the hallway toward the terrifying sounds.

But she didn't make it very far before the source of the noises came to her.

Olivia, running.

Destruction in motion.

Somehow, she had been turned. Her humanity peeled away and discarded to reveal a howling beast. In a burst of inhuman speed, she blazed down the hallway. Her face was smeared with blood and her fangs were unsheathed, stained scarlet. She screamed with rage.

Olivia was still wearing the loose jeans she had on when the Bertrams had taken her away. But that was the only similarity between then and now. Her chest was bare, flecked with blood, small breasts bouncing as she ran.

Kylie saw her in slow motion as she raced down the hallway, arms pumping, knees rising and falling in perfect rhythm. She had been truly transformed. All her sickness swept away as if it had never been. And with the virus wiping away the wreckage that cancer had left behind, Kylie saw Olivia how she must have been before it all started.

Her cheeks were rounder, but not softer, a hardness flashing behind her eyes. And her body. Kylie blinked in the face of this metamorphosis. Arms sleek with muscle, belly flat and hard, both small breasts symmetrical again, the left one whole and unscarred. The air of fragility about her, gone.

Kylie barely recognized her as the young woman she'd ravaged with her fangs. Her neck was completely healed and her body moved with a strength and power it never had before. Olivia ran through the halls snarling incoherently through her new fangs while the Bertrams chased her. But the soldiers didn't fire their weapons. They didn't seem to know what to do, how to handle one of theirs who had been turned.

Olivia raced past her mother, ran to Kylie's cell, and ripped away the door as if it was no more significant than tissue paper. She used the remote that Kylie noticed for the first time to free her from the shackles and chains, ignoring her mother all the while.

"Come!"

At least that's what Kylie thought she said. Olivia's mouth was hinged open, the lips pressed apart by fangs she seemed to have no control over. She grabbed Kylie by the hand and sprinted away from the humans, past the cells, some empty, some filled with other chained vampires. Vampires who had spikes through their bodies, the tissue healing around the metal object in an agony that never ceased. One youngling was sucking her own arm, drinking the blood that spilled from the wound.

They ran down a long tunnel leading up steep stone steps and into the musty darkness of a cave that seemed like it had no way out.

"Wait!" Kylie shouted. "We're not strong enough to dig through that!"

But Olivia didn't pause. She tapped a hidden button and a secret door in the rock opened. They tumbled out into the woods and the smell of earth and growing things. Kylie ran behind Olivia, following her when she darted for a pile of leaves and twigs covering a familiar black Jeep.

Working quickly, they ripped aside the camouflage then jumped in the Jeep that already had the key in the ignition. Then they were flying, speeding through the woods at a pace the human Kylie would have considered suicidal.

But she held on to the handgrip above the door and clenched her teeth, prepared for a crash at any moment. She shot Olivia a sideways glance as the SUV rumbled over rocks and dirt and downed tree limbs. Her teeth rattled in her head when the Jeep seemed to find every rock and rut in the woods. Branches swatted against the top of the SUV as they sped past low trees. Insects exploded against the windshield, their yellow guts splashing across the glass like paint. The wind roared through the open windows.

Kylie trembled, her butt hopping up and down in the seat as the Jeep rumbled through the woods. Inside that place, she had been afraid. Truly afraid. She could honestly say that after being turned, she was never afraid of anything that walked the earth. No other vampire. Certainly no humans. But being captured by Olivia's family proved to her there was more pain and suffering and terror out there than she ever thought. Kylie looked over at the newly turned Olivia. The vampire who'd wanted to be turned all along. She was beautiful.

Olivia gripped the wheel in two gray-knuckled fists, her eyes staring straight ahead beyond the windshield. She looked terrified but determined. And her fangs had retracted back into her mouth. If Kylie didn't pay close attention, she could almost fool herself into thinking it was lipstick that made her lips so red and wet.

"Shit!" Olivia said as a branch slapped the side of her face through the open window. But she only ducked her head instead of closing the window. Her new senses, Kylie thought. She wanted to feel something—the danger of their flight, the gushing wind—rather than the human safety she'd experienced all her life. Kylie was only too aware of that feeling and what it could lead to.

"You didn't have to save me," Kylie said softly.

She grit her teeth when the Jeep hopped over a particularly large log, smacking her head against the roof.

"Yes, I did." Olivia shouted to hear herself above the wind. "This is my fault."

Damn right it is.

Kylie looked away from her, wanting to shout and scream at her for the betrayal, but knowing it wasn't the right time. When would be the right time then? A voice demanded at the back of her mind. That was the voice that wanted revenge for the agony of lust and love she had felt for Olivia. Lust and love that had just been tools to get her to do exactly what Olivia wanted. Kylie clamped her mouth shut.

Seconds later, Olivia slammed on the brakes. They were still in the midst of the woods, but a river was only a few feet from the front of the Jeep. A wide, muddy green stretch of rushing water that looked deep enough to easily cover both their heads.

"Come on!" Olivia jumped out of the Jeep and dashed to the front of the SUV, staring across to the other side of the river. "We have to swim across."

"It's probably better to let the current carry us downstream and away from here." Kylie climbed out of the truck, not bothering to close the door. Her bare feet and legs sank into the damp leaves and dirt. "They'd expect us to cross and keep going."

"They'll soon have choppers in the air looking for us. It wouldn't do any good for us to go downstream. They'd see us in a minute. I know how they search."

"Yes, you do know, don't you?" Kylie snapped, unable to hold her tongue any longer.

She stared at Olivia, feeling the anger rise up in her swift and hot, like lust. She was distractingly beautiful, her bare breasts drawing Kylie's eyes.

Olivia was probably the one who had discarded the shirts Kylie had torn in her lust to get to her skin. The memory of that feeding filled Kylie, building her fury. That act had been the culmination of all of Olivia's deception. All that she had led Kylie to do from the instant she climbed into her apartment.

"I should fucking kill you," Kylie growled.

Olivia swung to face her, eyes narrowing. "For what, saving your ass?" Her hands rose up at her sides, fingers curled into claws. Her humanity was gone.

"You know damn well why. You tricked me into coming into your apartment. You manipulated me into falling for you."

A rush of emotions moved across Olivia's face, but she did not lower her clawed hands. "I won't spend the rest of my existence apologizing for what I did. Because I'm not sorry for it." She lowered her voice. "It's everything else that came after that I regret."

"What, having to bear the indignity of fucking me when all you wanted was my virus in your neck?" Kylie slammed her fist into the front of the Jeep, creeping closer to Olivia, desperately wanting the ache of the betrayal to go away. She'd do anything to end the agony of it. Her own claws came up. She crouched low, growling at the woman who was the source of all her pain.

"Don't be stupid!" Olivia shouted. Her eyes snapped fire and her killing teeth flashed out.

Kylie's animal rose hard and fierce inside her. Now she would get the chance to kill the pain.

"Are we interrupting something?" A low, rumbling voice flowed out at them from the darkness of the river.

Olivia gasped.

CHAPTER TWENTY-THREE

Kylie leapt back against the Jeep, a hand flying out to grab Olivia and drag her backward with her. A dark shape fully emerged from the river to stand on the bank. A half a dozen other shapes slipped up from the water, clambering silently to fan out on either side of the first figure. Silvija.

"What are you doing here?" Kylie stared at the clan in astonishment.

"Rescuing you." Silvija's mouth twisted in an ironic smile. She turned to Julia on her right. "Radio in. Tell her we have Kylie. Now we strike the humans." Silvija glanced briefly at Kylie's nakedness and without pausing, pulled off her T-shirt and offered it to her. She barely looked at the bare-breasted Olivia.

"No!" Before she could react, Olivia jerked from her arms to stand in front of Silvija. "Don't hurt them."

Kylie took the oversized shirt from Silvija and pulled it on, carefully watching Olivia. The shirt fell halfway down her thighs. Whatever special fabric it was made from already pulled most of the moisture from the shirt so that it felt nearly dry.

Silvija, with her powerful torso now bared in a sports bra, looked at Kylie. "Did you turn her?"

She vehemently shook her head. "No. It was someone else. Someone they killed." She remembered the vampiric scream, the sound of steel striking concrete through flesh, the thud of the body falling in separate pieces.

Silvija nodded once, and the others—Julia, Liam, Violet, Ivy, Rufus—moved in the direction Kylie and Olivia had just come from. All the vampires were dressed in black, blending in with the looming dark trees, the bushes, the shadowy landscape. In the distance, Kylie heard the blades of a helicopter.

"Stop!" Olivia grabbed Silvija's arm.

Silvija looked down at her with disdain. Even from where Kylie stood, she saw the killing frost in her eyes. Olivia quickly dropped her hand.

"Don't hurt them," she pleaded. "They didn't realize what any of this meant when they went after Kylie."

"Don't worry." Silvija's eyes glittered. "I'll make them understand the error of their ways." She stepped forward until Olivia had no choice but to move out of her way.

"Kylie needs blood!" Olivia shouted in desperation. "You should take care of her first. She's been tortured."

"Don't worry about Kylie." Silvija kept walking. "We take care of our own."

In a flash, Olivia was in front of her, clutching at Silvija's booted legs. "Please don't do this. Please. I'll do anything."

Kylie swallowed at the image Olivia made, kneeling at Silvija's feet with her sumptuous skin glowing under the moonlight, her breasts bare and beautiful, her full mouth red and trembling.

But Silvija only looked down at her with annoyance. "I have a woman who sees to all my needs. There's nothing you can provide for me or for the clan that we don't already have." She kicked Olivia aside, a blur of her booted foot that slammed her in her bare chest. She flew across the forest and smashed into a tree nearly twenty feet away with a dull thud. Olivia gasped, a hand pressed against her chest. Silvija kept walking.

Kylie helped Olivia to her feet. She staggered on unsteady legs, gasping and rubbing her chest as she stared at Silvija in horror.

"Not everyone in the clan is as gullible as me," Kylie said. "Or as nice."

"But they can't kill them. They can't."

"Silvija will do whatever she wants." But as much as Kylie knew that Silvija was planning to take them down, she couldn't deny the surge of satisfaction from knowing that soon the people who'd tortured and starved her would no longer be on the earth. She only wished that she was the one serving them their rough justice.

Just then, Kylie heard the chopper come closer. It hovered above a small clearing a few hundred feet away then landed. The radio crackled quietly on Silvija's hip, a frequency too low for humans to hear. Kylie heard her mother's voice then Silvija's response. She called the clan back with a low word.

"We'll finish this another time," Silvija said, emerging from the woods with the two-way radio at her lips. She spoke into the radio. "We're on the way now."

Olivia's eyed widened. Even with her newfound power, she looked like a bewildered child, bloody tears drying on her face as she wobbled from Silvija's kick. "What happened?"

"New information." Kylie stepped back to allow her to stand on her own feet. "We have to go now."

The vampires who had gone ahead of Silvija crept on silent feet from the woods, heading for the clearing where the helicopter sat waiting for them. Kylie deliberately turned away from Olivia to follow her clan toward the chopper, a fat black beast of a machine with her mother in the cockpit.

Belle sat with the large headset nearly obscuring her features. She wore black just like everyone else. Her gloved hands easily held the cyclic control stick as she waited for the clan to board. Kylie felt more than saw her mother's thorough gaze on her, examining every inch of Kylie as she ducked her head down and clambered into the machine. Belle nodded before fanning her eyes around her, watching for enemies lurking nearby. Silvija slammed the door shut when everyone was on board then climbed into the front beside Belle. The chopper immediately took off, ascending quickly into the night sky.

No one spoke for the duration of the ride back to New York. Kylie sat pressed between Ivy and Rufus, enjoying the simple feeling of their flesh against hers, a necessity she'd been denied for the past few days. She whimpered quietly at the thought of the things she had done and gone through since being in Atlanta. Losing her virginity. Nearly losing her second life. Killing Olivia.

"Fuck...."

Rufus put a hand on her shoulder, and she closed her eyes, simply grateful to be back where she belonged.

Chapter Twenty-four

As soon as the chopper landed on the roof, the clan shot into motion. Silvija wrenched open the door and jumped down, flicking up a wrist to glance at her watch then at Violet with a quick nod. Belle turned off the machine, threw off the headphones and yanked open the door to pull Kylie into her arms.

"You scared the shit out of me!" She squeezed Kylie so hard that her ribs creaked. For once, she didn't resist the love her mother was showing her, returning the exuberant hug with one of her own. "Don't do that again."

The slowing blades of the helicopter chopped the air above them. New York's night lights blazed in all directions, feeding rather than defeating the darkness.

"I'm sorry," Kylie said, her voice muffled in her mother's thick hair. She inhaled Belle's sea-salt scent and trembled in relief to smell it again. Her eyes closed. "I didn't mean for you to bring in the troops."

The other members of the clan squeezed Kylie's shoulder or arm as they walked away, leaving her alone with her mother. Silvija gave her a brief look before following the others with a reluctant Olivia in tow. She threw a frantic glance at Kylie, but Silvija firmly took her arm and pulled her away before she could say or do anything.

"You have nothing to be sorry for, baby. I'm just glad you're safe." Her mother hugged her again, then pulled away, looking into her face, smoothing her cool palms over Kylie's cheeks. "If they'd destroyed you, I would have gutted them all, no matter what Silvija said or what kind of weapons they had."

"I survived," Kylie murmured, overwhelmed by sudden emotion. *This* is what she had nearly lost. "I'm safe."

"And so are those humans, for the time being." Belle made a dismissive motion then touched Kylie's face again. "You need to eat."

"I will." But she knew that Silvija wanted a thorough debriefing. She wouldn't be able to eat or even change her clothes until then. "After."

"I left something for you in your room, when you're ready."

"Thank you." Kylie allowed herself to rest in Belle's arms for another moment, feeling her mother's strength and love that she had ignored for so long. "I…Thank you."

Belle cupped the back of her neck, eyes swimming with bloody tears. "Don't ever run off like that again. Okay?"

"Okay." Kylie found a smile as she pulled away from Belle. "Mama…"

She felt her mother go still at the word she hadn't called Belle since her second night as a vampire. Kylie clenched a hand behind her back and forced herself to continue. "I know I've made things hard between us." She bit her lip. "I've actually been a complete bitch."

Her mother looked at her in surprise then nodded. They both laughed, and tears slipped down Belle's cheeks before she could wipe them away.

"I was jealous of you and Silvija, and I was afraid of so many things. I'm not anymore." She unclenched her fist and took her mother's hand. "I've seen and felt things in the last few days that showed me how stupid it is to carry around bullshit resentments just because I can." She squeezed Belle's hand. "Forgive me?"

"I've already forgiven you, darling. I've just been waiting for you to forgive yourself." Belle smiled through her tears and gripped both of Kylie's hands.

The tension in her stomach dissipated. "Thank you."

Belle smiled. "Stop thanking me for just being your mother." She wiped away the new tears that managed to escape. "Now let's go to the debriefing room. We need to get a handle on this situation."

Kylie nodded and tucked away her own trembling smile. They left the roof and quickly made their way to the clan's meeting room. It was the safest room in the massive penthouse with thick sound and bulletproof walls and an elevator at the rear of the room that led directly to the helicopter pad or to the lobby of the twenty-five-story building.

It looked like any other meeting room with a large rectangular table that comfortably seated twelve, plain white walls, and a hidden panel in the front wall where they kept enough guns and ammunition to serve a small army. Silvija stood in front of her chair at the head of the table, watching the others who were already seated. Olivia sat at the chair to Silvija's immediate left.

She looked uncomfortable but determined.

I guess you didn't bargain on a new family with this new life, did you?

Kylie bit the inside of her cheek, the anger beneath her skin like a cold fire. She tried not to stare at Olivia.

They walked deeper into the room, and Belle claimed her seat at Silvija's right and pulled a chair close for Kylie to sit with her. Kylie hid her surprise, instead allowing herself to enjoy the unexpected closeness without wondering at an ulterior motive.

"Tell me," Silvija said.

She still hadn't put a shirt on. Her muscled arms and shoulders flexed as she braced her palms against the table. The black sports bra shifted from the weight of her breasts.

Kylie hesitated before she began thinking very carefully about her role in what happened and what her clan would do to Olivia if they knew just how deeply involved in the kidnapping she was. She felt her mother's eyes on her then a hand on her knee, a light squeeze. So she told them everything, leaving out only what Bertram had told her about Olivia's motives and how Kylie ended up in her apartment.

Silvija turned to Olivia who sat in the chair between her and Ivy. "Your family hunts vampires." It wasn't a question.

"Yes." Olivia shoved out her chin. "We've hunted you for generations, ever since my great-grandmother was seduced and drained and turned mad by one of you." She paused and pursed her lips. "By one of *us*. My great-grandfather was devastated and began training an army to destroy any vampires they found."

"And it wasn't long before they started actually *looking* for us, right?" Rufus spoke from his casual sprawl in the chair.

Olivia looked at him then did a double take, eyes widening when she seemed, for the first time, to recognize him from his other life as a rock star. She swallowed. "That's right."

"Your family is coming for us," Silvija said. "There's no doubt about that." She tapped a long finger on the tabletop as she watched Olivia. "The only doubt is whether or not you will help us to put them down."

Olivia visibly swallowed but did not look away. "I'll do what I can to help you both."

Silvija nodded with satisfaction, as if she'd expected nothing else.

"We found your family with the locator beacon in Kylie's phone. But that's technology everyone has these days. How did you get Kylie to come to you?"

Everyone in the room focused their attention on Olivia. She shifted under their stares but kept her gaze on Silvija. After all, she was the one asking the questions.

"I…" She pressed her lips together. "The Bertrams, my human family, developed a scent in the lab that attracts vampires."

"Why the fuck would anyone want to do that?" Liam stared at Olivia.

"To trap and decapitate us, silly," Violet supplied helpfully from her chair next to his.

The temperature in the room dropped several degrees as the clan waited for Olivia to continue.

She visibly swallowed. "I sprayed it in the curtains and on my balcony. I even wore it as a perfume when I went out."

"That's quite a risk," Rufus said. "You were lucky you didn't get drained and tossed aside."

"It wasn't luck." Olivia shrugged. "I knew what I was doing. And my family taught me to protect myself."

"That killer perfume didn't work on me," Violet said. "Or Silvija."

Belle looked at Olivia. "Maybe only the young ones like Kylie are susceptible," she said softly.

Silvija chuckled, but her eyes remained cold. "You brought us quite the specimen, little one." She tilted an eyebrow at Kylie before turning to the rest of the clan. "The Bertrams outnumbered us, but that wasn't the problem tonight. Our scout"—she inclined her head briefly in Belle's direction—"noticed they had rocket launchers. Radio scans showed they were getting ready to use them. Getting shot down would have greatly compromised our rescue mission," she finished dryly.

"What's the plan?" Violet asked, already sitting up at attention, her elbows braced against the edge of the table.

For the first time, Kylie noticed that Ivy was not in the room. She hadn't gotten into the helicopter with them even though she remembered seeing her on the riverbank. She frowned, wondering what Silvija was up to.

"First"—Silvija nodded in Kylie's direction—"escort our guest to one of the spare rooms where she can clean herself up. Then you take care of your own needs."

Kylie had been dismissed. She squeezed her mother's hand and stood, gesturing for Olivia to follow her.

"Wait." Rufus turned in his chair to face Olivia. "Before you go," he said. "Tell me who turned you."

For the first time, Olivia looked almost frightened. "It…it was my brother."

Kylie frowned. But Rufus only tilted his head toward her, wordlessly encouraging her to continue.

"He shoved me into the cell with Kylie, knowing she couldn't stop herself from feeding on me." Olivia drew a trembling breath. "I died then but woke up with another vampire's blood in my mouth. It was a young boy that my brother had forced to turn me. When Max was sure I was awake, he killed the boy in front of me."

Rufus nodded as if he already knew. "And this is the family you want to protect?"

Olivia looked away. Wordlessly, Kylie took her arm and led her to one of the bedrooms, refusing to feel pity for her about what her brother had done. She quickly left Olivia for her own room before she could say a word.

She shut her bedroom door behind her and pulled off the black shirt that smelled like Silvija, preparing to toss it on the bed. A sudden female scent assaulted her senses. She froze. Then noticed for the first time that she wasn't alone. There was a human woman in her room. A naked one.

She was suspended from the ceiling and tied up in a pretty design, the ropes twisted around her voluptuous body, pressing into her sand-colored skin, encircling each plump breast, her torso, and each spread thigh. A red ball gag parted her luscious pink lips. Between her thighs lay equally luscious pink and brown lips. Arousal dripped from the woman's pussy.

She watched Kylie cautiously. There was no fear in her face. Simply a waiting.

Her pulse thundered in her throat, a contrast to the calm façade she presented. The sound of that pulse made Kylie want to ravish her right then and there. The T-shirt dropped from her limp hand.

Her mother had chosen well, had chosen thoughtfully. The woman wasn't a pretty stick figure. She was delightfully plump, with thick thighs Kylie imagined would be soft and juicy under her teeth. As she watched, the woman dripped even more, the clear, viscous fluid dribbling from her pretty cunt, readying her for whatever her imagination had created. Kylie stared, wanting simultaneously to look away but also to keep staring. She felt guilty about the way her mouth watered for the woman's sweat and sex that smelled so delicious in the hot room.

"Well, isn't this nice."

Kylie jumped. She turned to see Olivia in her doorway.

She had showered, washed all the blood from her face and body, and brushed her hair, leaving her magnificent transformation even more apparent. Her skin glowed, richly dark with hints of red, and her short hair was thick around her beautiful face. The loose white tank top and black leggings she'd gotten from somewhere perfectly fit her slender body, the black fabric of the tights outlining the lean legs that posed with feline grace in the doorway.

She looked better than well; she was intoxicatingly lovely. The woman Kylie had been unable to resist before had been only a shadow compared to this radiant goddess in her bedroom. Olivia as a vampire was a powerful creature. A sleekly muscled panther waiting to spring.

Olivia closed the door behind her, and the mechanism clicked as it slid home. She looked at the human again, a single intrigued glance, then dismissed her.

"You smell even better than I remember." She walked close to Kylie, eyes raking her nakedness from hair to foot then back up again. "You smelled good to me before, but experiencing you like this, with these new senses, it's like being inside you." Olivia drew a deep breath, baring her sharp teeth, wetting her lips. "It makes me want to be inside you for real."

Something hot sparked in Kylie's belly. With Olivia watching her, she felt naked in a way she hadn't before. It was a vulnerability mixed with powerlessness, a softness to Olivia's hard, liquid to her flame. Arousal slithered under her skin. Her nipples tightened painfully. She restlessly shifted her thighs, trying to relieve the growing ache between them.

"You shouldn't be in here," Kylie said.

"Why?" Olivia crept toward her, sleek and predatory on bare feet.

"Because I don't want you in here." Unable to help herself, she backed away from the predatory gleam in Olivia's eyes. "You already got what you wanted from me. Get out."

Olivia made a low noise, one of amusement. "I haven't gotten what I want from you. Not by a long shot." She moved closer. Fast then slow, like she didn't yet know how to control her new vampiric speed.

"Leave," Kylie said.

Olivia grinned. "Make me."

"I don't want to play games with you, Olivia."

"I'm not here to play games with you, Kylie." She said her name teasingly, her eyes holding a new life's worth of darkness.

Time and movement sped up then slowed as Olivia approached her. Kylie was caught up in Olivia's inexperience of her new life, catching her in a blur of movement, a flash, before she was aware of her being close, closer than she should have been, her sharp teeth and sharper gaze close enough for her to touch.

Then Olivia did touch. She lifted a hand to Kylie's cheek. She flinched back, but Olivia followed. "You feel warm. Why is that?"

"It's an illusion," Kylie said, unable to look away from the dark eyes and flowing beauty in front of her. She was angry. She was furious, but that fury couldn't translate into movement. She couldn't make herself step away from the seductive darkness that was Olivia.

"I like it."

Olivia touched Kylie's throat, then drifted her hand down the smooth skin to her chest, a fang catching her own lower lip as she watched the movement. Kylie felt like she couldn't breathe, that she needed to breathe. She backed away again and found herself trapped between the wall and Olivia's warming body.

"God! I could just eat you up." Olivia's hand fell to her bare breast. Squeezed the fullness of it. "You're so beautiful."

A tremor ran through Kylie. "Don't."

"Don't what?" Olivia cupped her breast, brushed a thumb over her nipple. "Don't stop? Don't want you so much? Don't make you beg?"

A whimper of sound leaked into the room. Kylie thought it had come from her own throat, but as Olivia's fingers continued their maddening caresses, she realized it was the human woman. Bound and gagged and distressed. The scent of the human's arousal rose higher in the room.

Olivia smiled. "She's not the only one who's excited."

The words gave Kylie the strength to pull away, shove away the hand that was disintegrating her thoughts, making her wish and want and feel shame and regret and other things she was barely aware of to even put a name to.

"Beautiful, beautiful girl." Olivia whispered the words with a smile.

Then, moving quickly, she shoved Kylie back against the wall, pinning her arms. The wall was cold, solid. Olivia's touch felt hot, feverish on her skin. Olivia kissed her. The hot mouth on hers froze her where she stood. She was unable to believe what was happening.

The careful human that had once worn Olivia's body was gone. In her place was a ravening beast bent on taking what it wanted. Kylie longed to convince herself that she didn't want the same thing. But the hot mouth and firm grip stroked a deeper arousal between her legs, a plumping of pussy lips, heated wetness dripping down to coat her thighs. Her nipples were hard as agate, begging for a touch, a mouth, fingers. Anything.

Olivia's lips pressed against hers, gentle but insistent. She licked the corners of Kylie's mouth, the full bottom lip that fell open in response to Olivia's firm touch. The cool tongue slid into her mouth, licking the warming interior with firm intention while hands tightened around her upper arms, keeping her pinned to the wall.

Only her hands touched Kylie, controlling her movements, while her mouth slowly heated them up. Olivia pulled back and Kylie followed her mouth, moaning with need, wanting to keep that hot feeling. She hated that her desire ruled her so effortlessly. Hated that the cravings of her flesh made her so easily forget all the things that Olivia had done to her. But in that moment, she didn't care. She wanted that warmth. She wanted that satisfaction and firm control those hands on her arms promised. The rising temperature between them made the room seem hotter than before, melting. She whimpered.

"Damn," Olivia said softly.

She released Kylie's arms only to grab her wrists together, trapping them with one hand behind Kylie's back, forcing an arch to her spine. Her breasts thrust out. Her nipples tingled.

"I'm going to fuck you," she growled and buried her face in Kylie's throat. "I'm going to fuck you until we both die again."

Kylie moaned, closing her eyes. She remembered suddenly, from a lifetime ago, watching two women making love in their little apartment, how the woman's breasts had jutted out when her lover lashed her wrists behind her back, the noise she made then and how Kylie, still inexperienced in the ways of sex, had been excited to see her that way.

Olivia put a hand between Kylie's legs and groaned out loud.

"The way you smell is driving me crazy. I don't know what's happening to me." She groaned the words as if tortured, but she didn't stop the exploration of her fingers between Kylie's legs, the slow glide between her pussy lips, inside her, one finger. Two. "I can't stop myself."

And her fingers sped their motion, roughly shoving into Kylie. She bit her lip at the fullness inside her, the firm possession that made her belly clench with arousal and heightened desire.

"I'm sorry," Olivia moaned. "I'm sorry."

The bones of her wrists ground together from Olivia's firm grip. She hissed from the pain, mouth opening to protest. Olivia thumbed her clit, and she cried out with passion instead. Firm strokes of fingers inside her pussy, a thumb making hot circles on her clit, and before she knew it, she was gasping with pure bliss, her thighs stretching open, wider and wider, shoving her hips into the talented fingers, her head banging against the wall as the delight inside her climbed higher.

"You smell so fucking good."

Kylie didn't know if Olivia was talking about her or the human. She smelled Olivia, the blood heated scent of her cunt, warm and intoxicating and mixed with the clean cotton of her leggings. But there was the human's scent, a thick earthiness, as she watched Olivia fuck Kylie. Her pussy streamed with arousal and her hips twisted in the ropes.

Olivia licked Kylie's throat, sucked on the heating flesh while her fingers plumbed Kylie's depths, bringing her closer to her satisfaction.

Kylie clenched her eyes shut as the cum rose in her, a shattering that she felt would ruin her forever. Olivia sank her fangs into Kylie's throat, and she came apart. A hot gushing of liquid between her legs, her entire body fisting and releasing, tremors laddering through her body until she felt on the verge of collapse.

She panted, unable to believe the feelings rising up inside her. With Olivia fucking her, she felt alive again, getting breath back in those precious moments that heat flowed between them, when wonder existed between one touch and the next. Kylie leaned her head back against the wall as breath rushed past her lips, drying them.

She flinched as Olivia slid her fangs from her throat, licking the ravaged flesh. Her pussy clenched fiercely at the pain. Olivia's head rose and she looked at Kylie, her eyes nearly black with desire still unfulfilled.

"On your knees," Olivia growled.

Kylie didn't hesitate. She dropped to the floor, already pulling at the waist of Olivia's leggings, baring the slick cunt to her gaze and her mouth.

"Oh!" Olivia stumbled as Kylie's mouth latched on to her pussy.

Across the room, the human's noises of distress and pleasure grew louder, sounding tortured while she watched what was happening but could not be part of. Kylie drew the sounds into her, the woman's whimpers adding to her lust. Olivia's fingers clenched in her hair, pushing Kylie's mouth deeper between her legs. Kylie groaned at the salty wet flood on her tongue, the plump flesh flowering against her mouth.

"Fuck me, Kylie," Olivia commanded. "Put three fingers inside," she panted. "Do it now!"

She slid her fingers into the slick channel that eagerly welcomed them, coating her heating skin with lust. She moaned at the sensation of it, more intimate than anything she'd ever felt in her life, luxuriating in the squeeze of Olivia's pussy around her fingers. She did what she knew Olivia liked and curled her fingers up inside, stroking the welcoming area she found there, her mouth still working on the responsive clitoris.

Olivia stumbled, crying out, a hand grabbing Kylie's shoulder, fingers digging into bare flesh until Kylie cried out too. The drenched pussy bumped her mouth, its hair rubbing her lips, her chin, her nose.

She moaned again, the sound muffled in Olivia's pussy, the want flooding through her body like a healing elixir. Short fingernails dug into her scalp, urging her mouth on, encouraging her tongue deeper.

"Harder, baby." Olivia's voice was rough with wanting.

Kylie sucked harder on her fat clit, stroking between the plump lips with her tongue. Olivia's hips bucked and she made an incoherent noise.

Her hips moved faster. Her pussy fucked Kylie's mouth, and her fingers tightened in Kylie's skin. "Don't you fucking move!" Her voice fell away into incoherent sounds, thighs trembling beneath Kylie's hands, her flat belly flexing and releasing as she approached her peak.

"Kylie!"

She responded to the urgent sound of her name the best way she knew how. By fucking Olivia harder, thrusting deep, realizing that she didn't need to be careful anymore. Their sex before had been cautious and tender, Kylie taking care not to injure her. But now, she released the care she'd taken, thrusting her fingers deeper, faster, nibbling the clitoris that grew even larger in her mouth.

Olivia burst open on her lips. Hot fluid, viscous and salty-sweet flooded over her mouth and down her chin.

"Yes!" Olivia gasped, delighted laughter falling from her lips.

She reached down and dragged Kylie to her feet, kissing her. Kylie swooned in her heated embrace, her head swimming with the sensations they'd just shared. Her fingers still tingled from their home inside Olivia. She longed for that again, the fierce hunger that made her want to claw and scratch and bite and feel Olivia bleeding under her mouth and hands. She hovered with the unfamiliar violence of her lust, not knowing quite what to do.

But Olivia seemed to have no such problems with what they had done. She yanked up her tights as they kissed. Her tongue stroked Kylie's, her hands roving over her naked body, her ass, between her legs where she unerringly found her clit and pressed. Kylie shuddered.

Olivia drew back, smiling. "I'm so happy we're together like this."

For a split second, Kylie didn't know what she was talking about. Then she remembered the what and how of them getting to this point. She pulled roughly away.

Before she could say anything, Olivia tugged her back against her. "Don't start this again."

She bit Kylie's lower lip and linked fingers behind her back, lightly scratching her nails against the sensitive skin above Kylie's ass. Kylie shivered, her objections already flying away as Olivia's fangs broke skin and a trickle of blood flowed between them.

"You taste delicious, my darling. But I'm starved for something a bit more." She glanced over her shoulder at the woman trussed up in the rope. "Do you mind sharing her?"

Olivia didn't wait for her agreement. She simply tugged Kylie toward the woman. Her excitement was hot and pungent in the air, pussy still dripping, eyes as wide as saucers. Kylie's mouth watered.

It had been a long time since she'd last fed. She glanced sideways at Olivia, reminded instantly of who she had fed on, and where. Her appetite flagged. The anger resurfaced. Olivia, some sixth sense apparently engaged where Kylie was concerned, lightly pinched her side then slid her arms around Kylie's waist.

"You have my heart, Kylie." Olivia held her body still against hers, the dark velvet of her eyes caressing Kylie, her bare arms like the softest and strongest silk. "I know that doesn't erase the things I've done to hurt you, but I think it's important that you know." Her arms tightened around Kylie's waist. "I won't hurt you again." The corners of her mouth lifted. "Unless you ask me to, that is."

She stood, stunned in the circle of Olivia's arms at her declaration. *You have my heart.* It was on the edge of her tongue to tell her own truth, that even with the betrayal and the pain of the last few days, she loved Olivia in a way that defied reason. She loved her passionately and completely.

Olivia pressed a cool palm to Kylie's back. "I know, love." She smiled and kissed beneath Kylie's ear. "Now let's eat."

She took Kylie's hand and stepped toward their food.

"Hello, my pretty." Olivia grinned at the girl, showing all her teeth. If possible, the girl grew even more aroused, her juices flowing even more. Her red berry nipples were puckered in the warm room. Olivia touched between her legs, and her soft belly quivered, a moan gathered behind the gag.

"I think she already came," Olivia said with wonder, putting her pussy-wet fingers to her mouth.

She looked like the perfect fiend just then, as if she had been a vampire forever. She watched the girl like she would enjoy taking her blood, would enjoy taking her very life.

Olivia turned and reached out a hand to Kylie. "Come. Enjoy your gift."

She tipped the girl's head to the side, exposing the vulnerable curve of her neck, the thudding pulse. Kylie licked her lips, everything forgotten in the face of her overwhelming hunger. Her fangs shot out. Olivia made a soft noise.

"That's so fucking sexy," she murmured.

Kylie shuddered at her words, then sank her fangs into the human's neck. She sighed as the thick, richness rushed into her mouth, a river of the most perfect meal she'd ever eaten, the best sex she'd ever had, the last sunset of her human life.

Her eyes shot open when she felt Olivia's hand on her back. She was bent between the human's legs, licking at the quivering skin over the big thigh artery. "Bon appétit, my love." Olivia bit into the delicate skin, a moan singing from her throat as the blood flowed into her mouth.

❖

Hours later, Kylie stirred in the sheets when she heard the sound of a door opening. Her lashes, heavy from sleep, flickered open to see Rufus and Julia in the doorway. Julia chuckled.

"I think she's finally busted that cherry."

Behind her, Olivia gripped her hip, her head rising up from the pillow to see who had interrupted them. With a soft noise, she lay back down and pulled Kylie's hips even more into hers. She kissed the back of Kylie's neck and whispered something incoherent before she fell back asleep.

"That one is dangerous," Rufus said, watching Olivia. "I can feel it."

"Well, she wouldn't be Belle's daughter if she made things easy for us, would she?"

Then it was Rufus's turn to laugh. "Very true."

Kylie closed her eyes and felt sleep come back up to claim her as Rufus and Julia walked into the room. She heard the noises of them taking away the human, still alive and swimming in the aftermath of her satisfaction. They quietly closed the bedroom door behind them.

CHAPTER TWENTY-FIVE

Kylie woke up alone in her bed. She blinked and rolled over, her body half remembering the details of the last time it was awake: a delicate tongue licking the back of her neck, new fangs experimentally biting into her back and sending shudders of delight ricocheting through her entire body.

Olivia.

She sat up in a mild panic. Where was she? Kylie jumped up from the bed.

The space beside her was empty, but there was a lingering scent in the air that proved she had been there, that Kylie had not been dreaming. Olivia must have just left the bed since Kylie was waking now. She quickly pulled on the closest thing she could find and rushed out of her room, searching.

She quickly found Olivia's scent in the hallway not far from her room. Olivia was sitting on the floor in Kylie's robe in her favorite lotus position. Her slender figure was swallowed up by the thick white terrycloth, but the lotus bared her thighs and knees, and made Kylie wonder at what else was beautiful under the white cloth. She was talking with Julia.

They looked far too intimate sitting there together, talking quietly, the long hallway with emptiness stretching out on both sides, giving their meeting place a look of isolation, even conspiracy. What was Julia up to?

"Leave her alone," Kylie said, moving quickly down the hallway.

Julia, sitting with her knees together and wearing a skintight leotard that fit her from throat to ankles, looked up at Kylie with amusement. "Nice outfit."

Kylie looked down at herself. If she could have flushed with the easy display of embarrassment, her cheeks would have been darker with color. As it was, she looked away and shoved her hands in the pockets of the oversized, shimmering pink cat suit that fit her like clown pajamas.

It must have been whatever the human woman was wearing before they tied her up and left her as a present in Kylie's room. It sagged on her body, over-sized and bright pink, the collar drooping low over her small breasts, the thighs and belly of the outfit swallowing her figure.

Olivia smiled, a touch of mirth on that same mouth that had been sucking her clit only hours before. "It's fine, Kylie. We're just talking."

"Why am I not surprised that the two of you found each other? The betrayer and the bitch."

She spun around to go back the way she had come, then changed her mind at the last minute and took the hallway leading to the briefing room and Silvija's office. She had no idea why her feet pointed her in that direction. Kylie only knew that her mind wasn't quite her own. It felt out of control with thoughts she'd never had before. She stopped still. Jealous. She was jealous of Julia. And she felt stupid for it. Her mother would never have been prey to such foolishness.

She bit the inside of her cheek and turned to go back to her room and at least get rid of this absurd outfit. Then she smelled Silvija.

"Kylie." Silvija appeared in the doorway of her office. *Her wife,* a voice that sounded remarkably like Olivia's, reminded her.

Silvija wore a suit, gunmetal gray and fitted to her impressively tall body. Black high heels made her even taller, the hem of the skirt ending at mid-calf. As pretty as the suit was, it severely limited her movements. Silvija must be off to a different type of hunt tonight. She held a phone in her hand.

"I'm happy to see you getting along with the newest addition to the family." Humor flashed in her dark eyes. Was she laughing at Kylie?

She stiffened. "Why wouldn't I be?"

"I didn't think the sex, no matter how good it is, could make you forget all the things she did to you."

"She didn't do anything *to* me."

Silvija laughed without humor, her red lips barely moving. "You telling me what happened isn't that important?" *Because I already know*, was the implied conclusion to that sentence. "But have you been honest with your mother about what this woman had in mind for you when she lured you into her apartment?"

To have it put so plainly, that she was lured like a common and mindless animal, made Kylie hiss in anger. And embarrassment. "There are things mother doesn't have to know."

"You should tell her everything. The more honest you are, the closer the two of you will be to each other." Silvija's voice warmed a few degrees. "I know she wants that."

Kylie's eyes narrowed. "Does that mean you've told her that you're the one who bit me?"

Silvija's expression didn't change. The dark eyes stayed serene. Her posture in the doorway was straight, her tall and curvaceous body a domme dream in the gray suit and stiletto heels. But Kylie felt a rush of cold from her, a crippling rush of animosity that flowed over her. She froze under the implacable stare of Silvija.

"Back then, I had no choice about what to do. You would be dead and she would have been destroyed. I couldn't have that." Her shoulder moved in a shrug, no regret on her face. "It's been seven years and you're just now bringing that up. Why?" But before Kylie could answer, a smile shaped the full red mouth. "Of course. Pussy."

Kylie felt like her face was exploding. She opened her mouth to protest, to say anything and end her embarrassment, but again, Silvija beat her to it.

"I already told your mother that I was the one who brought you into the family. She wasn't happy with me that night." She smiled wryly, an understatement. "Or a few nights after that. But she's happy you're here with her instead of six feet under where she can't see your resentful little face anytime she pleases."

Kylie flinched. This was the first time Silvija mentioned the rift between Kylie and Belle. Usually, Silvija was coolly polite to

Kylie, watching with eyes that missed nothing but with lips that only censured her for things she did against the clan. Disobeying Silvija. Pursuing a human woman who could bring them all to ruin.

"The relationship I have with her is none of your business," Kylie snapped.

"You may be right, but Belle is my business. Her happiness means everything to me. And you've been making her very unhappy these last few years. Sometimes I wonder if it hadn't been better if I'd let you die in that basement." Silvija shrugged again. "Too late now."

The phone in her hand chimed softly and she looked down at it. Her smile came and went with equal swiftness, before she tapped the screen to accept the call.

"Anyway, the two of you are not to leave the house tonight. I don't care what you do here, just don't leave the premises." Then Silvija turned and walked back into her office. "Talk to me, Ivy. Are we all set?" She closed the door in Kylie's face.

She stood there, seething. Then growled low in her throat and went back the way she had come. Julia and Olivia were still in the hallway.

"Get dressed," she said to Olivia. "We're going out."

She went back to her room, threw off the over-sized, pink unitard, and started rifling in her closet for something to wear. She found the night's pair of jeans and T-shirt, socks, and jacket, threw them on the bed, and went into the bathroom to take a shower.

Her bathroom, like all the others in the house, was custom designed.

There were no windows and only one door. The room was nearly as large as the bedroom, and all of it was tiled with small one-inch squares in various shades of blue. Kylie's favorite color. On one side of the room was the tub, deep and luxurious with water pouring down from an antique-looking silver spout coming out from the wall. The same color tiles were slick under Kylie's feet as she walked to the basin, waist high and royal blue, a single elegant faucet dispensing water into her hands for her to wash her face.

She'd gotten rid of the toilet and used the space for more of the shower. The shower was a comfortable ten-by-fifteen-foot rectangle with twelve different shower heads attached to its three walls. All the heads were adjustable in terms of spray, rhythm, and amount of water they delivered. Two of the heads were attached to flexible arms and removable. Kylie had used them to wash her hair at one point before deciding she preferred hands-free showering.

"Damn, this is nice!"

Olivia stood in the doorway, admiring the fixtures, the plumbing, and Kylie naked in the middle of it all. She only glanced briefly at the bathroom's details before she focused her complete attention on Kylie, eyes eating her up like tongues of flame. Despite their history together, Kylie felt shy, wanting to hide her body from that focused and devouring stare. But she forced herself to keep her hands at her side.

"Very practical," Olivia murmured. "And big."

"I like to be clean."

"No kidding." Olivia walked under the various shower heads, still in her robe, touching one after the other but not turning on the water. "You like nice things."

"Yes."

Kylie had never thought about that but realized the clan had never lacked for luxury. Even when they had been in Jamaica when she was first turned, all of them in the small cabin near Montego Bay. Everything had been luxurious. The softest sheets. Plentiful clothes. Money to spend. Before the horror of it had really hit her, she was convinced she had landed in a fairy tale. It was disconcerting remembering those first few days, especially after just talking about her turning with Silvija. The end and beginning of everything.

"We're going out," Kylie said.

"The big one said we shouldn't leave."

Kylie turned in surprise. "Silvija talked to you?"

"Yes. She passed through the hall when I was chatting with the little one." The big one and the little one.

No names. Did she even plan on staying long enough to know anyone? Did she think this was just a pit stop on her tour through vampire land?

"It doesn't matter what she says, we're leaving." Kylie turned on the shower, putting the heat up as high as she could stand. Water splashed against the blue tiles, steam rose around them.

Olivia shrugged off her robe and dropped it on the floor. "Are you always so rebellious?"

She turned away from Kylie to examine one of the shower heads at waist level a few feet away. Kylie stared at her naked body, stunned again by its beauty; beauty Olivia wore and displayed so casually even before her breast had been made whole again. Smooth skin. Delicious nipples. Pussy with its triangle of neatly trimmed hair.

Kylie licked her lips, her hand sliding from the spigot and falling uselessly against her thigh. But Olivia seemed completely oblivious to her reaction. The steam from the hot water misted up around them, swirling around their bodies, winding in Kylie's hair, sliding into her nose.

"What will they think of next?" Olivia murmured with a pleased smile as she touched a shower head. Then she turned to look over her shoulder at Kylie. "We're not going anywhere."

The snap of command in her voice made Kylie look up. Then freeze.

"Come here."

Kylie shook her head. "What—"

"Come. Here."

Olivia wore the barest smile on her face. No teeth. Simply the faint stretch of her pinkened lips. She kept her gaze level, waiting.

Kylie felt a funny feeling in her belly. Butterflies. Hordes of them. Why was she nervous? It was just Olivia. But before she could process what her body was doing, what she wanted, she was crossing the few feet of space between them, walking slowly toward Olivia while a slow drumming awoke deep inside her. Her body cut through the steam billowing around them.

"So obedient." Olivia's smile widened. She stood with her hands on her hips, watching Kylie's slow approach. "Have you ever touched yourself in here?"

"Of course. I've showered here and touched myself all over." Then Kylie caught Olivia's meaning. Her lashes fluttered down, and she felt at sea, wondering why Olivia found it so easy to act as if everything was fine between them. She acted as if Kylie's anger didn't exist. She shook her head. "No. Never."

Olivia looked around with that same smile. "So much bounty, so little use." She touched Kylie's face. "Why do you want to leave the house so badly?"

"Because I'm free to do what I want," she said gruffly. "Why are you in such a rush to trot to whatever beat Silvija plays?"

"Because she's the leader of this family for a reason. Do you think she'd give an order if it wasn't necessary?"

"To me, yes."

"Why?" Olivia tilted her head to look up at Kylie.

"To punish me for being rude to my mother."

"And are you rude to your mother?"

"Sometimes. But not anymore." Belle didn't deserve her anger any more than Rufus or Violet did.

"Thank you for being honest." She teased the edges of Kylie's hair with her fingers, traced the whirl of her ear, and touched the line of her neck down to her shoulder. "Why were you being rude to your mother?"

"You know why."

"Yes, but do you?"

Kylie trembled, barely able to keep track of her thoughts as Olivia's fingers lightly touched her skin, bringing up heat and pinpricks of awareness, the drumming between her legs growing stronger. Steam wove around the bathroom, adding to the hypnotic effect of the water splashing against the tiles.

"That's okay," Olivia whispered. "We can talk about that another time." She floated a finger over Kylie's nipple. "I have more important things on my mind now."

Kylie longed to shove her away and tell her to stop telling her what to do, but the hands were light enough on her flesh that she wanted more. She wanted to see where all this touching was going to end. She bit the inside of her lip, aware of how wet she was, how hard her nipples were. As if she shared the same awareness, Olivia cupped her breast, finally, a firm touch, then stroked it.

Kylie gasped and squirmed where she stood, arousal dripping down her thigh, her nipples so hard that they hurt. Steam slid into her nose and open mouth.

"Touch yourself," Olivia said, her voice almost hoarse. She took her hand away from Kylie.

"What?" She was disoriented at the loss of sensation, blinking into the mist around them. She needed Olivia to touch her.

"Put your hand on your pussy. Like that first time in my bed."

Kylie did as she was told, gritting her teeth when she encountered her own cool wetness that thickly coated her fingers.

"Good." Olivia watched her with heavy-lidded eyes. "Good. Now lick your fingers."

Kylie hesitated. But at a look from Olivia, she put the wet fingers in her mouth. Salty and cool. Definitely not as good as what she'd already had from between Olivia's thighs, but the act was surprisingly erotic. She slid her fingers in her mouth, sucking off the juices. Her eyes met Olivia's and kept them as she slid her tongue around each finger, licking up the evidence of her arousal while her body continued to produce more.

"Oh, you're so good at that." The words were a low moan deep inside Olivia's chest.

They made Kylie tremble and want to be even better. Olivia moved closer. Kylie felt her own eyelids get heavy as Olivia's intoxicating scent crowded in on her. She took her hand from her mouth, anticipating Olivia's kiss, but Olivia's head dipped low. Her cool breath brushed Kylie's nipple an instant before her tongue lashed out and licked. Once, twice.

"Oh…."

A sigh leaked from Kylie's mouth and she stumbled on her feet. Olivia raised her head, grabbed Kylie's waist, and shoved her back against the shower wall. The steam heated tiles pressed into her back. The cool mouth covered her breast, and her eyes fell shut. Her hand fumbled to the back of Olivia's head.

Oh. God.

Until she'd been with Olivia for the first time, she didn't realize how sensitive her nipples were. These things that she had carried around with her for all her life became a source of such heady pleasure. She'd never tried to do it to herself, only waited patiently for the touch of Olivia's mouth or her hands that could take Kylie straight to the stars.

Olivia did it to her again. Covering her nipple with her mouth while her tongue circled and licked and nudged and fluttered and laved the hard nub, leaving Kylie moaning as she collapsed against the wall, her world narrowed down to the mouth on her, her body's reaction, the waves of bliss riding through her body. The steam in the bathroom was blinding.

"Open your legs."

Kylie immediately dropped her thighs open, panting in excitement, anticipating the press of Olivia's expert hands, her fingers manipulating her clit in a way that guaranteed that she would lose the power of speech for many, many minutes. But it wasn't Olivia's hand she felt.

Her eyes flew open and her scream of shock, of pleasure, pierced the cavernous room. Water. It was water. Olivia had a shower head in her hand, the water twirling in a powerful spray directly onto Kylie's clit. Sensation exploded into her pussy, a strong rhythm that made her gasp, then bite her lip against the tiny squeaks and screams that overwhelmed her. The water pounded at her as Olivia's mouth sucked and licked her nipple, first one, then the other, sucking and biting and soothing while the shower head drilled her hips into the tiles. Sensation twisted into her, building quickly, steadily. The orgasm came at her in a rush, quicker than any she'd ever had, the cum exploding from her hips like a bullet. The water continued to pound her flesh. Olivia's hand moved, and the water pressure changed, became lighter then built in strength, the rhythm variable and pulsing.

"Oh my G—!" Kylie screamed. "What are you—?" But she couldn't continue. She could only writhe against the slippery tiles while the water banged her into submission.

Olivia hummed against Kylie's breast, a fang sinking into the nipple with intent, and Kylie exploded again, the cum so intense that her belly cramped, she literally saw red as her head banged against the tile. She was vaguely aware of a cracking noise, the shower of broken tiles on her shoulders.

"That's it, baby." Olivia growled. "Come for me."

Then the shower head was gone, dropped to the floor, its hot water splashing on Kylie's feet. Olivia slid expert fingers inside her and lifted her head, her eyes piercing Kylie as her fingers fucked her deeply. Deep grunts leapt from her throat as her fingers rammed into Kylie.

"You feel so good, so tight." Olivia groaned deep in her throat, the words barely decipherable. "I could fuck you like this forever."

Each word punctuated by a deep and hard thrust, fingers bruising Kylie's pelvic cradle with each fuck, but Kylie didn't care. The heat between their bodies was amazing, the steam from the water and the shower rising around them, sliding into her mouth, her nose, her eyes. It was like they were fucking on another world. A world where life could be ending or beginning or non-existent, but where the only thing that mattered was the thrust and flex of Olivia's fingers inside her, the press of her heated flesh against hers, her mouth on Kylie's neck, clamping down but not biting. Holding her still for the slick and deep penetration into her depths.

The cum slammed into her with the force of a hundred fists. The scream she didn't even try to stop rolled out of her mouth in a piercing cry, amplified by the acoustics in the bathroom, thrown back into her ears until she felt like her entire body was a long, continuous scream, a piercing vibration of sound and destruction and power.

Wave after wave of sensation slammed into her body. Her pussy clutched tight. Olivia's hand retreated, and a rush of liquid spilled from her body, a geyser rivaling what was coming from the shower head abandoned on the floor. She slumped to the ground. Weakened. Depleted. Olivia stood over her with a pleased smile. She turned off the water and resituated the shower head on its hook.

"It's not time for you to rest yet," she said. "The night is young and I have plenty of energy to burn."

Olivia fucked her until she didn't want to leave the house anymore. Didn't even know why she had wanted to leave in the first place when there was a bed and a wall and a floor to fuck on.

As much as they had made love before Olivia was turned, this was the most intense, the hardest they'd ever taken each other, and Kylie loved it. Loved it and hated that she loved it. But she didn't allow those thoughts to plague her for very long. Or at least Olivia didn't. She fed Kylie orgasm after orgasm until she forgot that she had ever been hungry for sensation, forgot that Olivia had betrayed her. She forgot her own name.

CHAPTER TWENTY-SIX

Kylie slept the sleep of the happily dead. In the dreams that moved under her eyelids, scent and flesh combined. She was naked, in the woods, and running. Her bare feet pounded across the dirt while laughter floated behind her. Kylie laughed too. Hands clutched at her from behind and latched around her waist, pulling her against a firm and intoxicatingly scented body.

"Gotcha!"

Teeth nipped at her ear. More laughter, and the two of them were tumbling down into the dirt and leaves. Cool flesh warming, a mouth nuzzling hers. She sighed.

And woke.

The sigh followed her up from sleep. She turned over to see Olivia already awake and watching her. Olivia was heartbreakingly beautiful and whole, her eyes like searchlights. Kylie blinked away the last of her drowsiness, reluctantly leaving the remnants of the dream behind. Her skin still tingled from the dream kisses, she still felt a branch digging into her bare thigh, the hand slipping over her breast.

"What?" she croaked.

Her body felt pleasantly worn out from the full night of marathon sex with Olivia. Still aching in places, deliciously raw. Replete. Kylie stretched, blinked again, and sighed. Olivia obviously wasn't at the same place she was.

Olivia sat upright in the bed, legs crossed, hands clasped in her lap, forehead wrinkled with some worry.

"What's going on?"

"I can hear everything," Olivia said. She didn't seem pleased. "The sounds on the street. I can hear the man in the shop downstairs ask about getting change. In this house, I can hear people, your people, talking and fucking. I hear them and their noises and the words they're saying. I hear the breeze outside this window." Her eyes bored into Kylie. "The only thing I can't hear is myself." She pressed a hand to her chest. "Everything inside me is so quiet." She thumped her chest, once, twice. "Nothing moves. Nothing makes noise. Last night distracted me from it, but now it's all I notice."

Kylie sat up in the pillows, pulling two under her head and another under her back. Her mind floated briefly over the "distraction" of their full night and day together. Her clit stirred, but she forced her attention back to the matter at hand. "It's called being dead," she said.

Olivia flinched but didn't look away from her lover of the mercurial moods; fierce and seductive one moment, an uncertain innocent the next. Kylie shoved her thick mass of coils and curls out of her face.

"You can't go back from this," she said. "There's no taking back the change."

"I would never take it back." Olivia twined her fingers together in her lap. "This is better than the alternative." Her eyes clouded. "I wouldn't change it," she said in a stronger voice.

No. She wouldn't change how she had tricked Kylie into falling for her and falling into her bed. She wouldn't change how Kylie had suffered at the hands of her family.

"That's good to know," Kylie said softly. "I bet you'd be just as happy if the Bertrams blew up this house and burned my entire family to ashes. Is the prospect of that the only part of this 'relationship' with me that really got your panties wet?" Her eyebrow arched up.

Olivia's eyes narrowed. "That's not fair, Kylie."

"We're not talking about fair," she said. "We just need to deal with reality. You're one of us now. A bloodsucker." She growled. "Your people hate us. You played me like an idiot to get what you wanted. You're only here because you're afraid of dying. Nothing else."

"Kylie...." Olivia sat up even straighter in the bed. "I never meant to hurt you when I started this."

"But here I am." She pulled the sheet up to cover her bare breasts and crossed her arms over her chest. The burn marks from her electrocution had healed, but she would never forget the sensation of being fried by unending streams of current. The brightest and hardest pain she'd ever experienced. Ever. "The important thing is that you got what you needed out of this, right?"

"No! That's not fucking—!"

"Lover's quarrel already?" Julia stood in the doorway of the bedroom, looking deadly and gorgeous in tight white leather. Kylie could see a hint of something else underneath it, something black and skintight. A softer material.

"What do you want?" Kylie snapped.

"Such rudeness!" Julia laughed. "Anyway, the family is having an outing tonight. Silvija says you two should come." She laughed again, obviously tickled about something.

"What happened to me and Olivia staying put and not being allowed to leave?"

"Tonight is a new night." Julia bared her teeth. "It might be the night Olivia's humans come for us."

She spared them another laughing glance before stepping back outside the threshold of the bedroom. She left the door open.

"My family?" Olivia narrowed her gaze at the empty doorway. "They're coming for me?"

Kylie sucked her teeth. "Don't listen to Julia. She doesn't even know half of what she's talking about." The humans would come for them, but there was no certainty that it was tonight.

Kylie got up from the bed, self-conscious about her nakedness. Olivia quickly turned her head, a darting, birdlike movement, to watch her walk toward the bathroom. She felt Olivia's eyes on her ass.

"I'm going to take a shower," she said.

Olivia left the bed. "I'll keep you company."

Hot water on, Kylie climbed under the spray a moment before Olivia joined her in the bathroom.

"I just want to shower with you," Olivia said. "We can get back to our fight later."

A pulse of desire leapt to life inside Kylie. Why wasn't she able to hold on to her anger where Olivia was concerned? The betrayal burned, but each time Olivia touched her, it was as if she gave an antidote with each kiss, each touch, and each orgasm that flayed Kylie from the inside out. She savagely shoved the betrayal forward in her consciousness, trying to make it generate awful thoughts, revulsion. But at the sight of Olivia stepping across the damp blue tiles, magnificently naked, all Kylie wanted was to fuck.

But she needed to put some distance between them. "You could have waited for your turn. We don't have to pay for the water."

"It's not the water I'm thinking about," Olivia said.

She slowly walked the length of the bathroom toward Kylie, tracing a finger along the tiled walls. Steam twined around her long legs. A wicked smile played on her lips.

The water sprayed over Kylie from the dual shower heads, a steady and firm pressure of hot water that washed over her face and hair, her chest. From only a few feet away, Olivia looked at her, eyes nearly black in the blue tiled bathroom. Her skin glowed under the soft lighting, her eyes were luminous, her mouth full and hungry. Her lips parted slightly, but her teeth weren't showing, just the flicking wet motion of her tongue.

"We have to leave for this outing soon, right?" Olivia glanced briefly around the bathroom before she looked back at Kylie.

She nodded.

Olivia moved closer, obliterating the space between them, and kissed her on the mouth. She put her hands around Kylie's waist. "I want to kiss you," she murmured against Kylie's mouth.

"Don't." Kylie backed away. "You can't fuck me and pretend like everything is fine between us."

But that was exactly what Olivia seemed intent on doing.

Abruptly, Olivia gripped her waist. "Open your legs and put them on my shoulders," she commanded in the same instant that she was making it happen, effortlessly lifting Kylie up mid-gasp and bracing her back against the heated tiles that were wet from steam. Against her will, Kylie's thighs fell open around her face.

The shower jets splashed over her flailing legs an instant before Olivia's mouth claimed her pussy. Kylie bit her bottom lip and fluttered her eyes closed as sensation took her over. Olivia's tongue on her clit, firmly licking her, effortlessly calling up wetness. Heat.

"No…" She wanted to push Olivia away from her, rip apart the pink elephant in the room, but instead, she leaned her naked back into the wall, arched her pussy into Olivia's mouth, stretched her arms above her head. A moan breathed from her parted lips.

Olivia slurped at her wetness, slowly licking her pussy and sucking her clit with such succulence that it wrung incoherent sounds from Kylie's throat. Her palms slid against the tiles above her head, fingers bending and flexing, twitching as Olivia's mouth completely unmoored her.

Kylie felt delicious, liquid filled, throbbing with want.

Olivia moaned between her legs, the vibrations tipping Kylie closer to the edge. She felt like she was falling, tipping off Olivia's shoulders to the ground. But she didn't care. She groaned as the riot of sensation moved between her legs and Olivia's mouth made a thorough meal of her pussy. Her back slid up and down the wall with each hungry thrust of Olivia's tongue, water from the shower splashing on her legs dangling down Olivia's back.

A hand squeezed her breast, her nipple. She moaned.

So good.

Kylie grabbed the hand on her breast to keep it there. She had a sudden fear that the sensation would go away.

"Olivia!"

"Yes, baby?" Olivia moaned the answer between her legs, fingers sliding inside Kylie to take the place of her tongue, pressing into wetness until Kylie was panting with the effort of staying together while Olivia seemed intent on shattering her into tiny little pieces. "I won't let you fall." She fucked her deeply with her fingers. "I've got you." Her thumb circled her slippery clit. Then her mouth sucked, her tongue licked Kylie between the words. "Come whenever you're ready." Olivia's fingers stroked her deeply inside, fierce and firm and insistent. Tongue again. Fingers. Fire.

Kylie was ready. Her pussy clutched hard at the fingers inside, then she was coming, head slamming back against the shower tiles as she howled her release. She panted as if she had been running from the sun.

Olivia drew her mouth away, kissed her clit again, and licked the drip of juices on her thighs. Kylie shivered at the aftershocks that moved through her from the light touch.

"You taste like the best thing I've ever eaten." Olivia nipped at Kylie's trembling belly, gripped her waist, and lifted her down and back to her feet. "And I want to keep my mouth on you forever."

Kylie stumbled back against the tiles, blinking, shuddering still, her pussy soaking wet and satisfied. She grabbed the back of Olivia's neck and kissed her. She sighed at the flavor of pussy on Olivia's tongue, the sliding wetness of their mouths moving together. She slipped a hand between Olivia's thighs. She was soaked. She began to move her fingers.

"No," Olivia muttered. "Just…just turn around." Her words were deep and guttural. Desperate. Apparently, Kylie didn't move fast enough for her; she shoved her, whipped her around to face the wall, and gripped Kylie's hips. "I love your ass," she gritted the words into Kylie's shoulder. She positioned herself behind Kylie, her pussy, wet and heated and open on Kylie's ass.

She hissed something Kylie couldn't hear. Kylie braced her hands against the tiles, legs spread as Olivia slid her clit against the muscular weight of her ass, getting herself off. She groaned in her throat, fingers sinking painfully into Kylie's hips as her hand squeezed and tugged at a nipple. She steadily worked her clit against Kylie's ass.

"You're so damn sexy." Olivia groaned, tugging her nipple, grinding her hips. Cool breath brushed against Kylie's shoulder. "I can't believe I waited so long to fuck you." She pinched Kylie's nipple, rolled it between her thumb and forefinger. Kylie gasped and trembled, the arousal that was never far away, tumbling easily back into her body. She touched herself, slid her fingers between her legs, around the slick lips, her hard clit. She stroked herself to the rhythm of Olivia's hand on her breast.

"I should have taken you that first night," Olivia muttered into her skin. "God, you smelled so good then. So fucking good!"

Then she was gasping and coming, her entire body shuddering between Kylie and the steady gush of water from the shower. Kylie moved her hand frantically between her thighs, the sound of Olivia's orgasm, her body-deep groans pushed her toward her own conclusion. She screamed as she came again, a strong wave of sensation that began from her center and rolled out through the rest of her body, and kept rolling and rolling, not as powerful as the first but longer, making her entire body shake as if caught in a hurricane. Olivia's words. The feel of her pussy on her ass. Her mouth on her shoulder, the possibility of a bite, that stinging pleasure-pain under her skin that went straight to her cunt.

Kylie licked her dry lips and controlled her breath. With a hand still braced against the wall, she looked over her shoulder at Olivia.

"What do you mean you should have fucked me that first night?" she asked.

Olivia met her eyes, raking blunt nails along the skin of Kylie's inner thigh. She straightened and pulled Kylie upright. "I knew you were watching me before we talked." Her lashes fluttered down for an instant, then she pinned Kylie with her steady, dark gaze. "That night when I was fucking myself and you watched, I was thinking about you. I didn't know what you looked like, but I smelled your skin. I knew you were there in my place. And I wanted to fuck you."

Kylie blinked in shock. Olivia had known about her that entire time? She remembered all the things she'd seen, how she had felt uncomfortable spying on her. But everything she'd seen of Olivia, Olivia had meant her to see.

"Was there anything real about what I saw of you in Atlanta?" The raw pain in her voice embarrassed her, but she couldn't hide it.

"*This* is real." Olivia laced her fingers in Kylie's hair and tugged her gently closer. "And because of that, you know me better than anyone in the world."

Kylie shook her head and winced from the pain of Olivia's grip on her hair. "No, Olivia—"

"Girls, we know you're having fun, but Mommy wants us all to go now!"

Kylie flinched at the sound of Julia's voice from very nearby. She didn't bother to look in the doorway of the bathroom to see if she was there. She pulled away from Olivia's embrace.

"Let's get washed up," Olivia murmured. "We can talk more about this later."

❖

After they showered and dressed, they met the rest of the clan by the elevator then they all rode down to the street together. Everyone looked like their version of casual, Julia in her white leather; Rufus, Violet, and Liam in T-shirts, loose jeans, and Doc Martins. Ivy was back from wherever she had gone and wore a loose black sheath dress and sandals. Silvija in black slacks and a turtleneck. Belle looked like she was dressed for a walk on the beach in a pair of pink shorts, a black blouse, and gladiator sandals.

After a look at her mother, Kylie glanced at Olivia who stood by her side. Her lover, a stranger. Regardless of her anger about how she had been manipulated, she had to admit that Olivia looked gorgeous and confident in the long gray dress and red Converse sneakers she'd borrowed from Kylie's closet. Silver earrings shaped like gingko leaves, a gift from Julia, dangled from her earlobes. Olivia saw her watching and gave her a teasing smile, then brushed a hand over Kylie's back and ass. Kylie swallowed. She couldn't stop the sweetness that uncurled in her belly.

A car was waiting for them, a black stretch limo, idling on the street in front of the building. Silvija opened the front passenger door to sit up front with the driver, leaving everyone else to find a place in back. They all spilled in, voices chattering, laughing.

Kylie slid in next to Olivia but turned away from her. She felt like such a damn fool.

"I did what I needed to do, Kylie." Olivia touched her thigh. "You would have done the same thing."

"No!" Kylie growled under her breath. "I wouldn't have."

Everyone in the car seemed to be deliberately ignoring the disagreement Kylie and Olivia were having, paying attention to their own conversations or inner thoughts.

Rufus tipped his head in her direction. "You look nice, Kylie." He touched the zippered cuff of her black leather jacket, eyes moving slyly to Olivia.

His words captured the attention of everyone in the car until they were all staring at her and Olivia.

"Thanks." Kylie plucked at the knee of her jeans, looking away from their intrigued gazes. Her eyes collided with Olivia's and bounced away.

"It's probably from all that pussy she's been eating." Julia laughed and settled herself into the car.

Rufus chuckled, just as Belle pinched Julia. "Behave," she said with a glint in her eyes.

"Make me." Julia grinned.

But everyone seemed to be in a playful mood, happy to be getting out and doing something as a family. Even Rufus, who was the loner among them.

Even though she chided Julia, Belle wore a smile of her own. "You do look nice, Kylie. This suits you." She didn't say what *this* was, but she could tell by the wicked laughter in the car that she wasn't talking about Kylie's outfit.

The limo was luxuriously appointed. Leather seats, moon roof, and a bikini-clad woman near the bar. The woman smelled like herself. Deliciously human and filled with blood just ready to be taken.

"I like this car," Julia murmured, eying the bikini treat.

She was the first to approach the woman, who only smiled vacantly at them all. She was obviously drugged, but was free of bite marks. Probably a vampire virgin. One Kylie assumed they were free to kill.

"Drink only." Silvija's voice slid silkily through the speakers.

Julia paused, eyes glinting wickedly. "I haven't done that in ages, but okay."

She took the woman's wrist and kissed it. Then she sank her fangs in, teasing. The woman flinched but did not pull away, only closed her eyes, licking her lips as Julia continued to sip from her. Ivy came on the other side of the human, sliding between the woman and the bar, lifting her slight frame to sit in her lap. She drank in the woman's smell and tilted her neck to one side to lick the slender throat. But she didn't bite the woman, only smelled her and held her close, her hands loosely roped around the human's waist while Julia suckled from the small wound at her wrist.

Rufus glanced at the woman, seemed to think about whether he wanted to take part, then mutely shook his head and relaxed against the seat while the car pulled away from the curb.

It was a long ride. The car took them out of the city, beyond the lights of their Upper East Side neighborhood through Harlem, then White Plains. They'd been driving for a while, the buzz of soft conversation in the car keeping everyone occupied, when Silvija's voice came over the intercom again.

"Some of you may be wondering where we're going."

Across from Kylie, Julia only shrugged. She rested against the headrest, the woman's limp wrist draped across her lap, her thumb rubbing back and forth across the wound she had made in the woman's skin. She would go wherever Silvija told her, most of the clan would. No need to tell them where the journey would end and what it was for. Silvija inspired that kind of trust and loyalty. But even after seven years, Kylie was not quite there yet. She listened to what Silvija had to say.

"We're going on a hunt," she said. "Kill or get hurt. Eat what you catch."

Cheers erupted in the car. Julia giggled and clapped her hands like it was Christmas Eve. Grinning, she squeezed the human's cheek as if the woman was part of her glee. "This is going to be so much fun!"

"What's going on?" Olivia frowned in confusion.

Belle looked at Kylie with a raised eyebrow. It was her responsibility to acclimate Olivia to everything about her new life.

Kylie touched Olivia's wrist that lay next to hers on the leather seat. "It's just like it sounds," she said. "Silvija organizes them from time to time. They…" She cleared her throat as she thought about how to explain it.

"We hunt human criminals to the death in the middle of the woods." Violet curled up against her twin and barely raised her head to answer the question.

"Oh." Olivia's eyes widened.

Kylie couldn't remember if Olivia had ever fed to the death. She had been turned by another vampire who was now dead. That vampire fed her, but aside from their shared meal of the girl in Kylie's room, was that the only time she had fed? She touched Olivia's wrist again.

"Are you—?"

"I'm fine with it," Olivia said tersely. Then she softened her tone, turning over her hand to clasp Kylie's fingers. "It'll be fine."

Kylie nodded. Before she'd been turned, Olivia talked about how she would have no problem killing or with drinking until her victim's death. Now that boast would be put to the test.

"Don't worry your pretty little head about this outing of ours," Ivy said with a thin smile at Olivia. "I have a suspicion that you're going to really enjoy yourself."

The car turned off the paved main road and onto a bumpy, dirt path through the trees. Moonlight illuminated the branches already losing their leaves to autumn. The trees seemed to close in on them the farther into the woods they drove.

Julia giggled with anticipation, trading the occasional verbal barb with Belle while the others shared quiet conversation or closed their eyes, keeping their thoughts to themselves. Kylie kept her fingers twined with Olivia's.

When the car stopped, it was at a large, two-story cabin in the middle of a clearing. A place Kylie had never been before. The moon hung low over them, silvery and fat, showing every leaf, every animal, every curling worm. Silvija stepped from the car just as the cabin door opened.

A beautiful woman, a vampire, stepped outside. She had sable skin and a lushly curved body in a flowing black shirt and Turkish pants. She bared her white teeth in welcome.

"Thank you for accepting our invitation to play on our property, Silvija."

"Thank you for offering, Olu. This came at the perfect time."

"I'm glad." They clasped hands then stood still to look deeply into each other's eyes. Finally, Silvija smiled again and drew the woman into a warm embrace. "It is good to see you again, old friend."

Kylie looked away from the intimate hug, half-expecting to see her mother with a squirming, jealous look on her face. Instead, Belle was talking with Violet about perimeter security, elbows cupped in her palms, eyes roving around the woods.

The other beasts were chatting easily with each other, some stretching, others looking around the moon-bright woods with brilliant and easy smiles. Rufus ambled over to where Kylie and Olivia stood.

"Although you probably haven't heard it yet, welcome to the family, Olivia." He made no move to embrace her, but his attitude was one of welcome, hands shoved into the pockets of his loose jeans, a smile on his lips.

"Thank you." Olivia surprised Kylie by stepping forward to offer her hand.

Rufus didn't seem surprised at all. He simply clasped her hand in his and patted her shoulder. "It will get easier," he said.

He gave Kylie one of his enigmatic smiles and turned toward the woods, quickly disappearing among the dense trees. No one seemed to mind.

Olu turned from Silvija to address the rest of the clan. The mood in the clearing became instantly charged. Kylie felt the focused attention of every being in the clearing like electricity over her skin, the anticipation tightening her belly, her shoulders tensing under the leather jacket.

She released a nervous breath and clenched her fingers. She was excited. Eager. But she didn't know if it was because of the hunt or the added equation of her lover being with her. A lover who had tricked and manipulated her at every turn. A lover she still loved. Beside her, Olivia sharply focused on Olu.

It had been at least a few months since the last hunt, a gathering Silvija regularly organized to keep the clan sharp, well fed, and entertained. They never knew when the next hunt would be, or where, or how many prey would be on the loose. Or even what weapons they wielded. Once, one of the hunted had turned a flamethrower at them. He hadn't lasted long.

"Welcome to the hunt." Olu addressed everyone in a deep and sensual voice, slightly accented with Nigeria by way of Britain. "You can start whenever you like. The prey is already in the forest, armed as they had chosen at the beginning. You are chasing approximately twenty dangerous human criminals. An assortment of rapists, murderers, and politicians." Olu grinned, showing off a dimple in her right chin. "Their weapons are a surprise, but there's nothing there you shouldn't be able to handle. Obviously, you must catch them all before sunrise or lose the hunt." She nodded briskly, looking around at the gathered vampires. "If there are any questions, the time to ask is now. If you don't have any questions, the path into the forest is yours to choose." She paused, looking at each vampire as if waiting for a question. Her eyes landed on Olivia, pausing the longest. But Olivia said nothing. "Very well," Olu said. "Good hunting."

Kylie shivered, her teeth aching at the promise of a chase and capture and satiation. She reached for Olivia, the thrill of the hunt obliterating her earlier anger and dismay. Kylie felt the touch of Olivia's fingers as Olivia reached for her too. Olivia turned and met her smile.

Around them, the clan moved in barely a hush, a sound she knew wasn't audible to human ears. Silvija turned to look at Belle, then gave her a long and intimate smile before she strode into the woods. Belle came up behind Kylie.

"Be careful," her mother said. "They're human, but they're still dangerous." She told Kylie the same thing every year. But this was the first year Kylie actually believed her, and it was only because of her experience with Olivia's family that she understood for the first time what her mother had been trying to tell her.

"I will," she said.

Belle touched Kylie's face with a cool hand. "Now go. Kill something." Her gaze encompassed Kylie and Olivia both. "It'll make you feel better."

Then she loped off into the woods in the same direction as Silvija. Kylie turned in time to see Ivy peel off the thin black dress and sandals, drop them on the front steps of the cabin, then race into the woods.

"What does she plan to do?" Olivia asked. "Fuck them to death?"

Kylie shrugged. "I don't know what she does. All I know is she comes back happy and nearly bloated with blood."

"In that case, how come you're not running around naked?"

"I don't like to get dirty," Kylie said.

Olivia hummed under her breath. "Yes, you do like it clean, don't you?"

It was impossible for Kylie to miss her sharp smile in the moonlight, the naughty glint in her eyes that conjured the memory of what they had done together barely two hours ago. Kylie shoved her hands in her pockets, disconcerted by the memory and the ease with which Olivia brought her back into that moment, back into the bathroom with the feel of the wet tile at her back and Olivia's heating mouth on her pussy. Kylie cleared her throat and shifted.

"Ready?"

"Almost," Olivia said with a grin. She bent, ripped a hole in her dress, then tore most of the hem away, turning the maxi dress into a mini. She dropped the extra fabric on the step of the house next to Ivy's dress. "Now I'm ready."

Kylie swallowed. "Okay. Let's go."

They walked into the heart of the woods together, Kylie aware of the shortened length of her dress and the fact that she wore nothing under it. The breeze brought Olivia's scent of spice and sex and sadness to her nose like the finest intoxicant, the most potent aphrodisiac she'd ever experienced.

"Do you ever catch anyone?" Olivia's words were a soft whisper in the dark.

"Yes."

"Do you enjoy it?"

Kylie thought of the primal stretch of her limbs as she ran her prey to ground, her senses awakened, her teeth elongating in her mouth in anticipation of the kill, adrenaline pounding through her body. Chase. Kill. Conquer. Feed.

"Yes," she said. "I enjoy it very much."

Something in her voice must have said more than even she intended. Olivia looked at her. "Is it better than sex?" It felt like the question was a distraction from Olivia's fear of what was to come next. The hunt. The kill. But that didn't stop the words from affecting Kylie. She stumbled over her own feet.

Is the hunt better than sex? Could she even compare the two acts? Kylie shook her head, unable to answer.

Olivia laughed softly. "I must not be doing it right."

Kylie ducked her head and walked ahead of Olivia into the woods. As soon as the clearing faded from sight and the darkness of the trees and overhanging branches closed in on them, Kylie felt a little differently. Moved differently. Even Olivia seemed changed in her eyes, this woman whom she lusted after with a fierce passion but also didn't quite trust.

Kylie growled in denial.

"What? Do you see one of them?" Olivia's voice was low, a whisper negating her earlier bravado.

She was nervous about killing; Kylie could see that now. But she wondered at it. Wondered why. Hadn't her family bred her for violence and death? Hadn't she seen countless vampires lose their lives at the hands of her brother, her mother, the rest of her family? What was this then to the amount of violence it took to actually kill a vampire? It was more than a few shots fired. Much more effort than twisting a knife once or twice. It was certainly more work than snapping a man's neck.

"No," Kylie said. "I don't see anything."

They crept through the woods together, Kylie's senses heightening with each step. The scent of the woods was all around her; she could smell the loamy fertility of the dirt that moved beneath her feet, and the sap, sticky and bitter, dripping from the trees overhead. She smelled the breeze and the perfume it carried, of night-blooming flowers, and the mossy taint of the river nearby.

From not too far away, she could smell something sour, an unwashed man trying to hide high in a tree among the leaves. His breathing was under control, but he was frightened.

Kylie grabbed Olivia's hand and drew her deeper into the woods, toward the man, cautioning her with a harsh squeeze against saying anything. Olivia was quick. Maybe she had hunted before as well. Kylie slid her a considering look, wondering what else Olivia was not telling her about her past human life.

The smell of the woods was like blood. Rich. Life giving. Wet and dangerous. And her prey was hiding in the very center of that. Fool. She could smell him. The man was hidden nearby, and the thought of him so close and the things she would do with him, made her shiver. She lifted her nose and pulled in more of his scent.

"Do you smell that?" She kept her voice low.

"Yes." Olivia smiled with all of her teeth.

"Do you want him?" Kylie asked.

"Yes." Her voice was silken and deep, barely audible.

Kylie nodded once and slipped through the woods with ease, the human man in the tree the immediate object of her desire. His smell didn't get any better as she grew closer, only a confirmation of his unwashed, fear stink.

This one could control his breathing, the impulse to run, but he could not control the cold sweat that broke out on his body in waves. Or the way his hand tightened and released around the gun.

She shrugged off her jacket and dropped it on the forest floor, understanding not for the first time, Ivy's impulse to be naked in the woods while she tracked her prey. Clothes seemed like such a bother at times, snagging on branches or knives when the skin was easy to care for, the steel passing cleanly through it, the prey closer, feeling their fear as they dropped down beneath teeth and fangs. Kylie growled, pleasure and hunger for the hunt rising in her like smoke.

She moved faster, eyes scanning her surroundings, ears plucking at the sounds nearby. Yes, she could hear nearly all of the prey. A couple were truly afraid, speaking in frantic whispers as they pointed guns out into the dark, hands trembling and hearts pounding. But most were steady, waiting patiently in the dark for the chance to strike.

Branches plucked at her T-shirt, her jeans, at her face. But she moved steadily past these minor obstacles, focused on the one above. Kylie stopped.

She saw him. Nearly twenty feet up in camouflage pants and jacket. Hints of thin, pale hair. The rifle held in steady hands as he sat with his back solidly against the trunk of the massive tree, eyes tracking the forest, a professional who had killed before. He was slender but smelled like he enjoyed a healthy diet of sex and good food.

She felt Olivia behind her, stealthy and quiet in her short skirt. It was her scent that Kylie caught then. She remembered how well it mixed with the salty taste of her pussy, with Kylie's own scent as they trembled and slid together in bed.

Focus! She bit down on the inside of her lip to force herself to pay attention to what was happening now. Fuck later. Hunt now. But Olivia was distractingly close. She eased back, intent more on getting away from Olivia than taking down her prey.

In the tree, the man shifted, his night vision lenses tracking to where she stood. She froze and was pleased when Olivia did the same. The man muttered something and firmed his grip on the rifle. She heard the sound of his teeth grinding together and smelled the sweat rolling down the back of his neck. They stayed still for a beat of forty, sixty seconds. Then he looked away. Kylie ran toward him.

As she loped across the forest floor, making the barest whisper of sound, a piercing scream broke the silence, then a laugh. Another human brought down under teeth and claws.

The man above Kylie almost pissed himself. His finger spasmed against the trigger, squeezing off a burst of bullets. Kylie lifted her head, sniffing. There were at least five dead humans now, their blood thick and delicious in the air. She reached the tree where the man hid and climbed swiftly up, her fingers digging into the thick, cool bark of the tree.

She avoided the large branches and the obvious handholds, using the covering of leaves to her advantage. The smell of moss and the sap from the bark under her fingernails drifted to her nose. Damp leaves brushed her face.

Her prey was so busy looking around the rest of the forest that he paid no attention to the tree where he sat. Olivia stayed hidden.

Kylie quickly clambered up the tree trunk, shot up through the leaves in front of the man. He wasted no time on surprise, only quickly swung the rifle toward Kylie, his pale eyes wide but determined to keep his life. But she was too close and the rifle was too long. She grabbed the rifle and flung it away.

"Is that all you got?"

An instant later, she felt him move. Then a knife slid into her belly. She gasped at the sudden and familiar pain. "Nice one," she grunted.

Kylie broke his hand. He howled and tried to shove himself back. But she yanked him up by the collar of his camouflage shirt, the yellow patch on the breast pocket catching the moonlight. He gasped and fought her hold, but she gripped him tighter, teeth bared in pain.

"That wasn't very nice now, was it?" She threw him out of the tree. "Catch!" she called down to Olivia.

Olivia caught him before he hit the ground, plucking the heavy human neatly out of the air as he fell face-first, and flipping him over then slamming him into the ground on his back. Kylie expected a small noise of triumph, a grin, anything to show she was pleased how her new reflexes were coming along. But instead, Olivia leapt back with a sharp cry that sounded almost like a name.

Kylie jumped down from the tree, landing a few feet from Olivia. The man at her feet huffed in pain as he tried to scramble away. The heels of his boots kicked up the dirt and dead leaves. Olivia stared at her with a horrified expression.

"What did you do!"

Chapter Twenty-seven

Kylie stared at Olivia, not understanding what she was talking about. "I didn't do anything to him, yet." She stepped toward the man. "I was actually just getting started." She curled her hands into claws, allowing the slow rise of her beast.

Olivia shoved her back. "Don't touch him!" Her scream rose through the forest, frightening a pair of owls on a branch nearby. They flew off in a frantic flutter of wings. "Alec?" Her hand trembled as she reached down for the human, but she didn't touch him. She looked up at Kylie, her eyes wide pools of misery and anger. "This is my cousin," she wailed. "My fucking cousin!"

Kylie was confused. "What the fuck is going on?"

"Were you in on this?" Olivia flew at her, shoving her back across the forest floor. Her palms thumped hard into Kylie's chest. "Did you know about this? Did you?"

She just kept shoving at Kylie until Kylie's back was against a tree, the thick trunk slamming into her back again and again as Olivia slammed her hands into Kylie's chest, her face a mask of blood tears and rage. "Why did you do this? I thought you were going to leave them alone!" She wasn't crying, but everything about her screamed sadness and pain. Betrayal.

"Who?" Not knowing what was going on, Kylie didn't try to fight her off.

"How could you do this?" Olivia screamed.

"Now you have some idea of what our little Kylie felt then?" Silvija was suddenly there. Or at least her voice was, but Kylie couldn't see her.

Olivia stopped shoving Kylie and whirled, trying to face Silvija. "It wasn't like that." Her teeth snapped out, loud in the clearing. The man at her feet stared up at her in horror, going even paler. He cowered away from her, but she didn't notice.

"I'm not interested in your version of how things went down." Silvija's voice seemed to shift around them, moving so much that Kylie couldn't get an exact idea of where she was. "The GPS and recorder on her cell phone told us everything we needed to know." A hint of humor in the sepulchral voice. "Maybe a little too much."

Kylie's face prickled with embarrassment as she realized the significance of what Silvija said. The clan had tracked her to the Bertram compound. They had retrieved the information from the phone. They had heard and seen…everything.

She froze, understanding then what Silvija had done. The Bertrams in the underground compound. She had somehow captured them all and had them out in the forest fighting for their lives. Kylie stared at Olivia, the destroyed look of her. At their feet, the man in combat fatigues stared up at her with his ashen but defiant face.

"Silvija—" Kylie began.

"Kill him." Silvija appeared out of a splash of moonlight, tall and powerful in her black turtleneck, slacks, and boots. Her thick hair was braided in a coronet at the top of her head. She looked truly like a queen. Their leader. Her eyes flashed dark fire when she looked at Olivia, at Kylie. "I won't say it again." Her voice was tempered steel.

Belle stepped from the darkness, the queen's bride. "We are a family here, despite anything else you may have been led to believe." Twigs snapped and dried leaves whispered under her heavy footsteps. "We always take care of our own. And I will always take care of my daughter." She looked at Silvija, then at Kylie.

Despite the sharp pain in her back and chest, Kylie flung herself away from the tree, whatever damage Olivia had done already healing. She stared at the man cowering in the dirt with his broken hand, his automatic rifle tossed uselessly a few feet away. She crouched over him and gripped his mouth shut, ready to drain him dry.

A spray of bullets peppered the ground inches from Kylie's feet. "Leave him alone!" Olivia growled, raising the rifle higher.

"Fire those bullets into one of us and you won't live long to regret it." Silvija appeared at Olivia's side, silent as misery. She made no move to take away the rifle although she could have easily done so. "For now, you are one of us. For better or worse, Kylie has chosen you. But you fire that gun and you are as dead to me as your great-grandfather." Silvija's voice deepened. "And I'll bury you just as deep." Then her eyes dipped away from Olivia, and she looked down at Kylie.

Kylie sank her fangs in the man's throat. One instant, he was still and listening for the executioner's decision, and the next, he was bucking under the razors of Kylie's teeth, gushing his iron-rich blood into her mouth. While Silvija was talking, he had grown increasingly comfortable, his breathing more stable, his eyes relaxing their terrified stare. He was afraid of Silvija but convinced Olivia would do something to save him. He probably didn't think that anymore.

He bucked under her, his screaming muffled under the brutal grip she had on his face. Olivia hiccupped with fear and swung the rifle back to Kylie. Kylie, who in the midst of feeding on the man's terror-sweet blood, was very aware of Olivia's finger lifting to stroke the trigger of the rifle.

A gun barked once in the clearing. Not Olivia's. Olivia screamed and jerked as if struck by a bolt of electricity. She dropped to the ground at the same time that an ATV roared through the woods. Two humans were on the vehicle, one driving and the other gripping tightly to a handgun, firing again at Olivia who was already down and screaming as if her entire body were going up in flames.

Belle and Silvija leapt into motion, chasing after the bike and running in a zigzag pattern to avoid the spray of bullets that were apparently more than ordinary. Olivia's screams proved that much.

What the fuck had the Bertrams cooked up in their labs?

Kylie ran over to Olivia who was trying to tear at her skin where the bullet had entered. Her skin had already healed, but whatever was in the bullet was still inside her, making her scream.

"Make it stop," she howled. "Make it stop!"

Kylie flicked the switchblade from her pocket and cut into her shoulder. Under the red and bloody flesh ran a river of liquid fire. It skimmed through the meat of Olivia's body, burning as it went.

The leaves overhead shook with the force of her screams. Night animals howled in response to her terrified cries. Using the switchblade like a spoon, Kylie stuck it into her already healing flesh, scooping up the liquid flame. It didn't burn the metal, only slid, sinuous and strangely beautiful, along its length, then dropped from the silver blade cleanly as Kylie splashed it in the dirt away from Olivia. She repeated the action until all the yellow was gone from Olivia's flesh.

Olivia lay limply on the ground, panting, the pain falling from her eyes. She blinked up at Kylie with relief.

"What—what happened?" she asked.

"You tried to kill me," Kylie said tenderly.

Olivia sat up. "No. I—" She looked around the woods, the empty area where they were, the dead man a few feet away. She turned from him, eyes glazing again with tears. "My family," she moaned softly.

"Your family just tried to kill you," Kylie said. "Is that a thing with you people, the way you prove your love?"

Olivia pressed her hands to her face. "I don't know what to do. I don't know whose side to be on."

Kylie stood, brushing off her jeans. "Let me make it easier for you." She looked down at Olivia. "No matter how hard your love is, I'd advise you to pick the family that's not trying to put you into the ground permanently."

"And which one is that?" Olivia's gaze was steady.

Kylie turned to look into the woods where Silvija and her mother had disappeared. She began to follow them, when a cold voice stopped her.

"I've never liked the company you kept, Olivia dear."

Kylie spun to face the woman of her nightmares. Olivia's mother.

Bertram wore full camouflage, the jacket, pants, and boots fitting like armor. A machete was strapped to her thigh in a sheath, and she gripped a pistol in both hands.

Before Kylie could form the thought to leap at the woman and tear her to pieces, a shot blasted past her ear. Then a solid thump in the center of her chest. And another. Pain. More pain than she had ever felt in her life. Burning. Her insides were melting away as the agony ripped away all her reason.

She felt herself falling and could do nothing to stop the ground from rushing up to her face. She felt writhing agony. All the while, she was aware of more screams in the forest, humans being torn apart. She smelled at least two humans in a nearby shelter of trees with their weapons pointed at her and Olivia.

"No!" Olivia dropped to her knees beside Kylie. "Mother!"

She felt Olivia's cool hands on her shoulders, flipping her over to expose the wound the bullets made in her chest. "Stop this!" Olivia cried. "Stop hurting her."

"Hurting her?" The woman curled her lip. "You mean hurting *it*."

Just then, a man emerged from the woods with a chainsaw. His loose dreadlocks swayed with each step, his pale skin faded under the evening's silver light. It was the man from the underground prison, the one who'd been watching Kylie near Olivia's apartment. Moonlight glinted off the killing machine as he turned it on. The chainsaw roared in the woods, snarling and bucking in his hands. But Bertram didn't look at him. She was completely focused on Olivia.

She kept her gun pointed on Olivia. "Just because you let that thing fuck you doesn't make her any more human and you any less of a Bertram."

Kylie was melting away. She could feel her chest turning to liquid inside the cage of her skin, the acid burn spreading through her and eating her flesh at the same rate that her body healed itself. It was agony upon agony, like being slashed from the inside out. Kylie gasped as she writhed on the forest floor, gritting her teeth and refusing to scream, although she wanted to. God, she wanted to!

"But you made your choice." The Bertram soldier stepped closer, revving the chainsaw. "Bloodsucker."

Kylie was dimly aware of another soldier from the Bertram family covering him, protecting him as he crept toward her and Olivia, a grin of fierce and terrible joy on his face. There was a crack of sound in the forest, then a bullet hole appeared between his eyes. Bertram dropped to her belly and rolled away from her dead soldier just as another shot sounded. Then another, two bullets taking out both the soldier's eyes, three neat little holes made in quick succession.

The other soldier dropped to his belly and began firing into the woods. Soon, his gun fell silent. The dreadlocked soldier, already dead, swayed on his feet. Olivia pushed Kylie out of the way, rolling her body in the midst of her agony away from the falling chainsaw. The chainsaw fell with the soldier, sawing through his legs in a spray of blood, meat, and bone. He was too dead to care.

Bertram fired back into the silvery darkness, her eyes narrowed in concentration. All through the forest, Kylie heard screaming. Humans dying. But she had her own concerns. The fire burned all through her, liquid hell deep inside her chest and running down into her belly. Olivia knelt over her with the switchblade, slitting open her chest, thrusting the knife into the bloody cavity. It was then that Kylie did finally scream.

The heat of the acid, Olivia slitting her open again, the narrow blade scooping into her flesh, it was all too much to bear. Olivia hissed as she must have realized the blade wasn't enough to get rid of the acid left behind by the two bullets. She reached up and ripped an earring from her ear, using the silver leaves to sweep away the liquid fire from Kylie's flesh.

"Stop it, Olivia!" her mother shouted. "Stop it or I'll end you too."

"Then do it," Olivia said coldly. "I'm not going to leave her to die." She kept working frantically to get the burning liquid out of Kylie.

"It's already dead," her mother said. "And if you don't know that basic fact then you've forgotten everything I've taught you."

Olivia dug the silver earring into Kylie's chest, and Kylie screamed, releasing the agony into the night air. Her entire body heaved, jerking and dancing on the bed of leaves, dirt, blood, and bone. "I'm just like her, mother. She and I are the same."

"Don't say that. Don't ever say that."

Through the haze of pain, Kylie saw Bertram's indecision, her flinch of pain. Then she made a choice, Kylie saw it on her face as clearly as the moon. Olivia still had her back to her mother. She did not turn at the whisper of the blade leaving its thigh sheath, although she must have heard the sound.

Although Kylie sensed at least one other vampire out there in the woods near them, whoever it was didn't interfere.

Bertram rose swiftly to her feet, a look of disgust on her face. Olivia still swiftly scooped away the yellow fire, and Kylie grit her teeth to fight back her screams.

Bertram lifted the blade, swung it back, and aimed for Olivia's neck. Through the thick haze of her pain, Kylie grabbed Olivia and dragged her to the ground. Olivia's knees slid in the dirt, her body fell onto Kylie's. There was a scream, then the machete whistled over Olivia's head, embedding itself in the tree behind them.

Kylie rolled with Olivia, shielding her with her body as they rolled into the underbrush. She clenched her teeth from the rasp of dirt and forest flotsam in her open wound. She gasped with the effort and the pain, still clutching Olivia who seemed frozen from the shock that her mother had truly tried to kill her.

"Mommy?"

Olivia's hand trembled, and the shell earring fell on top of Kylie's bare chest, missing by inches the wound that was already closing up and expelling the foreign debris.

"I don't have a daughter anymore." Bertram grabbed the discarded rifle at her feet and swung it around at Olivia, squeezing the trigger.

But Kylie and Olivia weren't there anymore. Kylie held Olivia in her arms. Weakened by her emotions, Olivia could only cling tightly to Kylie, her nails sinking into Kylie's bare arms and neck as she ran swiftly with her across the forest floor. She was weak and slower than normal, but at least she could run.

"I'll never stop hunting you!" Bertram shouted. "I always fix my mistakes."

The breeze brushed against Kylie's face. Leaves crunched under her feet; the burden of Olivia in her arms felt heavier than it should. The pain throbbed inside her chest, but it eased with each step she took. Behind her, she heard an ATV start up and felt Bertram behind the wheel.

Olivia twitched in Kylie's arms. "Stop. Put me down." She was breathing heavily, her humanness coming out in the breath she couldn't control. "Please. Put me down. I can't just run away. She'll never stop looking for me."

Just then, the ATV exploded out of the forest, kicking up dirt and leaves. The engine growled. Bertram gripped the handlebars, her lips skinned back from her teeth, the ends of her braided hair fluttering in the breeze. She viciously bore down on them.

"Kylie, please." Olivia's tone was more command than request. "Put me down."

But Kylie didn't want to let Olivia confront her mother. There were only two ways that the confrontation could end, and she was afraid that either one would destroy Olivia forever.

Kylie settled her on her feet but did not move from her side. She set narrowed eyes on Bertram, ready to move in case she tried something. Bertram hopped off the ATV, a rifle held firmly in one hand.

Olivia faced her with hands clenched at her sides, her feet braced apart.

"You've never been a coward, have you? That's one thing I can always say about my daughter." Bertram's gaze hardened even more. "My vampire daughter." She said the words in much the same way someone else would say "pedophile." "I still can't believe you chose to become this rather than face what your wicked ways have brought you."

"Good people get cancer too, Mother."

Bertram raised an eyebrow. "But you're not a good person, are you?"

A look of profound sadness took over Olivia's face. Her chin trembled. Then she straightened her spine and took a hesitating step toward Bertram. "Mother, it will cost you nothing to let us go. Forget that you ever saw us."

"Forget my family's work? Forget who I am?" Her mother made a disbelieving noise and brought the gun up sharply.

Kylie shoved Olivia aside as a gun barked and spat its bullets. But it wasn't the gun in Bertram's hand. Bullets tore through her, as savage and unforgiving as teeth, tearing into her back and exploding out of her chest, taking chunks of flesh and muscle with them.

Olivia screamed and ran toward her mother. Kylie grabbed her away, trying to get her from the path of the bullets still rattling the woods. The bullets wouldn't kill but they would severely incapacitate them long enough for anyone to make the killing blow, take their heads, and set them on fire.

But Olivia didn't care. She fought Kylie to stay with her mother, biting and screaming. But Kylie had the experience of fighting much stronger opponents on her side. She clamped a hand over Olivia's mouth, grabbed her, swept her up into her arms, and ran deeper into the woods with her precious burden, away from the gun and the human wielding it. She hated running away but had no choice.

In her arms, Olivia fought her, bit her hand and twisted away, her eyes burning with rage and sorrow.

"No! Let me go!" She slashed Kylie's face with her clawed hands, drawing blood. "Let me go!" Tears rushed down her face.

Kylie cursed, blinded by the blood and Olivia's flailing. Pain lanced through her face from Olivia's slashing hands. She stumbled, and Olivia fell to the ground with a thud, then leapt up. She dashed away from Kylie, avoiding the quick latch of her hand. She ran through the woods the way they had come. Fast. Faster. Kylie chased after her, calling her name.

"Stop! Olivia!"

Wind raked her face and grabbed at her hair as she tore through the woods, chasing after Olivia's gray-clad form that dodged between the trees.

Kylie came to an abrupt halt as Olivia stopped ahead of her. A human with a rifle confronted Olivia. It was her brother.

Kylie saw him clearly. A tall man wearing dark camouflage, bulletproof vest, a full face helmet showing his eyes and narrow features through the thick glass of the visor.

"Max!" She bellowed her brother's name, her voice a hollow drum.

"Your pet bitch would have killed her anyway." But he still sounded shocked that he'd killed their mother. "She's going to kill us all."

Before he could raise the rifle, Olivia was on him. A leaping rush across the forest floor, the ripped hem of her dress flashing up, hard thighs flexing, hands curved into claws. She ripped the helmet from his face, nearly taking his head with it. He screamed as she knocked him to the ground and ripped into his throat, savagely tearing out chunks of flesh to get at the blood he carried. He screamed and thrashed under her. She screamed and bore down into him. Their voices rose up in the forest, growling and crying, howling and wailing.

"You killed her," Olivia sobbed as she drank from him, tore at him. "You killed my mother!"

But Max couldn't hear her anymore.

CHAPTER TWENTY-EIGHT

Olivia didn't say anything the entire ride back to the city. She lay slumped in the corner of the big car, dried blood on her face, her dress torn, her face shell-shocked. Kylie sat beside her, holding her unresponsive hand, simultaneously glad the Bertrams had been wiped out, but sad for Olivia. She couldn't imagine what she would do if she lost her family.

She looked around the car where the rest of the clan lay in total relaxation. Well-fed and happy, they draped themselves over each other, exhausted from the long night and the hunt.

Belle sat next to Kylie, her fingers laced with Kylie's while her head rested on Silvija's shoulder. Silvija was only wearing a black tank top and jeans, having discarded her blood-soaked sweater at the cabin. She stroked Belle's neck and lay back in the leather seat, staring out into the distance.

Julia was curled up on the floor of the car, resting her head on a pile of bundled up clothes. She seemed asleep. Rufus sprawled across from Kylie and Olivia, bare-chested, his hands making delicate motions in the air as he spoke softly to Ivy. Ivy who was now dressed in Rufus's T-shirt and nothing else. Liam and Violet were playing an endless game of rock-paper-scissors, bursting into laughter when one did something the other didn't expect.

Yes, this was Kylie's family. And she was grateful for them all, even Silvija.

Beside Kylie, her mother stirred. She turned her head. "Olivia."

Olivia turned away from the window to look at Belle. Dark tears had dried on her face, staining her skin. But even as she cried for the loss of her family, she was the most beautiful Kylie had ever seen her: skin glowing, the blood of her first kill pulsing like moonlight under her flesh. The killing had made her stronger. She just didn't realize it yet.

"We're your family now. You made that choice when you drew Kylie into your web." Belle looked approvingly at Olivia, like she appreciated her resourcefulness in getting what she needed. "We won't promise you a fairy tale, but we won't ever turn our backs on you. You're stuck with us forever."

Whether Olivia took that as a threat or reassurance was hard to tell. She nodded when Belle finished talking, a tight smile stretching her mouth. Then she turned back to the window. Belle squeezed Kylie's hand, then brushed her thumb across the still bloody knuckles. "Take care of her, darling."

Kylie nodded.

When the car arrived at the penthouse, the driver opened the door and the clan spilled out into the pre-dawn street that already held the smell of morning. Julia got out of the limo and stretched like a cat, grinning. "Home at last," she purred.

The gray sky and grayer landscape framed their dark figures as they stood on the sidewalk, beautiful beasts who had had a successful night's hunt and looked forward to a luxurious day's sleep.

Silvija slid her arm around Belle's waist and led the way into the building. Instead of following, Kylie stayed in the car. The driver, a pretty, long-haired boy in a suit, firmly shut the door and closed her inside the car with Olivia. He went back to sit in the front seat, turning on the music and staring straight ahead.

Olivia hadn't moved from her position by the window. Her forehead lay against the glass; her hands rested limply in her lap.

She turned to Kylie, dark eyes full of sadness, pinkened lips plump and blood-rich in the car's overhead light. "Do you think they'll try to kill me?" Her voice was hoarse.

"No, they won't," Kylie said. "That's not how this family operates."

Olivia flinched but did not respond. She looked down at her hands and twisted her fingers together. "I lost...I lost everything."

Olivia shook her head. "Of all the things I pictured when I came up with the plan to be turned, this…." Her words tapered off into silence. "They're all dead because of me."

Kylie knew what Olivia was feeling. She knew intimately what it felt like to lose her whole world and be set adrift. But she didn't bother offering any false platitudes; they wouldn't do either of them any good. "If you play with big dogs you're bound to get bitten."

Olivia's eyes flashed. "Don't be an asshole."

The corner of Kylie's mouth twitched. "Would it make you feel better if you bit me?"

"No!" Olivia quailed, the flare of anger gone as suddenly as it had appeared. She shrank back against the door, lashes fluttering as if she saw something behind her eyelids that horrified her, perhaps her brother struggling under her fangs, gushing red blood while she tore him to pieces.

It made Kylie angry to see her like that. To become this shrinking, regretful creature after she'd begged and connived to be like this. She followed her against the door.

"Yes." She grabbed Olivia's arm and her eyes flashed up, a narrowed gaze, a growl on her lips.

"What are you doing?"

"What are *you* doing?" Kylie sank her fingers into Olivia's flesh. "I nearly died for you. After all we've been through to get here, you don't get to be like this."

"Leave me alone."

"No."

Olivia tried to drag her arm away, but Kylie held on, yanking her closer until their mouths were only inches apart. "If you've made your choice like you say you have, then there's no turning back. If I have your heart then you don't get to break it for those bitches in camo who nearly turned me into vampire jerky and burned you from the inside out." She yanked Olivia's arm. "You damn well don't."

Pain flared across Olivia's features. She hissed. "I can do whatever the fuck I want!"

"Of course you can. You can manipulate and use and cry innocent because these are the things you want to do. Damn the consequences, right?" Kylie tightened her hand on Olivia's arm. "But know this: We were born in blood. We live in blood. Did you think when you wanted to be turned, you could escape that?"

Olivia blinked. Teardrops rolled down her cheeks, spilling onto her gray dress and adding to the blood stains already there. She gasped on a breath and sagged against Kylie, her forehead butting her collarbone.

"Shit!" She groaned and clung to Kylie, moaning low in her throat. "I didn't think it would be like this. I didn't." Her body shook and more tears splashed onto Kylie's shirt. "I ruined everything. I'm sorry." She gasped and shook. "I'm so sorry."

Kylie pulled her more firmly into her arms. She remembered saying something similar to her mother just a few nights before, and how it felt for her to come to that place. "I forgive you," she said softly, rubbing Olivia's heaving back. "Now all you have to do is forgive yourself."

The words echoed between them, then died away.

Olivia raised her head. Her eyes were red-rimmed and swollen, the tears still falling. She touched Kylie's cheek, wonder and pain on her face. "You are amazing," she whispered, her voice thick with sadness. "I don't know what I did to deserve you."

"You've just been yourself," Kylie murmured.

It seemed like the most natural thing in the world for their lips to come together.

Olivia tasted like blood and tears and misery. She tasted like perfection, her cool lips and tender fingers on Kylie's face. Kylie felt a tremor run through her and through Olivia as emotion rose up even more between them, a thick river of love and forgiveness.

The desire was slow to rise inside Kylie. She only wanted the comfort of Olivia's touch, the arch of her lean body against hers, an agreement that they belonged together and everything else was dust. She touched Olivia's cool flesh, felt it warming under her fingers, a gradual and throbbing heat that made her deepen the kiss, plunge her tongue in for more.

Yes, she wanted Olivia. She wanted her with the clan. She wanted her happy. Kylie had become hopelessly addicted to the way Olivia warmed her with the barest touch. But it was the love that had blossomed unexpectedly between them that she wanted most, the soft and hard feeling.

This was what she was reaching for.

Olivia moaned, a quivering and low sound that raked over Kylie's senses.

She drew a hissing breath and scraped her blunt fingernails over Olivia's hair and down the back of her neck. She gripped her hard, pressing that incredible body against hers. Olivia moaned again, and Kylie swallowed.

The enclosed car filled with the sound of Olivia's sighs, the whisper of flesh and clothes and leather as they lay down in the seat, mouths still pressed together, tongues entwined, bodies heating in the small space. Olivia's spicy and hot scent slithered around her, seduced her sharpest teeth from their resting place.

Her fangs curved against the plumpness of her lower lip, ready to taste, to feed.

Olivia slid her hand up the back of Kylie's T-shirt and sank her fingernails into the flesh there. Kylie hissed then turned them on the seat so that they were side by side with Olivia's leg thrown over her hip.

She felt so warm and vital, the need pulsing between them like a living thing, plumping the flesh between Kylie's thighs and hammering lust into her post-hunt flesh. She thought she had been satisfied. But with the lash of Olivia's moan in her ear, her hard nipples prodding at Kylie's through the two layers of cloth, the salty wet scent of her cunt under the dress, Kylie knew want again. Knew hunger. Knew the ache of her fangs pressing out and begging for a place to bury themselves.

Olivia called her name, closed her eyes, and turned her face away as tears leaked from between her eyelids.

"Touch me," she begged softly. "Please."

Kylie slid her hands under the short dress, spanning the slender but firm thighs, pushing the dress up as her hands rose, revealing the narrow hips, the thick bush of her sex, her belly, breasts. She tossed the dress and it landed somewhere behind her in the car.

Olivia was naked against her, the lithe body moving impatiently against the leather seats. She smelled divine, an intoxicating mix of the hunt, her scent, and the blood she'd taken. The pulse of desire inside Kylie grew stronger.

She kissed the length of Olivia's neck. Olivia grasped her hair and held her close, breathing and vulnerable, trusting Kylie with her pleasure, with her forgiveness, with her tears. Kylie licked her throat, traveling low to kiss her collarbones, the space between her breasts. Then she pulled a nipple in her mouth. Her tongue wet a circle around the puckered brown tip, licking it, stroking the velvet flesh while her own body drowned in its want. Pussy lips swollen, the tingling between her legs grew to a deep and insistent throbbing.

She kept her tongue on Olivia's breasts, licking and tasting them, taking her time to build sensation in a way she knew Olivia liked, using her tongue as a paintbrush to cover every inch of flesh on her breasts, her nipples, until Olivia's hands were tight in her hair and the sound of her breathing was heavier, harder, in need.

But Olivia didn't beg. Although her body was tight as a spring and her thighs moved restlessly against the leather, although the smell of her pussy was getting more and more lush in the air, she only waited for what Kylie could give her.

Kylie lifted her mouth from the succulent nipples and slid her hand between Olivia's thighs. She was soaking wet.

Olivia sobbed and gripped her hair. Then it was Kylie's turn to moan and fight the heated flare of want through her body, fed by the simple touch of Olivia's pussy, proof that she wanted her, the way the tight wetness eagerly swallowed her fingers. She stroked and Olivia threw her head back, moaned, circled her hips.

She tipped her knee toward the roof, inviting the deeper thrust of Kylie's fingers inside her, tilting her hips, sighing, a woman in the grip of lust. Of surrender. The smell of her pussy in the car was thick and heady, an addiction to her senses. Kylie heard herself grunting with each push of her fingers inside Olivia, a deeper stroke, a firmer fuck, her control reined tightly but the bliss of it no less intense.

Three fingers deep, she caressed the seductive button of Olivia's clit with her thumb, wanting to dip lower and taste her, feel the slow and inevitable build of her passion against her mouth. But more than that, she wanted to see Olivia's face.

Although Olivia tried to turn away, burying her face into the seat as the sensations took her, Kylie firmly held her jaw. She wanted to look at Olivia and see all of her. See what she wanted to hide, what she wanted to give. After a brief struggle, Olivia accepted Kylie's grip and stopped trying to turn her face away. Then Olivia was delirious in her pleasure, lips damp and parted, her throat shuddering with her breaths, eyes closed as incoherent half-words tumbled from her. She was beautiful. Wrecked by passion.

Kylie felt the sweat under her clothes as she fucked her, her sex swollen to bursting between her legs. Olivia moaned. Her pussy pulled Kylie's fingers deeper, her nails sinking into Kylie's scalp, painful, but dragging her closer to her own peak.

Olivia called out Kylie's name as she came, shuddering violently between Kylie and the back of the leather seat. She licked her lips, looking up at Kylie as if dazed. Kylie squeezed her clit once more then gripped her hips, pulling them firmly against hers.

"You're mine." Kylie growled and sank her fangs into Olivia's throat. Scarlet nourishment exploded over her tongue.

Olivia bucked under her, crying out as the red bridge of blood drew them closer. Kylie's body tilted off the edge of orgasm and fell. She was quivering and delirious, her pussy throbbing in her jeans. She lifted her head, licking her lips.

Olivia opened her eyes, pink rimmed but bright from her satisfaction. Her gaze was clear now, the sadness pushed aside for the moment.

"And you belong to me," Olivia said, her voice breathless but strong.

She moved her hands to the waistband of Kylie's jeans and undid the thick leather belt, the button, the zipper. She slid her fingers over Kylie's wetness and stroked her to trembling.

"Always."

About the Author

Jamaican-born Fiona Zedde currently lives and writes in Atlanta, Georgia. She is the author of several novellas and novels of lesbian love and desire, including the Lambda Literary Award finalists *Bliss* and *Every Dark Desire*. Her novel, *Dangerous Pleasures*, was winner of the About.com Readers' Choice Award for Best Lesbian Novel or Memoir of 2012.

Her short fiction has appeared in various anthologies including the Cleis Press Best Lesbian Erotica series, *Wicked: Sexy Tales of Legendary Lovers*, *Iridescence: Sensuous Shades of Lesbian Erotica*, and *Fist of the Spider Woman*.

Writing under the name "Fiona Lewis," she has also published a novel of young adult fiction called *Dreaming in Color*.

Find out more at www.FionaZedde.com.

Books Available from Bold Strokes Books

Desire at Dawn by Fiona Zedde. For Kylie, love had always come armed with sharp teeth and claws. But with the human, Olivia, she bares her vampire heart for the very first time, sharing passion, lust, and a tenderness she'd never dared dreamed of before. (978-1-62639-064-5)

Visions by Larkin Rose. Sometimes the mysteries of love reveal themselves when you least expect it. Other times they hide behind a black satin mask. Can Paige unveil her masked stranger this time? (978-1-62639-065-2)

All In by Nell Stark. Internet poker champion Annie Navarro loses everything when the Feds shut down online gambling, and she turns to experienced casino host Vesper Blake for advice—but can Nova convince Vesper to take a gamble on romance? (978-1-62639-066-9)

Vermillion Justice by Sheri Lewis Wohl. What's a vampire to do when Dracula is no longer just a character in a novel? (978-1-62639-067-6)

Queerly Beloved: A Love Story Across Gender by Diane and Jacob Anderson-Minshall. How We Survived Four Weddings, One Gender Transition, and Twenty-Two Years of Marriage. (978-1-62639-062-1)

Switchblade by Carsen Taite. Lines were meant to be crossed. Third in the Luca Bennett Bounty Hunter Series. (978-1-62639-058-4)

Nightingale by Andrea Bramhall. Culture, faith, and duty conspire to tear two young lovers apart, yet fate seems to have different plans for them both. (978-1-62639-059-1)

No Boundaries by Donna K. Ford. A chance meeting and a nightmare from the past threaten more than Andi Massey's solitude as she and Gwen Palmer struggle to understand the complexity of love without boundaries. (978-1-62639-060-7)

Sacred Fire by Tanai Walker. Tinsley Swann is cursed to change into a beast for seven days, every seven years. When she meets Leda, she comes face-to-face with her past. (978-1-62639-061-4)

Frenemy of the People by Nora Olsen. Clarissa and Lexie have despised each other as long as they can remember, but when they both find themselves helping an unlikely contender for homecoming queen, they are catapulted into an unexpected romance. (978-1-62639-063-8)

Timeless by Rachel Spangler. When Stevie Geller returns to her hometown, will she do things differently the second time around or will she be in such a hurry to leave her past that she misses out on a better future? (978-1-62639-050-8)

Second to None by L.T. Marie. Can a physical therapist and a custom motorcycle designer conquer their pasts and build a future with one another? (978-1-62639-051-5)

Seneca Falls by Jesse Thoma. Together, two women discover love truly can conquer all evil. (978-1-62639-052-2)

A Kingdom Lost by Barbara Ann Wright. Without knowing each other's fate, Princess Katya and her consort Starbride seek to reclaim their kingdom from the magic-wielding madman who seized the throne and is murdering their people. (978-1-62639-053-9)

Uncommon Romance by Jove Belle. Sometimes sex is just sex, and sometimes it's the only way to say "I love you." (978-1-62639-057-7)

The Heat of Angels by Lisa Girolami. Fires burn in more than one place in Los Angeles. (978-1-62639-042-3)

Season of the Wolf by Robin Summers. Two women running from their pasts are thrust together by an unimaginable evil. Can they overcome the horrors that haunt them in time to save each other? (978-1-62639-043-0)

Desperate Measures by P. J. Trebelhorn. Homicide detective Kay Griffith and contractor Brenda Jansen meet amidst turmoil neither of them is aware of until murder suspect Tommy Rayne makes his move to exact revenge on Kay. (978-1-62639-044-7)

The Magic Hunt by L.L. Raand. With her Pack being hunted by human extremists and beset by enemies masquerading as friends, can Sylvan protect them and her mate, or will she succumb to the feral rage that threatens to turn her rogue, destroying them all? A Midnight Hunters novel. (978-1-62639-045-4)

Waiting for the Violins by Justine Saracen. After surviving Dunkirk, a scarred and embittered British nurse returns to Nazi-occupied Brussels to join the Resistance, and finds that nothing is fair in love and war. (978-1-62639-046-1)

Because of Her by KE Payne. When Tabby Morton is forced to move to London, she's convinced her life will never be the same again. But the beautiful and intriguing Eden Palmer is about to show her that this time, change is most definitely for the better. (978-1-62639-049-2)

Wingspan by Karis Walsh. Wildlife biologist Bailey Chase is content to live at the wild bird sanctuary she has created on Washington's Olympic Peninsula until she is lured beyond the safety of isolation by architect Kendall Pearson. (978-1-60282-983-1)

Tumbledown by Cari Hunter. After surviving their ordeal in the North Cascades, Alex and Sarah have new identities and a new home, but a chance occurrence threatens everything: their freedom and their lives. (978-1-62639-085-0)

Night Bound by Winter Pennington. Kass struggles to keep her head, her heart, and her relationships in order. She's still having a difficult time accepting being an Alpha female. But her wolf is certain of what she wants and she's intent on securing her power. (978-1-60282-984-8)

Slash and Burn by Valerie Bronwen. The murder of a roundly despised author at an LGBT writer's conference in New Orleans turns Winter Lovelace's relaxing weekend hobnobbing with her peers into a nightmare of suspense—especially when her ex turns up. (978-1-60282-986-2)

The Blush Factor by Gun Brooke. Ice-cold business tycoon Eleanor Ashcroft only cares about the three P's—Power, Profit, and Prosperity—until young Addison Garr makes her doubt both that and the state of her frostbitten heart. (978-1-60282-985-5)

The Quickening: A Sisters of Spirits Novel by Yvonne Heidt. Ghosts, visions, and demons are all in a day's work for Tiffany. But when Kat asks for help on a serial killer case, life takes on another dimension altogether. (978-1-60282-975-6)

Windigo Thrall by Cate Culpepper. Six women trapped in a mountain cabin by a blizzard, stalked by an ancient cannibal demon bent on stealing their sanity—and their lives. (978-1-60282-950-3)

Smoke and Fire by Julie Cannon. Oil and water, passion and desire, a combustible combination. Can two women fight the fire that draws them together and threatens to keep them apart? (978-1-60282-977-0)

Asher's Fault by Elizabeth Wheeler. Fourteen-year-old Asher Price sees the world in black and white, much like the photos he takes, but when his little brother drowns at the same moment Asher experiences his first same-sex kiss, he can no longer hide behind the lens of his camera and eventually discovers he isn't the only one with a secret. (978-1-60282-982-4)

Love and Devotion by Jove Belle. KC Hall trips her way through life, stumbling into an affair with a married bombshell twice her age. Thankfully, her best friend, Emma Reynolds, is there to show her the true meaning of Love and Devotion. (978-1-60282-965-7)

Rush by Carsen Taite. Murder, secrets, and romance combine to create the ultimate rush. (978-1-60282-966-4)

The Shoal of Time by J.M. Redmann. It sounded too easy. Micky Knight is reluctant to take the case because the easy ones often turn into the hard ones, and the hard ones turn into the dangerous ones. In this one, easy turns hard without warning. (978-1-60282-967-1)

In Between by Jane Hoppen. At the age of 14, Sophie Schmidt discovers that she was born an intersexual baby and sets off on a journey to find her place in a world that denies her true existence. (978-1-60282-968-8)

Secret Lies by Amy Dunne. While fleeing from her abuser, Nicola Jackson bumps into Jenny O'Connor, and their unlikely friendship quickly develops into a blossoming romance—but when it comes down to a matter of life or death, are they both willing to face their fears? (978-1-60282-970-1)

Under Her Spell by Maggie Morton. The magic of love brought Terra and Athene together, but now a magical quest stands between them—a quest for Athene's hand in marriage. Will their passion keep them together, or will stronger magic tear them apart? (978-1-60282-973-2)

Homestead by Radclyffe. R. Clayton Sutter figures getting NorthAm Fuel's newest refinery operational on a rolling tract of land in Upstate New York should take a month or two, but then, she hadn't counted on local resistance in the form of vandalism, petitions, and one furious farmer named Tess Rogers. (978-1-60282-956-5)

Battle of Forces: Sera Toujours by Ali Vali. Kendal and Piper return to New Orleans to start the rest of eternity together, but the return of an old enemy makes their peaceful reunion short-lived, especially when they join forces with the new queen of the vampires. (978-1-60282-957-2)

How Sweet It Is by Melissa Brayden. Some things are better than chocolate. Molly O'Brien enjoys her quiet life running the bakeshop in a small town. When the beautiful Jordan Tuscana returns home, Molly can't deny the attraction—or the stirrings of something more. (978-1-60282-958-9)

The Missing Juliet: A Fisher Key Adventure by Sam Cameron. A teenage detective and her friends search for a kidnapped Hollywood star in the Florida Keys. (978-1-60282-959-6)

Amor and More: Love Everafter edited by Radclyffe and Stacia Seaman. Rediscover favorite couples as Bold Strokes Books authors reveal glimpses of life and love beyond the honeymoon in short stories featuring main characters from favorite BSB novels. (978-1-60282-963-3)

First Love by CJ Harte. Finding true love is hard enough, but for Jordan Thompson, daughter of a conservative president, it's challenging, especially when that love is a female rodeo cowgirl. (978-1-60282-949-7)

Pale Wings Protecting by Lesley Davis. Posing as a couple to investigate the abduction of infants, Special Agent Blythe Kent and Detective Daryl Chandler find themselves drawn into a battle over the innocents, with demons on one side and the unlikeliest of protectors on the other. (978-1-60282-964-0)